Second Generation

**Also Available in Large Print
by Howard Fast**

The Immigrants

Second Generation

HOWARD FAST

VOLUME I

G.K.HALL&CO.

Boston, Massachusetts

1979

Library of Congress Cataloging in Publication Data

Fast, Howard Melvin, 1914 -
  Second generation.

  "Published in large print."
  1. Large type books.   I. Title.
[PZ3.F265Se 1979] [PS3511.A784] 813'.5'2 79-10580
  ISBN 0-8161-6715-X

Copyright © 1978 by Howard Fast

Published in Large Print by arrangement with Houghton Mifflin Company

Set in Dymo Graphic Systems 18 pt Crown

This book is published by special arrangement with Eric Lasher

For Jerry and Dotty

CONTENTS

PART ONE

Homecoming

Pete Lomas' mackerel drifter was an old, converted, coal-fired steam tug of a hundred and twenty-two tons, purchased as war surplus in 1919. It cost him so little then that he was able to sell its oversized engine for scrap and replace it with a modern oil-burning plant. He named it *Golden Gate*, packed his wife and kids and household goods into it, and sailed from San Francisco Bay down to San Pedro. There he rented a berth for the tug and went into the mackerel business. His wife suffered from asthma, and her doctor determined that the San Francisco area was too damp. Lomas then decided to make the move to Los Angeles County, and he bought a house in Downey.

He laid out his drift nets with a three-man crew, and until the Depression came, in the thirties, he did well; and even after 1929 he managed to make a decent living out of his boat and to pay his crew living wages as well. Years before, he had worked for Dan Lavette as the captain of his fleet of crabbing boats on Fisherman's Wharf in San Francisco; and when, in 1931, he stumbled on Lavette on the dock at San Pedro, broke and hungry, he offered him a job. Now, in 1934, Dan had been working for Lomas steadily for three years.

Today, the first of June, 1934, Dan Lavette came off the mackerel boat at ten o'clock in the morning and got into his 1930 Ford sedan to drive to his home in Westwood, where he lived with his second wife, an American-born Chinese woman named May Ling, their son, Joseph, and her parents. Their small house was a few blocks from the University of California campus in Los Angeles, where May Ling worked at the library.

Dan was a big man, six feet and one inch in height, heavily built but without fat, broad in the shoulders, his skin tanned and weather-beaten by the sun and the salt water. He had a good head of curly hair, mostly gray, dark eyes under straight brows, high cheekbones, and a wide, full mouth.

To the two men who comprised the crew of the mackerel boat along with Dan and Pete Lomas, Lavette was a plain, soft-spoken, easygoing, and competent fisherman. He never lost his temper and he never complained, regardless of how brutal or backbreaking the conditions were, and that in itself was most unusual among fishermen. Of his background, they knew only that years before he had fished with Pete Lomas in San Francisco Bay. One of them was a Chicano, the other an Italian who spoke little English, and they were not inordinately curious. As for Lomas, who knew a great deal more about Dan Lavette, he kept his peace.

The Chicano, whose name was Juan Gonzales, while only twenty-two years old, was alert enough to realize that Dan Lavette was unlike any of the other fishermen on the wharf. He said to him one day, "Danny, how come a man like you, he's satisfied to pull fish?"

Dan shrugged. "I'm a fisherman. Always been one."

"You'll be an old man soon. I'll be goddamned if I spend my life on a fishing

5

boat, take home twenty, thirty dollars a week, and end up a poor bum on the dock.''

''I've been a bum on the dock,'' Dan replied. ''I like fishing better.''

Driving home today, Dan thought of that. Did he actually like what he did, enjoy what he did? It had been a bad night, cold and wet out on the water, and he had wrenched a muscle in his shoulder. His whole body ached, and he thought longingly of the hot bath that he would climb into the moment he set foot in the house. He supposed he was as happy as a man might be. He had made his peace with himself. Nevertheless, he was still a fisherman who took home between twenty and thirty dollars a week, and he was forty-five years old.

The morning mist and overcast had cleared by the time he reached Westwood. His father-in-law, Feng Wo, was in the garden, tending his beloved rosebushes, and he greeted Dan formally, as always.

''You are well, Mr. Lavette?'' He had never broken his old habit of addressing Dan as Mr. Lavette.

6

"Tired."

"You have a letter. From your daughter, Barbara."

Dan nodded. "I'll have a bath first."

He soaked in the tub, and strength and comfort flowed back into his body. In a few hours, May Ling would come home, and he would sprawl in a chair and listen to her recitation of what had happened that day on the campus. She dispelled the common notion that nothing but whispers are heard in a library; everything that May Ling looked at or encountered took on a marvelous and enchanting dramatic shape. Her whole life, every day of it, was an adventure in newness. This past night, out at sea, one of their drift nets had parted. Dan hated the drift nets, which trapped the mackerel by their gills. This time he spent an hour splicing the break, soaked to the waist, the dying fish threshing around his hands; still, he could not put into words what he felt, yet with the most ordinary occurrence May Ling brought a whole world to life.

Out of the tub, he toweled himself dry, relaxed, delightfully weary. The *Golden*

Gate would lay over until tomorrow morning while the nets were refurbished, so he had a long, lazy time of daylight ahead of him, and then a night when he could sleep himself out on a clean bed instead of huddling for an hour or two on the damp bunk in the cabin of the boat. He and his son would play a game of checkers. May Ling would be reading a book, looking up every now and then to catch his glance and smile at him. Hell, he thought, it was all and more than anyone wanted out of life.

Dressed in a clean shirt and trousers, he went down to the kitchen where the old woman, So-toy, his mother-in-law, had tea and cake waiting for him. The letter from Barbara lay on the table next to his plate. "You'll excuse me," he said to So-toy.

Still, after so many years in America, she spoke very little English. She simply smiled with approval as he opened the letter, then sat down opposite him at the kitchen table while he read. At first, he had been uncomfortable living with two people who worshipped him as uncritically as Feng Wo and his wife. Now

8

he was almost used to it.

"Daddy," the letter began — always that single word, as if it conveyed a significance beyond what any adjective could, yet a word she had spoken to him only at one meeting, a year before — and then went on: "School's over, but I had to write to you before I leave New York for San Francisco, because you will remember that every letter I ever wrote to you has been from here over the past eight months, and I want this to complete our correspondence for this semester. You always tell me that you are not much of a letter writer, and it's true your letters are short, but I do treasure them. And if anyone ever asked me about my father, and they do, you know, I could have said that so much of what I know of him is from his letters, which is strange, don't you think?

"Anyway, school is over. It was such a good year and I do love Sarah Lawrence, but really, I don't know whether I want to go back. Isn't that a strange thing for me to say? For the past week I have been puzzling over the way I feel and trying to make some sense out of it. Have you ever been very happy, but with a little worm of discontent nibbling away at your insides? I shouldn't ask you that, because I saw you with May Ling and I know how happy you are and that there are no worms of discontent eating at you, and it's worse because I don't for the life of me know why. Can one be happy and so terribly dissatisfied at the same time?

"But now when I look at what I have written here, it occurs to me that happy is not the right word. Jenny Brown, who is one of my roommates, gets very blue, and she can't understand why I am always so cheerful, and I guess that's what I really mean. Cheerful is a better word than happy to describe how I usually feel, because even when I feel that something is deeply wrong about the way I am, I don't get depressed about it. But I am going to take two decisive steps when I get home. I shall tell mother that I want a place of my own, and I also intend to find a job, and the latter may have to take place before the former, since it's up to mother whether my allowance continues.

Anyway, I feel a little ashamed writing to you about that, when my allowance is more than anyone deserves without working for it. All of this is just to tell you what to expect when I come down to see you, because it's so very long since my first trip to Los Angeles, and every time I think about that I get all wet-eyed and emotional. But I do promise you that very soon after I get home, I will drive down to Westwood.

"I can't tell you how much I want to see Joe again. It's so strange to have a brother you have only seen once in your entire life, and I liked him so much. How can one have two brothers as different as Tom and Joe? But of course I can answer that myself. I do love Tom, but he's such a stuffed shirt. You know that he's graduating from Princeton this year, and he's just furious at me because I wouldn't hang around with mother's family in Boston until the graduation, and I wouldn't because I don't think it would matter a bit for me to be there at the graduation and I don't intend to make that long train trip twice in one month.

11

"Anyway, two more weeks away was just too much. I am so eager to get home and to see San Francisco, and to see you and Joe and May Ling, who is just the loveliest person in the world, and her father and mother, who are just darling and much more like two people you read about in a book and don't ever meet in real life."

She signed the letter "Barbara," as if no term of endearment could add to what she had written, something Dan understood very well indeed.

"How is daughter Barbara?" So-toy asked him.

"Good. Yes, she's fine."

I have stepped into the pages of *Alice in Wonderland,* Barbara told herself; yet she had been here and lived in this San Francisco mansion before, and nine months away was not such a long time. She was playing a role, not they. She was having dinner in the pretentious dining room with her mother and her stepfather, John Whittier, and while it was true that the room was somewhat larger and more elegant than the dining room in the house where she grew up on Russian Hill, when her mother was still married to Dan Lavette, the difference was not all that great. The mahogany table was no longer. It was true that they had not had a butler on Russian Hill, but this was by no means her first dinner in the Whittier house, and the position she occupied between her mother at one end of the long table and John Whittier at the other was not particularly novel. Why then did she feel totally disconnected from this world, a stranger, an intruder? The plain fact of the matter was that she was a daughter of the very rich and had been from the moment of her birth, so how could she sit in judgment? But I am not sitting in judgment, she assured herself, I am simply very uncomfortable and filled with guilt, and I don't know why.

Jean was not an insensitive person, and Barbara realized that she had planned a simple but delicious dinner that would be quite different from the institutional food at school: a clear soup, then a planked steak with scalloped potatoes and asparagus, and ice cream for dessert, remembering Barbara's passion for ice cream. Knox, the butler, brought in the ice cream, a gallon brick sitting in a tureen of lovely pale ivory Limoges. He served a portion of the ice cream to each of them and then put the tureen down in front of Jean and left the room.

John Whittier was holding forth on the waterfront strike, which had been called in San Francisco just two weeks before Barbara's return. Whittier was not a conversationalist; he had small ability to listen to anything he was not saying himself; and when he spoke, especially in anger, he tended to be carried away and lose the threads of his discourse. It always helped him to be accusative.

"Don't tell me you can understand why they're striking," he said to Barbara.

"But I can."

"Because you don't understand one damn thing about it," he went on. "That's the trouble with a place like Sarah Lawrence. I told your mother that. It's not only a wretched substitute for education, it's a communist substitute. It's anarchy

— and I'm not saying that because of what it cost your mother and myself personally."

"Leave me out of it, dear," Jean said softly. "I left the bank this morning. I am through with business." She smiled.

"Hardly, my dear," Whittier said. "Like it or not, this family is the largest shipowner on the West Coast, and for two weeks we haven't moved one damn pound of cargo out of this port. Do you know what that has cost us?"

He directed this at Barbara. She shook her head, her eyes fixed on the mound of ice cream in the Limoges tureen. It was melting. No one noticed that it was melting. No one cared that it was melting.

"Would a million dollars shock you? Or does a million dollars mean absolutely nothing to you? What do they teach you back there in school? That Karl Marx was a saint? Or do we have our own living saint in Franklin Delano Roosevelt? Do you know what longshoremen are? Have you ever met a longshoreman? Have you ever smelled one?"

"John," Jean said.

"The dregs of this city, and we've put the bread in their mouths all these years, and this is our repayment — to be destroyed! And you tell me you can understand why they're striking —"

Listening to this, Barbara watched the ice cream melt. In back of her mind, there was the memory of Professor Franklin's Sociology II, where he made the point that the rich are incapable of understanding the rich. It had been a non sequitur then, and now suddenly it made sense. A gallon of ice cream, melted, could only be thrown away.

"Mother," she said, "the ice cream is melting."

Jean's slight smile remained unchanged. She was watching her husband, and Barbara realized that her mother heard nothing Whittier was saying, nothing she was saying. The ice cream continued to melt.

"As for Harry Bridges," Whittier was saying, "if there were law and order in this city, he'd be behind bars. Oh, yes, behind bars."

Barbara was in bed, reading Gertrude Stein's *Autobiography of Alice B. Toklas,* intrigued, fascinated by a world so distant and different, when the door opened and Jean entered the room. She wore a dressing gown of pale pink velvet and she had removed her make-up, and as far as Barbara was concerned, it only enhanced her face. If she were as beautiful as her mother, she would never touch make-up. She put down the book, and Jean came to the bed and sat down beside her. Jean picked up the book and glanced at it.

"Like it?"

"I like to pretend I'm in Paris."

"The question is, darling, are you glad to be back in San Francisco?"

"I think so. Yes."

"You mustn't mind John. He's terribly upset. People in his position develop a tremendous feeling of power. I know the feeling, and now, with the waterfront closed down as it is, he's utterly frustrated. This is hardly the best side of him."

"Mother —"

"It used to be 'mummy.' "

"I know. I'm twenty years old."

Jean was smiling.

"So you mustn't laugh at me."

"I wouldn't dream of laughing at you. But you're so very serious."

"Yes," Barbara agreed. "I guess I'm forcing myself to be serious because I have been trying to get up the courage to talk about this —"

"Baby, we can talk about anything. You know that."

"We can't," Barbara protested almost plaintively. "You're my mother. It's just not true that we can talk about anything."

Jean stopped smiling. "Try."

"All right. I want a place of my own."

"What do you mean by a place of your own?"

"My own apartment. I can't live here."

Jean sighed. "The truth is, you don't live here — I mean in reality, my dear. Think about it. You're away at school. It's only the few summer months. And your horse is down in Menlo Park, and you can stay at the club there whenever you wish — and if I know you, you'll be practically

18

living there. You do have your car, so I just don't understand what you mean.''

''You don't want to understand what I mean.''

''No, that's not fair. Put yourself in my position, Barbara. You tell me that you want an apartment of your own — but why? You're comfortable here. You have everything you could possibly want. You come and go as you please, and whatever you may feel about John, he certainly doesn't restrict your movements or impose any discipline on you.''

''That's not it.''

''Then tell me what it is.''

''This isn't my home. It never has been my home.''

''Why? Because you don't like John?''

''Please, please don't get angry with me, mother,'' Barbara begged her. ''You said we could talk. It's not easy for me to explain what I feel. There's a teacher at school, Professor Carl Franklin, who conducts a seminar in sociology, and he said the Embarcadero was a slave market, different, but no better and no worse than the old Negro slave markets in

19

the East, and I was so indignant I almost walked out of the class, because really, they don't think we're quite civilized out here."

"I don't see what that has to do with it," Jean said. "The Embarcadero is not a slave market. The longshoremen are well paid and their demands are utterly preposterous. And what on earth has this to do with your wanting an apartment of your own?"

"Like the ice cream at dinner," Barbara said hopelessly.

"What on earth! The ice cream at dinner?"

"Don't you see? There was that enormous brick of ice cream, and we just sat there and let it melt down while John lectured me about the strike. You can't do anything with ice cream once it melts. You throw it away, and it didn't mean a thing to any of us. It just doesn't. We can't think that way — I mean, we don't even understand what food is in a country where thousands of people are starving."

"But you do understand this," Jean said.

"Now you are angry with me."

"Barbara," Jean said calmly, "I am not angry. Not really. You're a very romantic child, you always have been. I'm well aware of the inequities of society, but we did not create them."

"I'm not a child, mother."

"I think you are. In many ways. You dislike John, and you compare him to your father. I don't think seeing your father has helped, and the romantic image of him that you have is far from the reality."

"Then I dislike John Whittier," Barbara said flatly. "I can't control who I like and who I dislike. Do you think it's pleasant for me to live under his roof?"

"It's my roof too. I happen to be married to John Whittier, and you are a part of a very wealthy family, like it or not. I have no intention of shedding crocodile tears or wallowing in guilt over what my father and his father created by their own sweat and wit. As for the apartment — well, we'll talk about that another time."

It had not been the best of days for Jean

21

Whittier, and now, looking at her daughter, the strong, lovely face, the pale gray eyes, the honey-colored hair, so like her own — and thinking that this was probably the only person in the world she truly loved — it promised to end even more wretchedly than it had begun.

It had been Jean's last day as president of the Seldon Bank, a great, unshakable financial institution, which her grandfather had founded in a wagon at the placer mines just eighty-two years before, and which her father had continued and cherished and nourished. At his death, six years ago, Jean — then Jean Lavette and not yet divorced — had become trustee for three hundred and eighty-two thousand shares of stock in the Seldon Bank, to be divided equally between her two children, Thomas and Barbara, twelve years later. With over seventy percent of the voting stock of the Seldon Bank in her trust, with the right to vote it, Jean had taken over the presidency of the bank, becoming the first woman in California, if not in the entire country, to sit as president of a major bank.

Now she was surrendering. No, as she saw it, not a surrender but an abdication. Willing or unwilling? She could not be certain. Until today, she had felt that she was certain, that she was taking a step out of her own free will, doing what was best for her and for the bank. Walking into the bank that morning, passing through the great marble-clad street section that fronted on Montgomery Street, she had been shaken by a sudden and desperate sense of loss. Which, she told herself immediately, was an understandable and emotional reaction. Essentially, nothing had changed. She still, as trustee for her children, voted the controlling interest in the stock; she would still sit on the board of directors; and at long last she would be able to return to the central interest of her life, her collection of paintings and sculptures, which she had so long neglected. It would be said, as it was perhaps already being said, that her husband, John Whittier, had persuaded her to take this step; and she admitted to herself that it was true in part — but only in part. It was her own decision.

23

Alvin Sommers, vice president of the Seldon Bank, had been waiting and watching for her that morning, and as he saw her enter, he hurried to meet her. He noticed that she was wearing what to his way of thinking was civilian dress, a bright flowered taffeta with pink velvet trimming, both cheerful and youthful, he assured himself. Even at the age of forty-four, Jean Lavette — he still thought of her as Jean Lavette — was, as the news stories so often observed, perhaps the most fashionable and attractive woman in San Francisco social circles. He himself, a small, dry man in his middle sixties with a small, pudgy wife, had long entertained his own fantasies about Jean Whittier; it was a totally frustrated, totally concealed love, lust, hate fixation, nourished on the one hand by her cold, distant beauty, and on the other by his resentment at the manner in which, after her father's death, she had taken over control of the bank. The fact that the bank had flourished during the first five bitter years of the Depression, when so many banks were in crisis or closing their doors, only increased his resentment. Now that time had come to an end, but he was still not certain that his own temporary ascendancy to the presidency would be made permanent, and he was thus more deferential than ever, more effusive in his greeting.

"My dear Jean," he said to her, "I've never seen you look so radiant. But what will we do now? We'll become a drab and colorless place."

"You will manage, Alvin. In fact, you will manage very well indeed. By the way, I told Martin" — Martin Clancy was the second vice president — "that I shall empty my office. You'll be moving in, I presume, and I hardly think you'll be comfortable with an Aubusson carpet of pale blue, or with the Picassos and Monet's *Water Lilies,* which you and Martin have always regarded as being a slur on the entire tradition of banking."

"No, indeed. You have a beautiful office."

He had to quicken his pace to keep up with her as she swept through the bank into the main lobby of the Seldon Building.

"Alvin, how old are you?"

"Sixty-five," he answered, thinking, What an outrageous question, and the way she asked it, like making a remark about the weather. But no comment followed it, and his inner debate on whether to follow her into the elevator like an obedient puppy dog was decided by her own motion. They were alone with the operator in the elevator reserved for the top three floors, where the bank's offices were.

"We set the board meeting for three o'clock," he told her. "Tentatively, that is. If you are free then?"

"No, I'm not. I'm meeting Barbara at the station, and that's at two-thirty, I think. But you don't need me, Alvin. I've drawn up the agenda. Martin will propose you and the board will vote it that way. You do know that, don't you?"

"I had hoped so. Thank you, Jean."

Since she didn't invite him out, he remained in the elevator. Jean admitted to herself that she couldn't tolerate him. That was a plus for her decision; she would not have to face Alvin Sommers every time she came to the bank. Yes, there was a whole list of positive things. Six years was enough. She had taken the step originally because it was a challenge. Or was it because her life was coming apart at the seams? Or was it because she loathed everything about the bank and everyone connected with it? That, indeed, was an odd thought, and a new one, and it might very well be so.

Miss Pritchard, her secretary, regarded her sadly. "I was not sure of your time today — everything is so upset. Will you see anyone?"

"I don't think so. I have a luncheon engagement, and it's ten o'clock already. I won't be in at all this afternoon."

"And tomorrow?"

"No tomorrow, Lorna. You know that. Finis." She patted Miss Pritchard's thin shoulder. "It's all right, and you must not worry about your job. Just take your two weeks' vacation and enjoy yourself," she said, wondering just how skinny, spinsterish, fortyish Miss Pritchard would go about enjoying herself. "Did I have any appointments? I didn't think so."

"No. But Mr. Liu called again. The man from the Oriental Improvement Society. He said he would call back."

"Then you talk to him. What does he want, a contribution?"

"I don't imagine so. I think it's part of their campaign to place Chinese and Japanese in jobs in banks."

"We're not taking on anyone, you know that," Jean said with some irritation. "If he wants to see anyone, he can see Mr. Sommers next week."

Provoked, and annoyed with herself for allowing it to show, Jean went into her office, closed the door, and stood there, looking around. It was a large office, twenty by thirty feet. The walls, once covered by walnut panels, were now painted in soft tones of ivory. The pastel blue Aubusson measured eighteen by twenty-four, and Jean thought wistfully of how splendid it would have been on the floor of her bedroom in the house she had lived in on Russian Hill, when she had been Jean Lavette. In the Whittier mansion — well, a pastel blue rug in the Whittier house was yet unthinkable. All in due time. She had already invaded her husband's house — which had once belonged to his father — with thirty-seven paintings, still only part of her collection, and now somehow she would have to find a place for the Picassos and the enormous Monet. It would mean a struggle, but she was determined that the Monet would hang on a wall in the Whittier house, and there were few decisions of Jean's that did not come into being.

She sat down behind her desk, a graceful eighteenth-century French piece that she had picked up in Paris, and surveyed the room. Actually, there was nothing more for her to do here; she was simply going through motions, but she could recall with satisfaction that she had never been a figurehead. She had run the bank and not only the bank; there were huge land holdings that her former husband had acquired, the largest department store in San Francisco, and other odds and ends of a small empire that had become a very large empire since her marriage to John Whittier. She had nurtured it. She had been wealthy before;

now, in this dismal year of 1934, she was a great deal wealthier.

"And totally miserable," she said aloud.

The telephone rang. It was her husband, John, explaining that something had come up and that he could not make lunch with her. "Can you go to the station alone?" he asked her. "The afternoon's just no good for me."

"I think I'm capable of getting to the station. Yes."

"You sound unhappy."

"Do I? I'm happy as a lark."

"Well, you'll be pleased to see Barbara again."

"Yes, of course." There was a long moment of silence, and then Jean said, "By the way, I've decided not to sell the house on Russian Hill. I shall keep it and turn it into a gallery."

"Oh. And when did you decide that?"

"Just this moment."

When she put down the telephone, she felt better. John hated the house on Russian Hill, just as he hated everything that related to Daniel Lavette.

As a matter of fact, John Whittier shared a sentiment held by his wife's former husband, Dan Lavette. It was less the house on Russian Hill that he disliked than the hill itself, the place, the ambience, the cluster of artists and writers who had given the hill a reputation almost as widely recognized then, in the 1930s, as that of Greenwich Village in New York. Those who knew John Whittier said that the only thing in the world that he loved, cherished, or respected was money — which was not entirely fair, for he respected Jean, his second wife, and certainly he respected the vast wealth that she represented. Whether or not he loved her, or had ever been in love with her, is a question which, if put to him, would have required for an answer a degree of introspection of which he was by no means capable. In his terms, she was a rewarding wife. She was tall, beautiful, dressed elegantly and in the best of taste, still youthful at forty-four, and in San Francisco terms at the very apex of society, the only daughter of Thomas and Mary Seldon; and Mary Seldon's mother had been an Asquith from the Boston family that still resided on Beacon Hill. All to the good. The various factors held together like an analysis of an impeccable blue chip stock. There were still other characteristics of his wife that John Whittier regarded as assets, but her involvement with the artists and writers of Russian Hill was not one of them.

He himself was a rather good-looking, tall, and somewhat overweight man of forty-six, with thinning blond hair and pale blue eyes. His father, Grant Whittier, now deceased, had been the largest shipowner on the West Coast, and the combining of the Whittier and Lavette interests had produced the largest single conglomeration of wealth in California; still, it nettled him that he should have to continue to pay taxes on a boarded-up mansion that was certainly the best piece of property on Russian Hill. Long ago, Robert Louis Stevenson had sailed out of San Francisco on one of the Whittier ships, and had afterward written a scathing little essay on how the ship was run; and while Stevenson had never lived on Russian Hill, his wife had, and Mrs. Stevenson's presence there contributed to making the place an anathema to the Whittiers. Even so small a matter as a piece in the *Chronicle* mentioning how much Peter B. Kyne, another resident of Russian Hill, was paid by the *Saturday Evening Post* for his stories, elicited an angry denunciation by Whittier against the large sums paid to writers in these depressed times.

His own home was in Pacific Heights, a twenty-two-room limestone mansion. It had been built by his father, and when John Whittier and Jean Lavette were married, they agreed that it would be their residence and that she would rid herself of the house on Russian Hill as soon as it was convenient for her to do so. Now it was to be a gallery — whatever that meant.

Whittier's musing was interrupted by his secretary, who told him that there was a collect call for him from Thomas Lavette, from Lambertville, New Jersey.

"From where?"

"Lambertville. Will you accept it,

Mr. Whittier?"

"Of course." He picked up his phone. The high-pitched voice on the other end was uneven, uncertain.

"John?"

"Tommy? Where the devil are you?"

"I'm in a frightful mess, John. Don't be angry with me, please. I didn't dare call mother. I don't want her to know —"

"To know what? Will you please tell me what happened."

"I'm in jail here."

"You are what?"

"Please," Tom begged him, "don't blow up at me. I'm miserable enough. I was drunk, and I smashed up the car."

"Are you all right?"

"I'm all right, but there was a girl with me, and they had to take her to the hospital. I don't think she's badly hurt. But they're holding me here for drunk driving, and I need five hundred for bail to get out —"

Whittier stared at the phone without replying. He had no children of his own from his first marriage — which had come late in life and lasted only three years — and he had no attitudes at all toward children. They were not of his world. It grated when he heard Jean refer to the children. As far as he was concerned, they were adults, a woman of twenty and a man of twenty-two. Between him and Barbara, there was a fence of thorns. Her kisses were cold pecks on the cheek, and communication was almost nonexistent. His attitude toward Tom was more neutral; it consisted of tolerance without affection, but the tolerance was not too elastic.

"John, are you still there?" the voice pleaded.

"How the devil did you get into a scrape like that?"

"God, I don't know. I just don't know. I wish it had never happened, but it did. I hate to come begging to you, but I need the bail money, otherwise I'll just sit here. I'll pay you back."

"All right. I'll wire the money. What did you say that place is? Lambertville, New Jersey?" He scribbled the name on a pad. "You'll need a lawyer. I'll have my people in New York find you someone in

Princeton. I trust you'll be in Princeton and stay there?'' he finished sourly.

"I will, believe me. I don't know how to thank you, John. It's very decent of you.''

"Stupid young fool,'' he said as he put down the phone. Then he called his secretary and instructed her to wire the bail money and to call his New York attorneys and have them find a lawyer in Princeton and have the lawyer get in touch with Thomas Lavette at the college. "We'll pay the costs,'' he added.

All of which he repeated to Jean, angrily and bitterly, before they sat down to dinner with Barbara. It definitely had not been one of Jean's good days.

Dressed in a woolen skirt, an old sweater, and the worn loafers she had used at school, Barbara took the streetcar down Market Street to the Embarcadero. On foot, she drifted slowly south from the Ferry Building, studying the striking longshoremen with curiosity and interest. Essentially, her mother was quite right about her romantic nature, and her mind gave every incident in which she participated a dramatic form and structure. She realized that she had never actually looked at the faces of men like those on the picket lines; the faces were worn, pinched, lined without reference to age. "Longshoreman" had a connotation in her mind of size, bulk, brute strength; but most of these men were no taller than she was, many of them shorter than she was, Mexicans and Orientals many of them, hunched over, pulling their jackets tight against the cold wind, holding their picket signs unaggressively, signs that called for a dollar an hour and for a hiring hall instead of the shapeup on the docks. Barbara had only a fuzzy notion of what a shapeup was, thinking of an auction system of some kind, which Dr. Franklin had referred to when he called the Embarcadero a slave market. Barbara went closer to read a sign covered with rough lettering, and the man carrying it stepped out of line, facing the sign to her and grinning a toothless, good-natured grin.

"Read it, sister," he said. "I'm in no hurry. I got all the time in the world."

The sign read: "I want a dollar an hour. I got three kids and a wife, and I average 15 hours a week. Can you make it on that? When we struck, my pay was 75 cents an hour when I worked."

He grinned again, stepped back into the picket line, and walked off. Barbara stared after him. She had thirty-five dollars in her purse, and her first impulse was to run after the toothless longshoreman and press all the money she had into his hands. No, that would be awful, perfectly awful, she decided. She walked along the Embarcadero, carrying the whole weight of poverty and suffering upon her shoulders. It made no difference to Barbara that every port on the West Coast was tied up, from Seattle down to San Diego; the entire guilt, in her mind, belonged to John Whittier and her mother, since they were the largest ship operator on the Coast — and thereby to her.

She came to a place where a truck was parked. The tail of the truck was down, and inside a sort of soup kitchen had been improvised; two men and a stout woman were serving coffee and doughnuts to the strikers. The lettering on the side of the truck read SCHOFIELD'S BAKERY, and under that a hand-painted card read BAKERY WORKERS. LOCAL 12. Barbara watched for a few minutes. Then she went to the woman and whispered uncertainly, "Do you take contributions?"

"We certainly do."

Barbara opened her purse, took out all the money she had, leaving herself only streetcar fare, and handed it to the stout woman.

"God bless you, honey," the woman said.

Barbara clenched her teeth and closed her eyes to keep back the tears.

"Are you all right, honey?"

Barbara nodded and walked away quickly.

At the age of sixty-six, Sam Goldberg was heavier than he had ever been. Six months before, at his doctor's office, he had tipped the scales at two hundred and twenty-five pounds, and since he was only five feet and eight inches, his physician told him flatly, "Keep this up, Sam, and you're inviting a coronary." Now, sitting in his office and munching gumdrops thoughtfully, he realized that the invitation still stood and that he was not terribly worried. His wife, who had always attempted to keep his weight in check, had died two years before. His partner, Adam Benchly — the firm was still Goldberg and Benchly — was a cadaverous Yankee who had died nine months ago at the age of seventy, and since then, Sam had been lonely and depressed for the first time in his life. The two young law clerks he had taken on to share the burden respected him and agreed with him, which only served to depress him further. Benchly had never agreed with him. They had fought and snarled at each other for forty years; now life without him was dull and uninteresting, and Sam Goldberg saw no good reason to refrain from either the gumdrops or the heavy, satisfying meals he ate each day at Gino's restaurant on Jones Street.

In any case, this was a new, different, and discouraging world, frayed at the seams and disintegrating. He and Benchly were of the immigrants, a special breed. Goldberg's father had come to California in 1852 to dig for gold and had ended up with a fruit stand in Sacramento. Benchly's father had jumped ship in San Francisco in 1850. He and Benchly had lived through a time when all was possible, and the possible was made real. Now the possible had been honed down to size.

Brooding over this and other matters, he was interrupted by his secretary's voice on the intercom, informing him that a Miss Barbara Lavette would like to see him.

He had to adjust, put things in their place, establish a perspective, and after a long moment of silence he said, "Yes, of course. Send her in."

He rose and waited. Time plays tricks, and his first thought as the tall, handsome young woman entered was that his secretary had gotten the name wrong and that this was Jean. The resemblance was striking. Of course it was Jean's daughter. He had not seen Jean for years, but certainly she was well past forty.

He came around his desk and took the hand she offered. Her manner was a curious mixture of shyness and confidence, and the slight, uncertain smile on her lips was very ingratiating.

"You're Danny's daughter," Goldberg said.

She nodded. "I should have called and asked you for an appointment, Mr. Goldberg. But I don't have any legal business. I want you to know that. I only wanted to talk to you and ask you some questions, and I know how busy lawyers are."

"My clerks are busy," he said. "I sit here and eat gumdrops and brood about the past. I'm delighted — Barbara. Can I call you Barbara? We shouldn't stand on formalities. I was your father's lawyer for twenty years, but it was not just being a lawyer, believe me. And you're Barbara. You have grown up to be a beautiful woman, my dear. The last time I saw you — well, you were six or seven. And now —"

"I'm twenty."

"That's a beautiful, beautiful age. And what about Danny? I know you saw him last year."

"I haven't been down to Los Angeles yet. I'll go soon. Am I intruding — on your time?"

"Intruding? My dear, this is such a fine, unexpected pleasure. It's almost twelve o'clock. Have you eaten yet? Or maybe you have a luncheon appointment?"

"Oh, no."

"Good. Then we'll go along to Gino's and we'll eat and talk."

"All right. I'd like that."

At the restaurant, sitting opposite her at a small table with a checkered cloth, Goldberg ordered spaghetti, a veal cutlet, and coffee. "We'll eat light. That's the fashion now," he said. He introduced her to Gino, who fussed over her and insisted that they have a bottle of wine on the house. "Danny's daughter," Goldberg told him.

"I know this place," Barbara said when Gino had gone. "He used to come here with May Ling."

"Does that bother you?"

43

"No, not really. It's just part of the whole thing that I'm trying to understand. When I went to see him last year — you know, I drove down to Los Angeles —"

"I know."

"I was so happy to see him, and I didn't really know him. I still don't, and I guess I don't know myself, either, and I'm so confused."

"I can understand that." He pointed to the food. "You're not eating."

"I'm not very hungry. Please forgive me."

"Nothing to forgive. I'm a fat man, Barbara. The reason people are fat is because they like to eat. So I'll eat and you talk."

"I have questions. Does it annoy you when people ask you questions?"

"That's a lawyer's stock in trade, if he can answer them." He chewed thoughtfully for a few seconds while Barbara waited in silence. "Go ahead and ask."

"Why does he work as a fisherman down there in San Pedro? He was a rich man."

Goldberg ate his spaghetti and regarded her benignly. Finally, having consumed the last mouthful, he said, "He wants to be a fisherman."

Barbara shook her head.

"He doesn't want to be a rich man," Goldberg said.

"That's not an answer," Barbara said pleadingly. "You're laughing at me, Mr. Goldberg."

"No, I'm not. You're asking me why Danny Lavette did what he did. I can tell you what he did, but not why. Anyway, I'm sure you know."

"But I don't know."

"Didn't you mother tell you?"

"My mother doesn't tell me things."

"You know about May Ling, the Chinese lady?"

"Yes — I know she was his mistress for many years."

"No, that's the wrong word. Your father wanted a divorce, and your mother refused. Over a period of twenty years, your father built a small empire — ships, land, the L and L Department Store, a hotel in Hawaii, and the first commercial

45

airline out here in California. When your grandfather died, he left the controlling stock of the Seldon Bank in trust for you and your brother. That was in nineteen twenty-eight, and the trust was to extend over twelve years. In nineteen forty, when the trust expires, the control of the stock will come to you. You'll be a very wealthy woman then, but I'm sure you know that."

"Yes, I know that."

"Meanwhile, your mother was named sole trustee in the will, with the power to vote the stock as she saw fit. She then decided to take over as president of the bank, something no woman in this country ever did before, certainly not with an institution the size of the Seldon Bank. All right, your mother didn't know one damn thing about banking, but she learned. She was not a figurehead; she had her finger in every pie, and she didn't do badly, believe me. For the next five years, that bank became her life. But I suppose you know that too."

"Yes," Barbara whispered, "I know that. What about my father?"

"He had a partner, whose name was

Mark Levy. The Levys had a chandler business down on the old wharf. Danny's father was killed in the earthquake. Danny had Joe Lavette's fishing boat and nothing else. He was just a kid then, but bright as hell, and soon he was operating three fishing boats, mortgaged to the hilt. He was always mortgaged to the hilt. Then he met your mother and fell in love with her, and nothing was going to stop him from having her and Nob Hill too. He and Mark Levy became partners — Danny was still a kid — and Levy mortgaged his business to finance the purchase of their first ship, a rusty old lumber carrier called the *Oregon Queen.* I still have a picture of it hanging in my office, and if you come back there with me, I'll show it to you."

"Do you know," Barbara said slowly, "I never met Mark Levy. All those years, and I never met him."

"Your mother didn't like him. He was a nice little feller, but your mother just didn't take to him. He's dead now, died in nineteen thirty. His son runs a winery up in Napa. Well, Danny and Mark stuck

47

together to the end. They were like brothers. Way back in nineteen ten, they hired a little Chinese feller by the name of Feng Wo to be the bookkeeper. People didn't hire Chinese in those days for anything fancier than a houseboy, but Feng Wo was smart as a whip. There was no way they could have done what they did without him. May Ling was his daughter." He took a deep breath and began to eat his veal cutlet. "It's a shame to let it get cold," he apologized. "I think a lot of your mother, don't get me wrong."

"I do too," Barbara said. "What happened?"

"I could go into this in detail and spend the rest of the afternoon talking about it, but the long and short of it is that when the Crash came in nineteen twenty-nine, Danny and Mark were overextended and their empire began to crumble. They were into the Seldon Bank for about sixteen million, and they couldn't meet their interest payments. Your mother called the loan, and that was the end of it."

"My mother did that?"

Goldberg stopped eating. "Now hold on.

It's not as simple as it appears. Your mother had no alternative, and in a manner of speaking, your father traded his edge for the divorce. He could have stayed on and run what the bank and the Whittiers took over, but Mark would have been out in the cold. Dan didn't want that. The truth is that he didn't want any of it. Something had happened to him. There's community property in this state, and Dan could have come out of it with half a million, just in personal property, real estate, and such. He didn't want that, either, and he signed a release giving everything to your mother. No one forced his hand. There are no villains in the piece, not your mother and not Whittier.''

''Yet you've just told me my mother destroyed my father.''

''No one destroyed your father,'' Goldberg said with just a trace of annoyance. ''I thought you knew all this. You saw you father last year. Did he look destroyed?''

''No.''

''Well, that's it then. What Danny did, he did. Not your mother or Whittier.''

"He was a rich man," Barbara insisted. "I know a little about community property. Whatever happened to his company, he could have remained a rich man. Why did he give it all to my mother?"

"I don't know." Goldberg sighed and shook his head. "Do you want dessert? You haven't eaten at all. Come on, have a piece of cheesecake." He motioned to the waiter.

"All right," Barbara agreed.

"Look, honey," he said, after he had taken his first bite of the cheesecake, "you're Danny's kid. He was like a son to me. But I don't know why he did what he did, and I don't want you to go home and throw this at your mother."

"I can't. She's not there."

"Oh? Do me a favor, eat the cake." She took a mouthful. "It's good, isn't it?"

"Yes, it is."

"Where's your mother?"

"She and John — her husband, Whittier —"

"I know."

"Well, they went east for my brother's

50

graduation. John will be back next month. Tommy and my mother are going on to Boston for a while."

"You mean you're alone in that huge barn of a place?"

Barbara smiled for the first time since they had entered the restaurant. "Oh, no, Mr. Goldberg. You can't be alone in that place."

"Honey, suppose you call me Sam. I'm a little older than you, but we're practically *mishpocheh*. That's Yiddish for family. I know ten words of Yiddish, and that's one of my favorites. Now, why can't you be alone there?"

"Because John has six servants with nothing to do, and when we gave up the house on Russian Hill, mother took Wendy Jones with her. She was our nurse, and now she's old and nasty and nosy. Anyway, I'm hardly ever there."

"I'm nosy too. Why are you hardly ever there? What do you do with yourself? Run around, drink too much?"

"You're scolding me," she said in amazement.

"Yeah." He grinned at her. "I guess I

51

am. Go on, eat the rest of your cake."

"I work at a soup kitchen," Barbara said. "I took today off. Most days I'm too tired to do much running around. I've been there two weeks, since my mother left."

"You work where?"

"The MWIU soup kitchen on Bryant Street."

"MWIU?"

"The Marine Workers, yes," Barbara said calmly.

"God Almighty! You mean Harry Bridges' outfit?"

"Yes."

"Does your mother know?"

Barbara smiled and shook her head.

"Well, she will, sooner or later, and sooner or later some wiseacre reporter will get on to you and spread it all over the front page of the *Examiner,* and that will certainly be a field day. My God, child, what has gotten into you? This isn't a lark. That's a brutal, dirty game they're playing down there on the docks."

"I only work at the soup kitchen. I'm not a communist. And they don't know my

52

name. I call myself Bobby Winter. It's easier if I keep the first name the same, and that's what they called me at school, Bobby Winter, because I loved the cold winters there. So they won't find out who I am."

"Maybe not in the next ten minutes," Goldberg snorted. "Why? Because you think John Whittier did your father in? He didn't. I told you that."

"No. No, really."

"What do they pay you?"

"Nothing."

"What do you do there?"

"Mr. Goldberg, you're shouting at me and scolding me as if I were some stupid, senseless little girl. You have no right to. I came to you to talk about my father, not to sit here and be scolded by you."

"You're absolutely right. I'm sorry."

"I hurt your feelings," she said.

"Absolutely. I hurt your feelings, you hurt mine. Now look, honey, you're the daughter of a man who is like my son. That gives me certain privileges. I talk to you this way because nobody else is going to. It just happens that John Whittier is the largest ship operator on this coast, and it also happens that he's married to your mother. You got sympathy for the longshoremen; so have I. Now I asked you what you do down there."

"I told you what I do. I work in the kitchen. I help to cook the food and serve it. I have an allowance of forty dollars a week, Mr. Goldberg —"

"Call me Sam, I told you," he interrupted. "If I'm going to yell at you, at least make me comfortable."

"All right. Sam. Do you realize that my allowance is more than twice as much as most longshoremen earn in a week?"

"It's five times as much as the average weekly wage in India, maybe ten times. What does that prove?"

"I'm not trying to prove anything. I don't need the money. I spend most of it on food for the kitchen."

"Do they know that?"

"I'm not a fool. I tell them it's contributions. I help to cook the food. I peel potatoes. I clean vegetables. I help with the serving, and sometimes I wash dishes."

54

"And you like that? You enjoy that?"

"Yes, I do!"

"Who's shouting now?"

"Well, you keep at me as if I'm doing something wrong. I'm not doing anything wrong. In fact, it's the first time in my life I ever did anything right or useful. It's the first time I ever worked. And if you saw the faces of those men, if you knew how hungry and wretched and miserable they are, you would understand what I feel."

The waiter came, and Goldberg took out his wallet and paid the check. Still holding the wallet, he looked at Barbara and said, "You got a boyfriend, honey?"

"No, not really. There was a nice boy at school who came down from Yale on weekends. His name was Burt Kingman and he lives in Philadelphia. But that seems like a hundred years ago. I know some boys here, but I haven't seen them since I've come back. Why?"

Goldberg smiled. "Why? Why, indeed. You're a nice girl, Barbara. Don't get into trouble. Down there on the wharf, you are going to change nothing.

Remember that."

"Not even myself?"

"Ah. That's where the trouble begins."
He took three twenty-dollar bills from his
wallet and pushed them toward her.

"What's this?"

"Buy more groceries. And remember,
the way you're going, it may be that you'll
need a lawyer. I'm not a bad lawyer."

After Dan Lavette's partner, Mark Levy,
died of a heart attack in 1930, his widow,
Sarah, continued to live alone in their big
Spanish Colonial house in Sausalito. Sam
Goldberg and his wife were frequent
visitors there, and when Goldberg became
a widower, he fell into a pattern of seeing
Sarah Levy on weekends. It was one of the
few defenses he had against unbearable
loneliness. The weekdays were endurable.
He could remain in his office and work
until seven or seven-thirty, and then
dinner at Gino's or some other restaurant
would kill the best part of the evening; but
the weekend stretched out as an
interminable period of nothing. So more
and more frequently after his wife's

death, he would invite himself to the Levy home on a Saturday or a Sunday. He had known the Levys for half a century, which, in the San Francisco of 1934, was an epoch that stretched back almost to the beginning. When Sam Goldberg had come to San Francisco from Sacramento, to read law at the offices of Colby and Jessup at the age of seventeen — as things were done in those days — he lived in a frame boarding house on the Embarcadero, opposite the Levys' chandler shop. As they were the only Jews in an overwhelmingly Italian neighborhood, he had come to know them well, and Mark's father had given him his first case, a salvage dispute that involved unpaid accounts at the store. He could remember, as if it were yesterday, the day in 1897 when Sarah arrived from New York, a lovely, slender, flaxen-haired girl, betrothed to a man she had never seen through the correspondence of the mutual parents, tagged and addressed like a parcel.

Now Marcus had been dead these four years past, a quick death from a massive

57

coronary, less to be pitied than his widow, whose daughter had been a suicide just two years before. Her single surviving child, Jacob, had married Clair Harvey, the daughter of Jack Harvey, who had been the first captain in the Lavette and Levy fleet of oceangoing vessels. In the early twenties, when the Volstead Act wrecked the American wine industry, Jake and Clair bought an old winery in the Napa Valley, and they had managed to survive Prohibition through the manufacture of sacramental wine, first for a handful of Orthodox synagogues in San Francisco, and subsequently for most of the synagogues in California and for a good many of the Catholic parishes. This had brought them to a modest prosperity, yet even with the repeal of Prohibition there was no great demand for wine. While Prohibition appeared to increase the national consumption of hard liquor, wine drinking became only a memory — and those who remembered now preferred the imported wines.

The winery, called Higate, lay in the Napa Valley a few miles north of

Oakville, nine hundred acres on the eastern slope of the hills, and now, driving to the Levy home in Sausalito, Sam Goldberg wondered, as he had so often in the past, why Sarah Levy did not accept Jake's invitation to live there, where there were three children, winery workers, life, and excitement, instead of in the huge Spanish Colonial house where she was utterly alone. As she so often told him, she would not inflict herself on her children. But what else were children for, Goldberg wondered. He had no children of his own. If he only had, how quickly he would accept such an invitation!

He decided that today he would raise this question with her, pointing out that for a vital woman of fifty-four years to bury herself here was both self-destructive and wasteful; but it was Sarah who brought up the subject of Higate. Clair had telephoned just this morning, asking her mother-in-law to drive up to the Napa Valley — if Goldberg were willing — and for both to spend the afternoon and stay for dinner.

"In which case, Sam," Sarah said to

him after she had greeted him and kissed him, "you will be my date."

"Nonsense. You are too young to be having dates with a man of sixty-six. Visits, that's one thing. Dates, no. Damnit, Sarah, you're a healthy, beautiful woman — too beautiful to waste away here doing nothing."

She smiled and took his arm. When she smiled, there was a reflection on her drawn face of the woman he had known twenty years before. Her pale yellow hair had turned white, but her eyes were the same bright blue and her figure had not changed. "I would always tell Martha," she said, "never to contradict a man who said she was beautiful. Of course, Martha was, wasn't she, Sam?"

"Very beautiful, yes."

"And I don't do nothing. I read. I knit. I tend my roses. I cook, sometimes."

"And you weep for Martha."

"Yes."

"Which is precisely what living alone here does to you. The past is over. You must —"

"Sam." She stopped him. "We won't

60

talk about where I live or why. Will you drive me to Higate?''

''Of course.''

In the car, Goldberg said, rather casually, ''Would you like to guess who walked into my office day before yesterday?''

''No. I don't like to guess things. But I would like to know.''

''Barbara.''

''Barbara? Barbara who?''

''Barbara Lavette. Danny's daughter.''

''No!''

''Yes. Yes, my dear Sarah.''

''She just walked in? Unannounced?''

''Yes.''

''Why? If you want to tell me?''

''I'm not sure I know why. She asked questions about what happened when Jean took over, but I'm not at all sure that's what brought her. I think she was reaching out.''

''What is she like?'' Sarah asked curiously. ''It's strange, isn't it, Dan's daughter, and Danny was like a brother to Mark, and I think I saw her only once, when she was a little child.''

"Splendid woman — tall, like Jean, looks a little like Jean — not as beautiful, but then, who is?"

"Indeed. She's twenty, isn't she?"

"Yes. Finished her second year at Sarah Lawrence College in the East. Now she's working."

"Where?"

"No wages. She's a volunteer at the Marine Workers' soup kitchen on Bryant Street."

"Barbara Lavette!"

"I thought that would get you," Goldberg said, smiling. "The world turns, doesn't it, Sarah?"

"It surely does."

Long, straight, narrow, a gentle fold between low green hills that only now and then become mountains, the Napa Valley is unique, even in a place like California, where there are a hundred thousand valleys and canyons; for of all the places where grapevines grow in America, only the name of Napa is absolutely synonymous with the word "wine." It is an old place only in terms of California, where nothing of European vintage is really old, and the first vines were planted there in 1840, by a man named George Yount. Yet, in the European tradition, most of the early wineries, established for the most part by German and Italian immigrants, were built of stone rather than wood, substantial stone buildings that very soon were covered over with broadleaf ivy, and if not actually ancient, they certainly gave the impression of being so. It was such a cluster of stone buildings that Jake Levy and his wife bought when he returned from service in World War I, and when they bought the place, it was little better than an antique and useless ruin.

Now, fourteen years later, the aspect of the place was quite different. The old buildings had been repaired and refurbished. The hillsides, abandoned during the first years of Prohibition, were now planted in gently curving and contoured rows of vines. Hedges and plantings graced the shapeless stone houses, and half an acre of garden was given over to the growing of table vegetables.

Goldberg turned off Highway 29 onto a dirt road that twisted over the hills to the stone-pillared iron gates of the winery. As he got out of the car and helped Sarah out, Jake, Clair, and their three children and two dogs came to meet them. Jake was a tall, heavyset man of thirty-five, his wife, a year younger, long-limbed, freckled, with a great head of orange-colored hair, a sunburned, good-looking woman indifferent to her good looks. The two boys, Adam, twelve, and Joshua, ten, were small, grinning replicas of their mother, carrot-topped and freckled, and Sally, the youngest, eight years old, had the pale eyes and flaxen hair of her grandmother.

With a touch of sadness and not without envy, Goldberg observed the warmth and excitement of the family as they greeted Sarah. He stood apart from the scramble of embraces, chattering children, and barking dogs. It was mundane and sentimental to see himself in relation to this, but he was a sentimental man. Then Clair noticed how woebegone and forgotten he appeared, and she went to him and took his arm and told him how delighted they all were to see him.

"It's been years," she said. "You and mother are all that's left to us of the old times."

"I wouldn't recognize the place. It reeks with prosperity."

"An illusion," Jake said. "Are you tired, either of you?"

"Not at all," Sarah replied.

"Why an illusion?" Goldberg asked.

"Because Americans have forgotten how to drink wine. If we were making whiskey, we'd be rolling in money. All the decent wine during Prohibition was smuggled in from France, and only the rich could afford it. Now they don't want our domestic wine."

"Which is as good or better than what they make in Europe," Clair added.

"Well, sometimes. Look, let me give you a tour of the place, Sam. I'll practice on you. Clair has a notion that we should open the winery to the public on weekends and let people taste our product and build up demand that way. It might just work if we could convince the big wineries to do

65

it, but we're too small to make much difference. We're going to have a valley meeting next week and propose it, but who knows? Anyway, I'll practice on you and mother."

"I've seen it," Sarah said. "Take Sam. I'll help Clair inside."

Jake led Goldberg off toward the stone winery buildings, the children trailing curiously. He pointed up at the sloping hillsides. "There are our newest plantings. Pinot Noir. Of course you might say that Zinfandel is endemic to this valley and it's what we're famous for. But I tasted Pinot Noir in France that was like the wine of the gods, and Clair and I decided that we'd produce a wine as good or better, and by golly, I think we have. You'll taste it later. We started with five hundred vines, and now we've got the best stand of Pinot Noir in the valley. Come back at the end of the summer when the grapes are ripe, and you'll have a treat, Sam. We don't irrigate up there. Some of the growers do, but for my money, you get a better grape if you make the vines fight for moisture. If you irrigate, the vines are loaded with grapes, and for your greed there's a poorer quality." Jake paused. Goldberg was regarding him in amazement. "What is it, Sam?" he asked.

"Your passion, sonny. I'm astonished."

"Why? Wine is a passionate thing. God Almighty, Sam, do you remember how we scrimped and starved and worked to have this place? It's my whole life. It's like I know every vine up there on that hillside by name and number and character."

Trudging alongside them, young Adam said, "He does, Mr. Goldberg."

"You've inoculated them," Goldberg observed dryly.

"Higate has. I sometimes try to think of what it means to grow up in a place like this and have Clair for a mother."

"You have a pretty damn good mother of your own."

"I'm not selling her short, Sam, only making a point. It's too hot to climb the hill and look at the vines. Come in here," he said, indicating the entrance to the largest of the stone buildings.

As he stepped out of the hot sun, the cool darkness blinded Goldberg at first, and he paused to let his eyes adjust and to breathe deeply of the cold, sour-smelling air.

"That's the smell," Jake said. "At first it's strange. Then it becomes a kind of perfume. What do you drink, Sam?"

"Scotch whisky."

"Of course. How long is it since you tasted a really fine wine?"

"I suppose the last time Jill and I were in France. Nineteen twelve. I'm not a wine drinker, Jake."

"You will be. Careful here." Followed by his three children, who were apparently fascinated by the very fat, bespectacled man who ambled after their father, Jake led the way down a set of stone steps into a cavernous cellar. There were rows and rows of wine — in bottles, in small kegs, and in large barrels. The air was cool and damp and heady with the musty smell of wine.

"The aging room. Over there" — pointing to the big barrels — "the sacramental wine. That's our bread and butter, Sam, if you can think of it that way. That's how we started and survived during Prohibition, first with old Rabbi Blum's synagogues and then with the churches. Now we produce about twenty thousand barrels of sacramental wine a year, port and Malaga, we call it, and not a bad imitation of the real thing. It's good, decent wine, if you like sweet wine. I don't. We don't grow the grapes for this stuff. We buy them down in Fresno. You'd think, with an assured market for twenty thousand gallons, we'd make money."

"Do you?"

"Not a nickel. Oh, we did make money back in twenty-eight and twenty-nine, but this Depression knocked the bottom out of prices. We break even. Come back at the end of the summer, and you'll find twenty men working here and in the fields. We meet the payroll and we're satisfied."

He pointed to the racks of bottled wine. "That's the Pinot Noir, the love of my life. That is wine," he said slowly, almost reverently, Goldberg thought. "We do about a thousand gallons a year, and we lager it, age it six months to a year in the bottle, laying it that way with the cork down. The cork stays wet and the wine

69

breathes and lives."

"Good heavens, it's become a religion with you."

"It tends to. Religion and wine have never been too far apart. That's how we pay our bills. Let me show you the rest of it — this is only the end product."

Jed led Goldberg from room to room, past the crushers, the fermenting vats, the storage tanks, and into the bottling plant.

"All this to make a glass of wine," Goldberg said wearily.

"This and more. Instinct and luck. Without that, you're doomed. Maybe we don't have the instinct, but we've had a lot of luck. Over here, Sam."

He led the way to the end of the bottling room, where half a dozen uncorked, labeled bottles stood. "Our tasting room," he explained. "We don't have a real one yet. We will someday. These are all the Pinot Noir. We test them as they age. Open them, and then let them breathe for a few hours." He poured two glasses of the dark red wine. "Try it."

Goldberg drank the wine slowly. The

last wine he had tasted was from the bottle Gino had brought to the table in the restaurant as his gift to the diners. He remembered the raw, flat taste of it. This wine was like liquid velvet, dry, slightly nutty, with a gentle, haunting fragrance.

"I don't know much about wine," Goldberg said.

"Do you like it?"

"If I knew anything about wine, I'd say it's pretty damn wonderful."

"You bet your sweet patooties. That wine, Sam, is going to conquer the world one day."

Willis Mackenzie, chief trainer at the Menlo Circle Club, at Menlo Park on the Peninsula, was something of an expert in the mores and ordinary habits of the rich and the children of the rich — in particular as they related to horses. Horses, as Mackenzie saw it, could be grouped with liquor, gambling, and desultory sex; they were less an indulgence than an addiction, less an interest than a demanding status symbol, to the rich of San Francisco and the

Peninsula what the automobile was to the upper middle class — and even more specifically so since the onset of the Depression.

To this, however, there were a few exceptions, people who loved horses passionately. Mackenzie, a tall, hard-faced man of forty-five years, separated such people from the others with a reluctant smile. He was a bitter man, who hated the people he served, who hated and resented the rich, and who desired and resented their well-kept, carefully groomed women. He put Barbara Lavette in the special category of those who loved and understood horses, and on this day, when she informed him that she wished to sell Sandy, her seven-year-old chestnut mare, he looked at her thoughtfully and then suspiciously asked her why.

"I have my reasons, Mac."

"Well, she's a damn good horse, a good bloodline on both sides. You got the papers?" he asked, wondering meanwhile how much he could pick up on the deal. A local deal was a problem. If he sold her outside the county, he could possibly pick up a few hundred.

"Right here," Barbara replied, taking them out of her purse.

"I didn't mean right now. You know there's an auction in August."

"I don't want to wait. I want to sell her now."

"Well," he said slowly, "I got a lady at Flintridge in Pasadena. She's looking for a good gentle mare."

"That would take time, wouldn't it?"

"A week or so. She'd want to see the horse."

"No. I want to sell her today."

"Well — well, now there's something, Miss Lavette. You don't just sell a horse like you sell a pair of pants. You got to find a buyer and you got to talk him around to it. You got to give him a run on the beast. No one buys a pig in the poke."

"Sandy's not a pig in the poke. I know you buy horses sometimes, Mac. What will you give me for Sandy?"

"You want to sell her to me?"

"I want to sell her today."

Mackenzie stared at her thoughtfully for a long moment. They were standing next to her car, a 1933 Ford station wagon, at the edge of the dirt road that led to the stables. Mackenzie looked at the car, ran a hand over the fender, and asked her, "What happened to your Buick?"

It was none of his damn business, Barbara thought. He was moving in. The careful wall of separation had collapsed. He had decided that she was in trouble, and he was breaking ground.

"Do you want to buy Sandy?" she said. She had no intention of talking about the car; there would be trouble enough with the car thing when her mother returned. The Buick convertible had been a gift from her mother on her eighteenth birthday, but it was nothing she could drive to the soup kitchen on Bryant Street, no way to explain a car like that, and anyway, the luggage compartment was too small for her purposes. She had sold it and bought the Ford station wagon.

"Let's go over to the barn and have a look at her."

"No. I don't want to see Sandy again. Will you buy her?"

"I'm just the trainer here, Miss

Lavette. I ain't got the kind of money you find in the club. I suppose I could buy her.'' He rubbed his chin and thought about it. "I'll give you four hundred for her.''

"Oh, no. You must be kidding. The saddle alone cost a hundred and fifty.''

"Throwing the saddle in?''

"Sandy's worth a thousand. You know that.''

He shook his head. "That's too rich for my blood. Throw in the saddle, and I'll give you five hundred.''

"Why, Mac? You know what Sandy's worth.''

"I told you, I'm just the trainer. You want to wait a week or two, this lady from Flintridge might give you seven hundred. Wait for the auction, maybe you'll get that much, maybe more.''

"Will you pay me cash? Today?''

"I'll pay you cash,'' he said.

Barbara drove north from Menlo Park, tears running down her cheeks and five hundred dollars in her purse. "I will not weep over a horse,'' she told herself. "I will not, I will not." Or was she weeping for herself and out of her own fear? After all, she had been nine months without Sandy, and giving very little thought to the animal, if the truth be told. It was the act of selling her, and selling her to that miserable Mackenzie, that chilled her — even more than the act of selling her car, her emerald pin, and her gold bracelet. In time they would all return, her mother, John Whittier, and her brother Tom. Her mother noticed everything. She would come directly to the point. "Why, Barbara, did you sell that beautiful Buick roadster and buy that wretched Ford?" The fact that it was a very special and splendid birthday gift made the surreptitious sale even more heinous. "And where is your bracelet? And what else have you sold? And what kind of trouble are you in?" Barbara was a poor liar and badly versed in the art. She would simply tell the truth, and then whatever might happen would happen.

She told herself that she had done nothing wrong. She had acted out of love and compassion. Or had she? Or was the action taken out of loathing for her own way of life and everything that had surrounded her? If so, it was a very sudden loathing. A few months ago she had been a reasonably content college student. Then she had returned to a home that wasn't hers, yet now she wondered whether even the house on Russian Hill had ever been hers in any real sense. Or is any home of the parents the home of the child? Now she was pitying herself, and that sort of thing simply disgusted her. Her mother's friends pitied themselves; she could remember overhearing their conversations, recalling her own annoyance at the wives of millionaires who pitied themselves in the America of the nineteen thirties.

She hadn't gone to Bryant Street by accident. She loved the waterfront, the Embarcadero, the docks, the fishing boats, the big steamers, the freighters, the great luxury liners. It was all part of the mythology of her strange childhood, of the father she had never really known. This had been his place, where he started as a hand on his own father's fishing boat, out of which he built his empire of wealth and ships. And then he left it, abandoned it; and not comprehending that, Barbara made a quixotic act of nobility out of it. To have and surrender, to find something real, to sacrifice meaningfully — all this raced around inside her tinged with romantic dreams, novels she had read, discussions with her friends at college, and piled childishly into a confusion and despair at odds with her basically cheerful nature.

And then one day she stood outside the soup kitchen on Bryant Street, just stood there and watched as the striking longshoremen lined up to be fed. She had a vivid imagination, and her romantic notion of the working class had been shaped mainly by the novels of Jack London and Upton Sinclair. All of which led to her meeting Dominick Salone.

He had paused next to her and said, "Lady, is something wrong?"

He was her own height, skinny, the dark flesh of his face drawn tightly over the bones, deepset, dark intense eyes, a small nose, a head of black, unruly hair, and, curiously in one so young, a nest of wrinkles at either end of his wide mouth. He couldn't have been more than twenty-three or twenty-four. He wore blue jeans and a stained green woolen windbreaker over a T-shirt.

She just stared at him.

"Because you're crying, lady."

"I am not."

"Sure as hell you are. We got sympathizers, lady, but mostly they don't cry."

"I'm not crying."

"O.K., O.K." He shrugged and turned away.

Barbara touched her cheeks. They were wet. Then she called after him. "Mister!"

When he turned around, she was wiping her face with a handkerchief. He stood there, staring at her, and then she walked over to him.

"Could I ask you a question, mister?" she asked uneasily.

"My name's Nick. Nick Salone. Don't call me mister."

She was taken totally aback by his reply. She stood silent for a moment or two, and he said, "Well?"

"My name's Bobby."

"All right, Bobby, ask."

"What?"

"You said you wanted to ask me a question."

She nodded at the kitchen. "How do you run it? I mean, where does the food come from?"

"What's with you, sister? You work for a newspaper or something?"

"You're suspicious of me."

"You're damn right. I'm suspicious of anyone who looks like you."

"What do you mean? How do I look?"

"Oh, Christ," he said. "Let it go. You want to know where the food comes from? It used to come from the union funds, but that's gone. Washed out, used up. So it comes from wherever we can beg, borrow, or steal it."

"Oh." She said, almost primly, "Would it be all right if I brought you some food — as a contribution? I wouldn't be hurting anyone's feelings?"

"Hurting our feelings?"

"I don't know about these things," she said lamely.

"No, you wouldn't be hurting nobody's feelings."

"Where would I bring it?"

He pointed to an alley alongside the storefront. "That leads back to the kitchen. Just bring it to the kitchen."

That was how it began. Walking the few blocks to a grocery store, it occurred to Barbara that here she was, in the twenty-first year of her life, yet never before had she entered a food store to buy anything more than a bag of pretzels, or cookies, or sausage for one of their late-night feasts in the dormitory back at school. She had never gone out to buy food as food, food to feed people who were hungry. Now she had about twelve dollars in her purse, and she had not the faintest notion of how much food one could buy for twelve dollars.

The man behind the counter in the small grocery store had a walrus mustache and wet blue eyes. It was half an hour past noon, and there were no other customers in the store. The proprietor watched her, appraising her dubiously. Finally, when she continued to stand there without speaking, he said, "We don't sell no cigarettes, miss."

"I don't want cigarettes." She had read somewhere that beans possess a fine balance of nourishment, and in any case, beans and working people made some connection in her mind. "How much are beans?" she asked.

"Beans?"

"Yes, beans."

"What kind of beans? I got lima beans, navy beans, pea beans, kidney beans, Mexican beans — what kind?"

"I don't know," she said unhappily.

"You ever cooked beans?"

"No."

He was studying her suspiciously. They were all suspicious of her. She acted wrong, she looked wrong, she dressed wrong; and she was becoming acutely aware of this. Nevertheless, she pursued her course doggedly.

"If you were to cook beans, what would you cook?"

"I don't give cooking lessons."

"What are navy beans?" she asked
desperately.

He reached down and held up a handful.
"These."

"All right. Give me twelve dollars'
worth."

He stared at her.

"What's wrong?" she asked.

"Lady for twelve dollars you can buy a
hundred-pound sack."

"I can?"

"That's right."

"Then give me ten pounds." Something
recognizable caught her eyes. "How much
is that salami?" she asked, pointing to
where a row of them hung behind the
counter.

"Twenty cents a pound. Each link is
five pounds."

Loaded down with all the food she could
carry, she made her way back to the soup
kitchen on Bryant Street, went into the
alley and through the open kitchen door,
where she set down the food, and fled.
After that, two days passed before she
could gather sufficient courage to return.
Meanwhile, she informed herself. She

went down to the kitchen of the house on Pacific Heights and addressed herself to Mrs. Britsky, the Polish cook who presided over the place, asking her where most of the food money was spent — with the excuse that she was preparing a paper for her return to school.

"Meat, meat," Mrs. Britsky replied emphatically. "There's a Depression, but that don't mean they give it away. Always, your mama wants French style. Entrecote, fifty cents a pound; saddle of lamb, fifty-five cents; leg of lamb, forty-nine cents. You can die from such prices."

"But isn't there cheaper meat?"

"Cheaper meat for the Whittiers, go on!"

"Not for them. Just for my information. What would a poor family do? What would they buy?"

"You can buy beef heart for ten cents a pound, good meat if you cook it right, chuck for twenty-five cents, pork for thirty cents, breast of lamb for twelve cents."

"Where do you buy it?"

"Darling, in a butcher shop, where else?"

Afterward, Barbara wondered whether any of it would have happened had she not been alone in the big house, with her mother and John Whittier and Tom away in the East. Partly, it was a game that had possessed and intrigued her, and that she found so much more exciting than the parties she was invited to and the dates with boring, empty-headed young men; and in another part it was her own vendetta against John Whittier, who owned half the cargo ships that made San Francisco their home port; and in still another part it was her quick, romantic sense of compassion and pity.

For her return to the soup kitchen, she bought a cheap, imitation leather purse and wore an old sweater, a plaid skirt, and brown loafers. She brought twenty pounds of soup meat. She knew that she was playing a game and that it was a little girl game, that she had hidden herself behind a sort of Halloween mask, but that knowledge did not make the game less exciting. Dominick Salone was there that

85

time, sitting on a fruit box and peeling potatoes, and after his initial surprise at seeing her, he grinned. The kitchen was a makeshift affair at the back of the store, and the cooking was done on an old coal stove. There was one other woman in the place, a stout Mexican woman whose name was Irma, and four men besides Salone, all of them longshoremen. They made a big fuss over the meat, and Salone introduced Barbara to the others. That was when she told them her name was Winter. She had also invented her own cover story, that she was a bookkeeper in the big L & L Department Store, and that she worked the four-to-twelve-midnight shift, closing the books for the day's sales. The L & L store on Market Street had been founded by her father, Dan Lavette, and his partner, Marcus Levy, and she had at least a vague knowledge of its operation. The job, as she invented it, accounted for her free time during the day, and she explained the money she spent for food as money collected from workers at the store.

That day she offered to help Dominick

peel potatoes, and afterward she shared the beef stew that fed the striking longshoremen. That was the beginning.

It was a beginning threaded through with illusions. One illusion concerned the nobility of the longshoremen. She invested them with qualities that she felt she had found in her father, uprightness, quietude of suffering, morality. Another illusion concerned Dominick Salone, again as a variant of her father, who had started as a fisherman and had married a daughter of the Seldons of Nob Hill. Still another illusion concerned what she felt was a cloak of invisibility that she had thrown about herself, making the game of being another person with another life and background all the more enticing. The relationship with Salone had gone no further than their exchanges in the kitchen and then one day he walked with her down to the docks at the end of Townsend Street and pointed out Harry Bridges to her. Bridges, leading the strike, was Salone's hero, not a "phony," not "some lousy smart aleck" making a career out of the labor movement, but a plain longshoreman like himself. "The best goddamn man I ever knew in my life," Salone said. "There's nobody else like Limo, nobody."

"Why do you call him Limo?" Barbara asked.

"He's a limey, from Australia."

Looking at Bridges, Barbara realized how much like Dominick Salone he was, skinny, the same height, a narrow hatchet face, large pointed nose, dark hair that was combed flat over his head, held tight in the wind by Vaseline — contrasting both of them with the boys she knew in what was still called in the city the "Nob Hill set," the tall, well-fleshed, well-fed, athletic young men who kept horses at Menlo Park and sailed their boats on San Francisco Bay.

"You think a lot of Bridges, don't you?"

"I told you — the best man I ever knew."

They walked along in a world that was only a few miles from her home, yet another world entirely, looking at ships that her stepfather and her mother owned, ships tied to the docks and walled off by

88

the lines of bitter-faced pickets. Salone talked slowly, throwing out the words in bits and pieces, sometimes glancing at her, but making no move toward her, no advances, not even taking her hand.

As for what she felt about him, if anything at all beyond the curiosity his strangeness and difference aroused in her, Barbara simply did not know. And now, weeks later, driving north from Menlo Park after she had sold her horse and wept for the horse and for herself, she still knew no more of the reality of this thing into which she had plunged. She remembered Oscar Wilde's story "The Happy Prince," about the gold- and jewel-encrusted prince whose statue loomed high over some European city, and the sparrow who brought the prince stories of poverty and suffering. Each time, the prince surrendered a bit of gold or a jewel to be sold to ease the misery of the poor — until finally only the leaden core of the statue remained. She made the comparison with herself, and then was wise enough and sane enough to burst into laughter at her own sentimentality.

"What a dreadful, impossible ass I am!" she said aloud. "I don't blame mother for losing patience with me."

She was honest with herself to recognize that in selling everything of value she owned — jewels, trinkets, car, and now the horse — she had experienced more satisfaction and plain excitement than ever before in her life. It was really a very easy game. She had never known hunger, never wanted for money to exist, and each night she went home to the great barn of a mansion on Pacific Heights.

At the age of seventeen, Joseph Lavette was six feet and one inch in height and weighed one hundred and eighty pounds. The coach of the football team at University High in Westwood in Los Angeles singled him out and pressed him to try for the team. Joseph refused. He was a gentle, soft-spoken boy, introverted and not very physical, in spite of his large, heavily muscled frame. The coach, loath to relinquish what he considered a prime physical specimen, went into a lecture on the natural football abilities of the

American Indian. It was an understandable error. With his black, slightly Oriental eyes, his straight black hair, and his brown skin, Joe might well have been taken for an Indian; and Lavette, a French-Italian name, might well have been something out of the Northwest.

"I'm not an Indian," he said. "I'm Chinese. It doesn't work the same way. We make rotten football players. Anyway, I just haven't got the time."

"With a name like Lavette?" the coach snorted.

"My father is Italian. My mother is Chinese."

The time he hoarded so preciously was spent with books and with his grandfather, Feng Wo. He was a voracious reader, and he consumed everything he could get his hands on, almost without discrimination. As for his grandfather, two years before this, Feng Wo had decided that although he himself would live out his life on this land of the barbarian, it by no means meant that his grandson must of necessity grow up as a barbarian. Whereupon he

91

raised the subject quite formally and very politely at the family dinner table, stating that if Mr. Lavette agreed, he would like to teach his grandson, Joseph, to read, write, and to speak that most ancient and commendable of all languages, called Mandarin. Being Chinese, Feng Wo did not ask for the opinion or consent of either May Ling, Joseph's mother, or Joseph himself.

"Chinese! Are you kidding?" Dan said. "In the twenty-five years since you first came to work for me, I never learned more than ten words of Chinese, and that includes being married to May Ling. Nobody can learn Chinese."

"Except five or six hundred million Chinese," May Ling said sweetly. "And that includes myself. Father taught me Mandarin, and I picked up enough Cantonese and Shanghainese to get along in that as well. So *sa qua trey bun.*"

"What the devil does that mean?"

"Best left unsaid," Feng Wo told him. "My daughter has many bad habits."

"Why don't we ask Joe how he feels about it?" Dan said.

"I like the idea," Joe said.

"Oh, not so quickly," May Ling put in. "You really don't know what you're getting into, Joe. If father's going to teach you to read and write, it means learning about five thousand ideographs — pictures, symbols. It's picture writing, you know. Not like our alphabet at all."

"Then that does it," Dan said. He had never completed high school himself. Most of what education he possessed had come from May Ling, out of books she had persuaded him to read and out of the gentle flow of her knowledge that he had absorbed almost without knowing it. Nevertheless, he was fanatically eager for his son to be educated, well educated. The drive to do what you do better than anyone else was still present in him. "Where's his schoolwork? Where is anything else? And who is he going to talk Chinese to?"

"To me," May Ling said gently. "To my mother and father — and who knows who else? Why don't we let him decide?"

"I could try it," Joe muttered uncertainly.

A year later, he was able to write a two-page letter to Barbara at Sarah Lawrence, which she exhibited proudly to her friends and which was translated for her, not by any member of the faculty, but by a Chinese laundryman in Yonkers.

Now, early in June of 1934, Joseph Lavette came home and informed his mother and father that he had been chosen to give the valedictory address at the commencement exercises of his high school. Dan, who was still in his work clothes, who had picked up May Ling at the library only a few minutes before, listened to his son in silence, nodded, and then went up the stairs to his room. Joseph stared at his mother.

"Is he angry at me? Isn't he pleased?"

"Of course he's pleased." She threw her arms around Joseph and kissed him. "He's as pleased and proud as I am. It's a wonderful thing."

"Then why —?"

"Give it a little time, Joe. He's a strange man. I think this is the most wonderful thing that ever happened to him, but he can't cope with it."

"Why? I didn't ask for it, but God, I

wanted to please him. I thought he'd be excited —"

"Don't say any more. Not now. One day we'll talk about your father. He was too long away from you. The Chinese have an old saying that unless a man is to be doomed, sooner or later he must turn to himself and ask the question of why he exists. And find the answer. Your father tries, desperately. He's not like any other man I ever knew. Do you understand me?"

"I don't think so."

May Ling went upstairs to the bedroom. Dan was standing in front of the window, looking out.

"Well, Danny?"

He turned to her. "I hurt him, didn't I?"

"He'll understand."

"Do you?"

"Perhaps."

"I didn't know what to say. There was nothing I could put into words."

"It's not so astonishing, Danny. He's a bright boy, and he worked hard. He's well liked. But whatever he does, he feels it falls short of what you expect from him."

95

"My God, does he feel that?"

"I think so."

"He's my whole world," Dan said.

"He shouldn't be," May Ling said, a note of asperity in her voice. "You're only forty-five years old. How can he be your whole world? He has his own life to live, and so have you. Did he ever tell you what he wants to do? Did you ever talk about it? Did you ever really sit down and talk to him?"

"What does he want to do?"

"He wants to be a doctor. He doesn't think we can afford it."

"We damn well can!"

"Then why not start by telling him that?"

Leona Asquith, Jean's aunt, was seventy-two years old. She was a widowed lady of moderate wealth — moderate if one excluded her house on Beacon Hill, where the eighteenth-century and nineteenth-century furniture and paintings were both authentic and priceless. Her living room held an unfinished Athenaeum Washington, which some experts held to be prior to the Stuart Washington in the Boston museum, and in her library there were two authenticated Vandykes. Jean, who had already gained a national reputation as a sponsor and patroness of the Ashcan School of American painting, and who was one of the first eager buyers of John Sloan, Kuniyoshi, Reginald Marsh, George Biddle, and so many others, had no real interest in acquiring early American paintings for herself, but she did dream of a coup whereby she could bring the Asquith collection to a San Franciso art museum. This was one of the reasons she would go out of her way to spend time in Boston with a woman who regarded California as only slightly less barbaric than a wilderness to the south known as Texas.

Her husband, John Whittier, on the other hand, loved Boston, at least the circle in Boston in which they moved, because its rigidity and folkways gave him a sense of comfort and belonging. At dinner in the Asquith house, the night before his departure for San Francisco, he expressed this and assured Mrs. Asquith that only the circumstances of the waterfront strike could make him cut short his visit. Jean and Tom were to stay for another week, much to Tom's annoyance.

"Oh, no," was his first reaction when she told him that she expected him to remain with her in Boston, to be her escort, and to be very charming to his Aunt Leona. "I am bored. I am fed up to the ears. Mother, I've done four years at Princeton. I've paid my dues. This is the dullest, dreariest place on earth."

Jean looked at him thoughtfully. He was tall, slender, blue eyes under straight brows, a shock of straight brown hair that he parted on one side, a wide mouth, and a long, thin nose — very good-looking in a lackadaisical manner, almost indolent. There was apparently nothing in him of Dan Lavette, nothing of many generations of Italian fishermen, and Jean couldn't decide whether that pleased or displeased her.

"This is the place of your ancestors. I should think you'd be curious. I've always loved Boston."

"I'm not curious."

"And you haven't paid your dues — not quite."

"Oh?"

"It cost us almost three thousand dollars — hospital bills, five hundred to the girl to keep her quiet, and bribing a district attorney. Altogether, quite disgusting, but otherwise you would not have graduated."

"My God, did John tell you?"

"Of course he did. I saw no reason why he should pay the costs."

"It was the one rotten scrape I got into. I admit I had too much to drink, and it happened. That's all. Someday I'll pay back the money."

"I'm sure you will," Jean said gently. "Meanwhile, a few weeks in Boston is not too much penance. You'll still have most of the summer before you go into the bank."

"Then that's decided, that I go into the bank? God damn it, don't I have one thing to say about it?"

"Yes. Certainly. What would you like to do with your life?"

"Do I have to do something with it right this minute? Can't I have a few months to think about it? You and John may imagine that I just bummed away my years at Princeton, and I know all the smart-alecky wisecracks about the eating clubs, but if you look at my marks, you'll see that I didn't do half bad. I didn't spend four years getting drunk."

"I know that, and I did look at your marks. Many times."

"I just don't see myself sitting in a bank eight hours a day."

"Tommy," Jean said, "one day, not too many years from now, you and your sister, Barbara, are going to be very rich. The stock that my father left in trust for you will amount to many millions. In effect, the two of you own the Seldon Bank, one of the largest financial institutions in America. You know that. It's not just money. Power goes with it, and some respect for the power and some knowledge of how to use it. That's all I mean. Take the rest of the summer to decide. I'm not pressing you. But meanwhile you can be very helpful."

"All right, I'll stick it out. And do what?"

"Aside from being my escort and enduring some dinner parties and a few visits to the Boston Museum of Fine Arts, I would like you to be very charming and delightful to your Aunt Leona. We're her closest relatives, and I want her collection of paintings. I intend to turn the house on Russian Hill into an art museum. I'm not sure that I want her paintings there. My own taste runs to other things. But they're invaluable, and having them would give me tremendous leverage."

Tom shook his head. "I don't understand that. If you don't like them —"

"I do like them. They're splendid. But I want to found a museum of modern art. I could give these to some established museum and trade off, and at the same time there would be a Seldon Gallery of these paintings. There are ways to do it. I'm tired of hearing about the Crockers. The name of Seldon is just as important."

"Our name's Lavette, mother — except that yours is Whittier now."

"And we're still Seldons. I'm not asking

101

any great task of you. Take Aunt Leona to lunch at the Copley Plaza. Be pleasant. That's all I'm asking."

"I suppose I can do that."

"I suppose you can."

Aunt Leona Asquith was delighted with the invitation. She came downstairs, where her great-nephew was waiting, wearing a dress of beige crêpe de Chine with white satin cording, a short cape of summer ermine draped over her arm against a possible chill, and a broad-brimmed, cream-colored Panama hat. Tom, like most men of his age, accepted older women without actually seeing them. Now, suddenly, he realized that his Aunt Leona had a very trim figure for her seventy-two years, and that once she must have been an exceptionally attractive woman.

"Dear boy," she said, once they were seated in the back of her chauffeur-driven Packard, "this is really very considerate of you. Oh, I know that your mother blackmailed you into it. Nevertheless, you are the most handsome escort I have had in years. Your mother, like so many

102

modern women, has found a substitute for sex. By the way, have you read Havelock Ellis?''

Bewildered, Tom shook his head. "No, I'm afraid not."

"A pity. You must. What was I saying? Yes, a substitute for sex. What do you think of John Whittier?"

"Mother seems to like him. She married him."

"He's a parody of what he appears to think Boston society is all about. Of course, he hasn't the faintest notion of what Boston is. Your great-great-grandfather, my grandfather, was in the rum trade with Jamaica. It was better than the slave trade, and it permitted his brother to be both wealthy and Abolitionist, and grandfather was a pillar of the Congregational church. Nevertheless, he had a black mistress in Jamaica, and according to the family mythology, he birthed five black children there — aside from his proper family here in Boston. By the way, do you ever see your father?"

Confused, taken aback, Tom replied

103

that he had not seen Dan Lavette since the divorce.

"Why?" his aunt asked pointedly.

"I don't know," Tom said uncertainly. "He was never very close to me."

"Do you like him?"

"I don't know. Barbara does. She saw him last year. He's living in Los Angeles —"

"Yes, with his Chinese mistress, whom he married. Good heavens, you talk as if you were John Whittier's son. I met Dan Lavette once. Don't mumble."

At the Copley Plaza, in the dining room, the headwaiter greeted Leona Asquith by name and kissed her hand. At the table, she said to Tom, "Do the ordering, Thomas. I think it ought to be broiled lobster for both of us. Whatever elements of civilization have crept into that West Coast of yours, lobster is something they do not have. We'll have a Chardonnay to go with it." She was slightly deaf, and like so many slightly deaf people, tended to make her already high-pitched voice even more strident. It embarrassed Tom to have her conversation overheard by the

104

tables around them.

"A substitute for sex, did I say that? Yes. She does it with those wretched pictures she collects, and being president of a bank. Thank heavens that's over. And now she wants my collection, and you are to be very charming to me."

"Oh, no, no. Not at all," Tom protested, dropping his voice as if pleading with her to drop hers.

"Don't mumble, Thomas. It's quite transparent, but then, people are transparent, all of us, although we all pretend to ourselves that we are well hidden. So you're trapped here and bored to tears."

"No. I'm not bored, Aunt Leona." Which was very much the truth. At the moment, he was nervous and bewildered, but not bored.

"You need a girl," she said flatly.

He stared at her.

"Well, you do like women, don't you?"

"Yes. Certainly."

"How long will you be here now?"

"Another week or so, I think."

"That's not time enough for anything.

Do you want a drink?"

"I think so."

"You do mumble so. Order a martini for each of us. A week, you said. Well, I know a very respectable lady who runs a bawdy house. I think I'll send you there."

"Oh no," he said to himself. "I am not hearing this. It's not happening."

"Yes," she said. "That's decided. It's what you need, and you'll stop looking so wretchedly sour. Now I want you to tell me about this John Whittier your mother married. Tell me all about him."

Barbara carefully backed her Ford station wagon into the alley on Bryant Street, then went into the kitchen and asked for help to unload. It was eleven o'clock in the morning on the third day of July in 1934, and already the makeshift stove was smoking hot, piled with pots of stew to feed anywhere from two hundred to five hundred men. The kitchen was dirty, steaming, the garbage cans overflowing and spilling onto the floor, with two longshoremen washing tin cups and bowls and arguing about a third man who was,

106

according to their definition, either a fink or a pimp. Dominick and another longshoreman by the name of Franco Guzie were slicing stale, three-day-old bread. Volunteers from the bakery workers' union bought the unsold bread, paying for it out of union funds, and delivered it twice a week to the various soup kitchens the maritime strikers had set up. Sometimes it amounted to several hundred loaves, sometimes only a few dozen.

Salone looked up as Barbara came into the kitchen. Guzie shouted for a little quiet. "What have you got, Bobby?" Dominick asked her.

She was looking at the garbage. "Don't you ever clean this place?"

"It gets done," he said. "Is that what you come for — to tell us the place stinks?"

"No. I have a load outside."

"Come on, Franco," Dominick said.

She led the two of them out to the station wagon. "Jesus Christ," Guzie whispered. "What the hell have you got there?"

"I was down on the Peninsula, so I picked it up off the roadside stands," Barbara said proudly. "A lot cheaper there than here. Two hundred pounds of potatoes, two hundred pounds of onions, two bushels of cabbage, two crates of carrots, a hundred pounds of squash, and five hams. I got the hams at Tulip Farm in Belmont. They wanted twenty-five cents a pound, and I got them down to twenty. What do you think of that?" She was pleased with herself, as eager for praise as she had been as a child doing something noteworthy and deserving.

"What do we do with smoked ham?" Dominick said sourly. "You can't put it in stew."

"Who says you can't?" Guzie demanded. "Gives the stew a flavor. God damn it, Bobby, this is a bonanza. You're some lady, kid, you're some lady. I wish we had ten like you, ten like you. Don't pay no attention to this punk."

After they had carried the food inside, Barbara parked her car. Then she came back to the kitchen, put on an apron, and began to clean up. She hated this kind of work, yet she took a perverse satisfaction in forcing herself to do it. Dominick had finished slicing the bread. He stood watching her as she swept the garbage together and stuffed it into the cans. The smell made her gag.

"Take the cans out of here," she said to him. "This shouldn't be here with the cooking. You know that."

"Now you're running the joint."

"What? Oh, don't be an ass, Nick."

" 'Don't be an ass.' That's real classy talk. I'm sorry, duchess. I beg your pardon."

"Knock it off," Guzie said, and he picked up the can and carried it out.

Fat Irma Montessa, the acknowledged boss of the kitchen, shouted at Barbara, "Bobby, you forget about the cleaning, because with these pigs here, you can't keep nothing clean. The feeders are here, and we got to start serving. You want to help me?"

At the front of the store, standing behind the table next to Irma who was ladling the stew into tin bowls, passing out the bowls to the line of strikers and adding bread and chili pepper for those who wanted it, Barbara said to her,

"What's come over Dominick?"

"Men turn lousy, sweetie. Up and down. It's in their nature. Too much strike."

"It's not like him."

"Sure it is. What do you expect from a guinea longshoreman?"

Barbara had never heard the expression before. She finished serving the meal. She had been up at six that morning to drive down to Belmont for the food, and by now the sour smell of the stew filled her with nausea, so she went out into the alley for a breath of fresh air. Dominick was there, puffing on a cigarette.

"You're in a lovely mood today," she said to him.

"Yeah."

"I didn't mean to call you an ass. I lost my temper."

"Who the hell are you?" he asked angrily.

"Who are you?"

"I'm a guinea longshoreman, name of Dominick Salone."

"That's the second time today I heard

110

that word," Barbara said. "What does it mean?"

"What word?"

"Guinea."

"Oh, Jesus Christ! You don't know what a guinea is, you don't know what a fink is, you don't know what a goon is. You give me a load of horseshit about working at L and L and collecting money, and you drive a car that nobody makes eighteen a week could afford, and you talk the way some pisspot society dame talks. You spend the day here and you tell me then you go out and put in an eight-hour shift at the store. That's bullshit, and you know it."

"What if it is?" Barbara said tiredly.

"I just don't like to be conned."

"What do you think I am? Some kind of labor spy?"

He threw away the cigarette and grinned. "If you are, they're scraping the bottom of the barrel."

"Thank you."

"I didn't mean it that way."

"I know you didn't. Look, Nick, nobody else here worries about who I am. Nobody else objects to my buying food, and

111

nobody else cares where the money comes from. Nobody even objects to the way I speak."

"Yeah."

"So?"

"So I'm crazy. Since the first time I seen you, I can't think of nothing else. Ah, shit!"

"That's expressive."

"I'm sorry. God damn it, you're not like any dame I ever knew. I didn't need this. You come in here with your heart bleeding, and you do your lady bountiful act, and then back to wherever the hell you come from —"

"Come on, Nick."

"Don't patronize me!" He turned on his heel and stalked back into the kitchen.

She started to follow him, then stopped herself and shook her head, and she stood there staring at the cracked asphalt of the alleyway. He was not playing a game. No one there was playing a game. "And I'm not," she pleaded to herself; but then, had she nothing to do with the fact that he was in love with her? A skinny, undernourished, uneducated Italian

112

longshoreman had fallen in love with her. A brief, romantic flow of imagery flashed into her mind — her father's conquest of her mother, the fishing boat captain from the wharf making his way up Nob Hill — and then she shivered and threw it off. The thought — which she had never actually entertained before — of being trapped down here in this bleak, dreary hopeless abyss of workingmen was not pleasant. She felt no more for Dominick Salone than she felt for Franco Guzie or any of the other longshoremen. He interested and intrigued her, and she had been direct and open with him. At first, the longshoremen had frightened her; they were different, they spoke another language, they wore old clothes, and very often they were rank with body odor. But then, after only a few days of working around the kitchen, she discovered that they were amazingly correct in their behavior toward her. They always apologized for strong language used in her presence, they forbore any of the sexual innuendoes that were commonplace among the set of her own class, and all in all, they treated her with respect. It had simply not occurred to her that Dominick or any of the others might become emotionally involved with her.

She stood there in the alley for a few more minutes, trying to decide whether to go back into the kitchen and talk to Dominick again. Then she decided that it was best to leave it alone at this point, and she walked to where she had parked her car, got into it, and drove back to the Whittier house on Pacific Heights. She was tired; she would spend the afternoon curled up in a chair reading a book.

Knox, the butler, opening the door for her, said, "Mr. Whittier would like to see you, Miss Lavette."

"Oh? When did he get back?"

"Just about an hour ago."

Barbara went into the breakfast room. John Whittier was sitting at the table, dining on bacon and eggs and reading a newspaper. He rose as she entered and kissed her perfunctorily on the cheek.

"Sit down, Barbara. Will you have some lunch?"

"I'll have coffee," she said.

"Help yourself. There's a pot on the teacart there. I thought we'd have a chat, just the two of us. I never subscribed to the myth that servants don't have ears. They damn well do, and big mouths also."

"Did you have a good trip?" Barbara asked, bringing her coffee back to the table.

"Good enough. The wretched train takes forever."

"And Tom and mother — are they well?"

"Well enough when I left them. Your mother is determined to work your Aunt Leona for those dreary pictures that adorn her house. Did you know about her scheme to turn Russian Hill into a museum?"

"She mentioned something about it in a letter."

Her conversation was listless. Whittier looked at her thoughtfully. "Are you well, Barbara?"

"Perfectly well. Just a little tired. I thought I'd spend the afternoon with a book."

"Well, that will be a change."

She looked at him, wondering what was coming now.

"Apparently it's the first afternoon you decided to spend at home."

"What does that mean?"

"According to Knox, you've been out each morning and back each night since we've been gone."

"Really. Is it part of Knox's job to spy on me?"

"He's the butler. It's his job to know what goes on in this house."

"Then you have a faithful servant. That should please you, John."

"I don't think that tone is called for, Barbara."

"And I don't think I have to account for my time," she said coldly. "Thank you for the coffee." She rose and started to leave.

"One moment, Barbara." She turned to him, trying to control herself, trying to repress the loathing she felt for him. "What happened to your car?" he asked.

"Why don't you ask Knox?"

"I did. He says that your Buick disappeared, and that now you're driving an old Ford station wagon."

"Then you have your answer. Now I'm driving an old Ford station wagon." With that, she grabbed her purse and rushed out of the room, through the house, and out the front door. The station wagon was still parked in the driveway, where she had left it. She got into the car and suddenly burst into tears. She cried for a while. Then she felt better, relieved of what had been pent up inside her. She dried her eyes, turned the ignition key, and started the car. As she left the driveway, she saw in her rearview mirror that Knox was standing at the door, watching her.

She had no destination in mind, no thought except a compelling desire never to return to John Whittier's home. She drove through the park, and she found herself on 19th Avenue, heading south.

Joe Lavette was curled up on his bed, reading, when Dan came into his room and sat down at the foot of the bed. He had rehearsed what he was going to say several times, and now he came directly to the point. "That day," he began, "when

117

you came home and told us that you had been made valedictorian of your class — that day something happened inside me. I can't explain it, and I can't explain to you why I couldn't say anything. I can only say to you that I was so damn proud that if I had stayed there or tried to talk about it, I would have just gone to pieces, and that's nothing that I wanted you or your mother to see. I couldn't explain that to you, and I couldn't explain it to your mother, either. I've led a strange life, Joe. You know about that. Did you ever wonder why I work as a hand on a fishing boat?''

Joe stared at him uncertainly. "Yes," he said at last.

"Why didn't you ever ask me?"

"I couldn't ask you something like that."

"You know," Dan said miserably, "I have to get up my courage to talk to you. Not just to talk to you. But to talk to you like this."

"Why? Why, pop?"

"I don't know. Jesus —" He stared at the bedspread and then looked up and met his son's eyes. "I love you so much. How

118

many times I wanted to say that, and I couldn't say it. I loused up fourteen years of your life. All the time when you needed me, I wasn't there. And now I feel so damned empty, hopeless."

Joe reached out and put his hand on his father's. "Pop," he said softly, "all that stuff about college and medical school — it's not important."

"It's important."

"No. No, it really isn't. I see you come in after eighteen hours on that boat, so tired you can hardly stand up — it breaks my heart."

"Oh, no. No. Look, kid, I'm not an old man. You must not feel sorry for me. God damn it, no! I won't have that! Do you know when my life began to make sense, not much sense, but some sense?"

Joe shook his head.

"When I got enough guts to do what I wanted to do, what I had to do, when I was able to walk out of that house on Russian Hill in San Francisco and throw it away and want no part of it. Being a fishing hand — that's all right. I had to breathe a little. I could have dug ditches or cleaned toilets. It would still let me breathe a little. So if you want to go to college and medical school, you go. If you want to dig ditches, dig ditches. As long as you know what you have to do. It took me too long to find out.''

After dinner that evening, after Joe had gone up to his room, leaving Dan and May Ling alone in the living room, May Ling asked Dan, ''What did you say to Joe?''

''We talked.''

''I'm glad. It changed you, both of you, I mean the way you are with each other.''

''You noticed that?''

''Wouldn't I?'' May Ling smiled.

''You're a damn smart Chinese lady.''

''Thank you, Danny. Not for deciding that I'm smart, but for talking to him. Are you going down to San Pedro tonight? It's such a cold, wet night. I can't bear the thought of your going out on that boat.''

''I'm not going.''

''Oh?''

''I asked Pete Lomas for a week off, without pay.'' When she made no comment, Dan said, ''We can afford it.''

''Of course we can.'' Then she added,

120

"We're not poor. It's time you had a vacation."

"I'm not taking a vacation."

"What is it, Danny?" she asked gently. "Do you want it again?"

"Do I want what?"

"The power and the glory."

"No. I want enough money to send the kid to medical school. Pete offered to sell me a half share in the boat. I don't want that, either. He's getting too old to fish. So am I."

"We have enough money. My father —"

"I won't take your father's money. It may not seem like it, but Joe is my son."

May Ling rose and walked over to him and kissed him. "Dear Danny," she said, "I love you very much. Do whatever you have to do."

"That's what I said to the kid."

"I suppose it's all you can say to anyone. Come to bed now."

They had started upstairs when they heard the car pull into the driveway. They paused, and then the doorbell rang.

"It's eleven o'clock," May Ling said. She waited on the staircase while Dan went down into the living room, turned on the lights, and opened the door. Barbara stood there, smiling wanly. Dan stared at her, trying to make a reference of time and place, and then she was in his arms. He held her tightly, wordlessly. May Ling came down and closed the door behind her.

Then Dan let go of her, and she turned to May Ling and took her hand in both of her own, and said, "Dear darlings, both of you. I can't believe I'm here. I drove all the way down here from San Francisco and never stopped for anything but gas, and I kept having the nightmare that you wouldn't be here and the house wouldn't be here, because nothing ever stays the way it is — and now I'm starved. I haven't eaten all day."

It was past midnight. They sat in the kitchen, Barbara and Dan and May Ling, and for an hour Barbara had eaten her fill and narrated the history of her life during the six weeks since she had left Sarah Lawrence College. "So here I am," she said, "and every day since I got back to California I told myself that I would come down here to see you, and that's simply the way it was. I sat in my car outside that hateful house, and then I began to drive, and I just kept on driving. I should have come before, but each day I worked in the soup kitchen, it became more and more the center of my existence, and now I won't go back to John Whittier's house. I'll never go back there. That's over."

"Do you have any money?" Dan asked her.

"That makes no difference," May Ling said quickly. "She doesn't need money to stay here with us."

"I have a hundred dollars or so in my purse. That's left over from what I got for Sandy. You do forgive me for that," she said to Dan. "It's rotten to sell a gift — she was so beautiful — but I had to. Anyway, I have an allowance of forty dollars a week. The bank takes care of that. They send it to me, or I can pick it up there."

"You're still under age," Dan said. "Jean could cut off the allowance."

"She wouldn't do that. Mother's not vindictive."

"To what end?" May Ling asked. "Barbara's old enough to live alone."

"It's not that simple. Jean is Whittier's wife, and sooner or later, someone's going to uncover Barbara at that soup kitchen. That will make one hell of a front-page story, and they'll both hit the ceiling. Are you going back there?" he asked his daughter.

"I have to," Barbara said. "I can't walk out of it now. As crazy as it sounds, my forty dollars a week and whatever else I add to it keeps that place going. Oh, they get other food, but not enough. You can't imagine how poor those men are, how hungry. I know the union has other kitchens, but this one is my own burden."

"Why?"

"I don't know. I keep asking myself that. I feel guilty, but why doesn't Tom feel guilty? No, it's not only guilt. It's because, because now everything is very real. I romanticize it, but believe me, daddy, I know where I am and I know what I'm doing. I don't look at it through rose-colored glasses. Those longshoremen are crude and ignorant and very often nasty, and I'm not even sure I like them or like being around them. But they're right, and they're fighting for their lives, and that waterfront is a filthy slave market — and I am not talking out of hearsay. For almost six weeks, I've been there and watched it and listened to them. Do you know what the shapeup is?''

Dan nodded.

"Of course you do. Well, they're not nature's noblemen. A lot of them are just drifters and plain bums, but they're human, and they work on the docks because there's no work anywhere else. Well, they shape up on the docks at dawn, even before six o'clock in the morning, and they stand there shivering in the cold until the foreman comes to hire his gang. And he takes those who kick back to him out of the pitiful few dollars they earn, and sometimes they don't pay in money but with a brass check, which the longshoreman has to cash in some wretched bar. And every bartender is a nickel man —''

"What's that?'' May Ling asked.

"It means that the bartender takes a

nickel out of every dollar's worth of the brass check he cashes, and he won't take the brass check unless the longshoreman buys a drink first, and the trick is to get them drinking. When it's over, they have nothing, and their wives and kids can starve. And each day it's the same, shape up and pray to God you'll be lucky enough to find a day of work, even for a brass check. And if they're lucky enough to be paid in real money, they can work nine or ten hours for four dollars. They talk to me. They tell me about men who have dropped dead from exhaustion. There's the loading hook, and they have to keep up with that hook, without even the time off to empty their bladders. You know, the people from the bakery union bring us their stale bread. I've seen longshoremen empty the tin bowls of stew we cook for them into tins cans they bring with them. All they eat is the two slices of bread each man gets. The rest goes home to feed their kids. So I'm not being romantic, am I? When I think of the Embarcadero now, I always think of it as they do, in one single phrase: the shithole of creation.

And the ships tied up there belong to John Whittier and my mother.''

''Suppose they belonged to me,'' Dan said. ''Some of them did once. How would you feel then?''

Barbara thought about it for a while. ''They were your ships once?''

''Some of them. I didn't use the shapeup. I used steady gangs. They worked better that way.''

''If they were your ships,'' Barbara said, ''I don't think I'd feel much different.''

''The point is that you're Jean's daughter and Jean is Whittier's wife. It has to explode. Do you want that?''

''I don't care.''

''What about college?''

''I don't know whether I want to go back. I really don't know.''

''I want you to go back,'' Dan said.

''Daddy, listen to me. I'm not the same, and I don't think I'll ever be the same again. I don't truly know who I am or what I want, but I can't imagine myself back there at Sarah Lawrence.''

''I think,'' May Ling said, ''that we're

all too tired to imagine anything properly. I think, Danny, you should call Whittier and tell him that Barbara is here, and then we should go to bed. We'll open a cot for you in the living room, Barbara. Is that all right?''

"I'm so tired I could sleep on the floor."

"Did you know," Joe said to Barbara, "that to read and write Mandarin properly, one must know at least five thousand ideographs?"

"Well, that letter you sent me at college —"

"Full of errors."

"Yes, that's what Mr. Ming said."

"Who's Mr. Ming?"

"A laundryman in Yonkers."

"Oh, no."

"But he was the only one who could translate it, Joe." She burst out laughing while he stared at her tragically. "Oh, I'm sorry, Joe." She threw her arms around him and held him as he tried to pull away from her. "No, I won't let go until you say you forgive me."

"O.K. But don't laugh."

"Only because you're trying so hard to impress me, and the fact is that I am enormously impressed. Valedictorian. Chinese. Mandarin. Medical school. You're so smart it terrifies me, and you're one of the few boys I know who is at least five inches taller than I am."

"You're laughing at me again."

"I am not."

They were in his grandfather's rose garden. There, in a space of a few hundred square feet, Feng Wo had created a controlled wilderness of more than thirty varieties of roses — hybrid teas, Chinese tea-scented roses, evergreen and Polyantha, and manicured hedges of rugosa backed by frames of burning red ramblers. Now, in the early morning, the wet blooms gave off a powerful, heady fragrance that made Barbara feel that she had indeed awakened into a kind of a dream world.

"Do you know," Joe said, "I saw you once long ago. I guess I was only ten years old. That would have made you thirteen. We were still living in San Francisco, and I walked all the way to the house on

Russian Hill and stood there, across the street.''

"Then you knew where we lived?''

"A kid knows everything. They don't understand that. I must have stood there for almost an hour, and then you came out and got into the car. A big Rolls. You had a chauffeur who wore a gray uniform. You were wearing a white fur coat, and you had long hair then. I thought you were the most beautiful thing I ever saw in my life. I think I fell in love with you, and I was very disturbed by the notion of being in love with my own sister.''

"That's the nicest thing I ever heard.''

"It's all crazy, Barbara. I can't get used to the idea. This is the third time in my life that I've seen you. It makes no sense. And now, if you don't go back to the Whittier place, what will you do?''

"How do you know I won't go back?''

"I sat on the stairs last night and heard the whole thing.''

"Why didn't you come down?''

"I don't know. I was in my pajamas. I don't know. I suppose it was none of my business, but I heard it all. I think you're great. I wish you'd stay here — at least for a while, at least long enough for us to get to know each other a little.''

"I'll come back. I promise you.''

"Don't get hurt. Please. Don't let anything happen to you.''

She kissed him impulsively. "You are absolutely darling, and I'm just glad that you're the way you are. Nothing will happen to me, Joe — except that I may grow up a little.''

A few minutes later, May Ling called them into the house for breakfast. They were all at the kitchen table together, except for So-toy, who was very old-fashioned and would not sit down until after the men were fed. Feng Wo surrendered his Oriental inscrutability and responded with unconcealed delight to this tall, lovely, rosy-cheeked woman who was his beloved Dan Lavette's daughter, and Dan himself sat there, entranced with joy that these two children of his were together in the same house at the same table, chatting so easily with each other. In May Ling's mind, Jean had always been the "snow lady,'' her own somewhat malicious definition. May Ling was a very wise and compassionate woman, and now she fought down any impulse to resent Barbara or to see in her anything more than a physical resemblance to her mother. It was not easy. She forced herself to be very gentle, very concerned, begging Barbara to remain with them for at least a few days.

"I have a small study," Feng Wo said, "which I really do not need. My daughter considers me a scholar because I have published some translations from the Chinese. Let us turn it into a bedroom. You will be very comfortable."

"That's so kind. Thank you," Barbara said. "But I must go back. I've taken on a job that may make no sense to any of you, but I must finish it."

"It makes a lot of sense to me," Joe said. "Only I wish you'd stay. Please stay, Barbara."

She left at ten o'clock that day, Wednesday, the fourth day of July. Dan walked out to the car with her. "I'm here," he said, "whenever you need me. I'm not much good at saying these things, but I love you very much. *Vaya con Dios*. And come back — soon."

Barbara drove north without hurrying. She was still wrapped in a dreamy, delightful sense of well-being, encased in the warmth of the family she had just left. Never in her own home had she experienced this same sense of family, of support, of plain, uncritical approval and admiration; and the excitement of finding a brother who was both a stranger and a blood relation was quite wonderful. She tried not to compare him to Tom, telling herself that it was unfair, yet the comparison inevitably entered her mind again and again.

She stopped for gas and for lunch at a roadside stand, and then she drove on. It was late afternoon when she reached the peninsula and began to compare prices at the roadside vegetable stands. She bought sacks of potatoes, onions, and carrots and four bushels of oranges. The kitchen workers had reacted with annoyance the first time she brought oranges. "What the hell good are they in stew?" But she persisted in her own campaign to get the longshoremen to take them home for the children, holding forth again and again on the virtues of vitamin C.

It was almost seven o'clock when she turned into the alley on Bryant Street, only to find that the soup kitchen was closed for the day. She parked her car near the St. Francis Hotel, locked the doors, and hoped that no one would break into it. Then she checked into the hotel, and having no luggage, she paid for her room in advance.

She called the Whittier house from her hotel room. Knox answered the phone, and when she asked for Mr. Whittier, she was informed that he was out for the evening. Knox added that Mr. Whittier had been quite disturbed by her absence the night before, despite Mr. Lavette's call.

"I want you to assure him that I am perfectly all right. I spent last night at my father's house in Los Angeles, and if my mother telephones, she is not to be alarmed. I will stop by the house sometime tomorrow."

Then she went downstairs to the coffee shop and ate two ham sandwiches, a glass of milk, and a piece of pie. She brought a newspaper back to her room, hoping to catch up with the progress of the strike, but once in bed, she found that the words blurred and that she couldn't keep her eyes open. By nine-thirty, she was sound asleep.

Barbara awakened with the first light of dawn in the hotel room, at about five o'clock in the morning. She felt wonderfully rested and refreshed, and at first she just lay in bed languidly, enjoying the adventure of being naked between the sheets in this strange hotel room, away from her home, free at least for the moment to do as she pleased when she pleased. Then she remembered her car, filled with food and parked on the street. She leaped out of bed, considered taking a shower, wavered, then darted into the shower, dried herself and her hair as best she could, swished soapsuds in her mouth in lieu of toothpaste, and then pulled on her clothes, shrugging away the fact that she had not changed in three days. She should have washed her underthings and stockings the night before. Well, she had forgotten. So much for that. The dark blouse, the cardigan sweater, and the plaid skirt were durable and quite clean. The saddle shoes she was wearing did not matter. She grabbed her purse and dashed out of the room.

The lobby of the hotel was empty except for a clerk, who dozed behind the desk. The restaurants had not yet opened. It didn't matter. She wasn't hungry, and there would be time enough to eat after she had unloaded her car at the kitchen. Usually it did not open until seven o'clock, but Barbara decided that she would drive her car into the alley and then sit there, guarding her load of food, until someone arrived to open the doors. She walked down Stockton to Market, and as she was crossing the street, a file of a dozen mounted police trotted by, their horses' hoofs making a strangely loud tattoo on the empty street. They looked at her strangely. A block away, there were two men. Otherwise, no one.

Her car was parked on 4th Street, and she breathed a sigh of relief to find it was untouched. It was a quarter after six. She got into the car and drove to Bryant Street and into the alley. There, to her surprise, the kitchen door was open, and the sound of men's voices came from inside. As she cut her motor, Guzie and Salone came out of the kitchen, and Salone called out to her, "God damn it, Bobby, where the hell have you been?" But there was no rancor in his voice, and evidently the squabble of the day before yesterday had been forgotten.

"I drove down to Los Angeles to see my father."

"You sure picked the day."

"Everyone gets a day off," she said testily, "even longshoremen."

"Sure. Sure. Maybe it's good you weren't here. All hell broke loose on Tuesday."

Barbara got out of the car and started to let down the tailgate. Salone helped her. Guzie began to unload the sacks of food.

"What happened?" Barbara asked.

"That sonofabitch Joe Ryan sold us out. That lousy bastard, calls himself a labor leader, comes here from New York and sells us out."

"That was two weeks ago," Barbara said.

"All right. They were only waiting for Whittier to come back from wherever the hell he was. Tuesday, they decide to bust the pier on Townsend Street. Seven hundred cops and goons, riot guns, tear gas — the works. We had maybe six, seven hundred guys there, and they roll through us with a line of trucks like tanks."

"Did they break the strike?"

"Like hell they did!" Guzie said. "The trucks got through onto Pier Thirty-eight, but then we held the lousy goons for four hours, and then they broke it up. All right, they got one lousy pier open, and now the papers are screaming that the strike's busted. It ain't — not by a long shot."

"Bobby, today's the day," Dominick said. "They laid us off for the Fourth. They're so stinking patriotic, they don't want to break nobody's head on the Fourth of July, but the scuttlebutt is that today they gonna open the whole waterfront. We got every member of the union out for

138

today, and the seamen too. That's the way Limo laid it out when Ryan tried to sell us — the seamen and the longshoremen together or nothing. So today we gonna have a thousand seamen and a thousand longshoremen on the docks, and let them try to bust that up. The point is, Bobby, we want to borrow your car. We need cars. All hell is gonna break loose. We need the cars for command posts, first aid stations, maybe ambulances, food. This picket line ain't gonna stop. Nobody goes off, nobody gets relieved. So we figure to load sandwiches and coffee, and we got some bandages and iodine. We been cleaning up the room in front here, and we're supposed to have two doctor-volunteers — they'll cover the place. So you can stay here and help them when the trouble starts. Honest to God, you can trust us with the car —"

"It sounds like a war."

"That's right. Maybe. So what do you say, kid?"

"You can have the car," Barbara said, "but I go with it. I don't want anyone else to drive it."

"Kid, that's crazy. You don't know what can happen down there."

"You can have the car for whatever you need," Barbara said firmly. "But I drive. I know the car. The clutch is ragged. You put someone else in there, and in a pinch he'll stall it."

"I can drive anything," Guzie said. "Anything."

"That may be. But if you want the car, I drive it."

Dominick nodded. "O.K., O.K. We ain't got time to argue. Let's load and get rolling."

They loaded the station wagon — a milk can of hot coffee, a bushel basket of tin cups, another of wrapped sandwiches, a box of rolled bandages and adhesive tape, two bottles of peroxide, and a quart bottle of iodine. By now, dozens of longshoremen and seamen were pouring into the alley. Barbara went into the kitchen, gulped hot coffee, and munched on a piece of stale bread. The longshoremen crowded in, and she found herself pouring coffee and hacking pieces from a salami. The bread was gone now, used up in the making of sandwiches, and with wonder Barbara watched the half-awake men making a breakfast of salami and black coffee. It did not matter. They were victims of a pervasive and consuming hunger.

Irma Montessa arrived, and she shouted for someone to take a basket of oranges and put it in the station wagon. "Stupid bastards," she said to Barbara. "All they know is meat and potatoes."

From outside, Dominick yelled, "Bobby, Bobby! Let's get it on the road!"

She pushed through to the door. Out in the alley, forty or fifty strikers, some of them with picket signs, were crowded around the station wagon. They were rubbing their hands, hopping up and down to keep warm, grinning at her as she came out. Many of them knew her, and they shouted things like, "Hey, Bobby! Here's our girl!" and "You'll tell 'em, Bobby!" as they opened up for her to get through to the car.

She heard one of the men say to Dominick, "The goons are forming up across Fourth Street. They say they're going to make a cordon from the depot to

Market Street.''

''Listen, you guys,'' Dominick shouted. ''We go down Bryant, slow. So stay around the car. If the cops try to stop us at Fourth, we push through. We get the car inside the police line and as close to the docks as possible.''

Dominick climbed into the car next to her, and Barbara started the motor, easing it into low gear and moving slowly out of the alley, the longshoremen walking in a group around the car. It was eight o'clock, and already the city appeared to be converging on the waterfront. Empty of cars, Bryant Street was spotted with clusters of people — strikers, sympathizers, kids, curious citizens. On the other side of the street, a solid knot of a dozen men moved toward the docks.

''Goons,'' Dominick said.

Moving at a walking pace, the Ford's motor whining in low gear, they were approaching 4th Street. Barbara saw the line of police stretching across the street, almost shoulder to shoulder. The kids and the curious were being barred, a crowd of people beginning to fill the street. She was

142

also able to see herself in perspective: Jean Whittier's daughter, driving a car loaded with food and medical supplies into a police barricade. She was frightened and excited at the same time.

"Are you O.K., kid?" Dominick asked.

"O.K.," she said. "I'm fine," with just the slightest quaver in her voice.

"Don't stop unless I tell you to. Just keep it going at the same speed."

They were now about fifty feet from the police line, and the crowd of strikers around the station wagon had increased to several hundred. The tight group of men that Dominick had specified as "goons" now moved into the street on a diagonal toward the strikers. A police officer moved to meet them. Another police officer began to make his way through the strikers to the station wagon. A young man with a press card in his hat pushed in among the strikers and yelled at Barbara,

"Hey, lady, what's your name?"

"Roll down your window," Dominick said. "Keep it down."

"Not closed?"

"Down. Down."

The strikers were at the police line now. "Move it, move it!" Dominick yelled.

"That wagon don't go through!" an officer shouted.

Barbara kept the car moving, and the police line gave. Several of the policemen drew their sidearms, and then an officer who appeared to be in charge waved his arms, and the policemen dropped back, opening the way for the strikers and the station wagon to move through.

Barbara's heart had stopped beating. "Thank God," she whispered. Dominick grinned at her. The man with the press card in his hat swung onto the running board.

"Lady, you got guts. What's your name?"

"Buzz off!" Dominick yelled. The strikers pulled him away. Then he said to Barbara, "Just right on down as close to the Embarcadero as we can get." They passed 3rd Street. In her rearview mirror, Barbara could see the police re-forming their line and holding back the increasing crowd of spectators. "We're in," she said to herself, "but how do we get out?"

"Turn left here," Dominick said, "and pull over to the curb."

Longshoremen and seamen were filling the street. Barbara eased the car through them up to the curb, and then she kept her hands on the wheel for fear that if she lifted them they'd shake violently. Dominick reached over and cut the ignition. "Good kid," he said. "You got lots of stuff."

Now she saw the crowd open up to let Harry Bridges through. His hair was slicked back, his blue eyes alive and darting from face to face. Two other men, heavyset, moved on either side of and behind him. He came over to the car and said,

"Hello, Nicky. Got some boodle?"

"Coffee, sandwiches, and medical stuff."

"Good. Who's the kid?" he asked, nodding at Barbara.

"It's her car. She's a good kid."

"Yeah." He stared at Barbara thoughtfully for a moment, then he said, "What's your name, miss?"

"Bobby Winter."

He called over his shoulder, "Hey, Fargo!" Fargo pushed through the crowd, a big, slope-shouldered, heavy-bellied man in his forties. "Fargo was a medic during the war. Fargo, that's Bobby behind the wheel. Bobby, you show him where the stuff is, and maybe if you want to, lend a hand."

Suddenly, their attention was diverted by a roar of men shouting and swearing, a gush of anger and profanity such as Barbara had never heard before. An apparently endless line of red trucks was moving down Harrison Street. The men swarmed toward the trucks, and at the same time a group of a dozen mounted police, backed by a hundred more on foot, moved in to bar their way. Barbara glanced at the little fox-faced man. He didn't stir. The longshoremen rushed the trucks, climbing onto the motors and trying to get into the cabs, and the foot patrolmen rushed the strikers, swinging their long nightsticks wildly and viciously. The mounted police spurred their horses into the strikers, lashing from side to side with their clubs, and now police

146

reenforcements came running from across Harrison Street, darting between the slow-moving trucks. More seamen and longshoremen poured into 2nd Street, running toward the trucks, but by now the police were able to form a solid line across the street while others dragged the strikers from the trucks and clubbed those caught between the police line and the trucks.

"Lousy, bloody bastards," the fox-faced man said, and he walked toward the mass of strikers who were falling back before the police. The cops were shooting over the heads of the strikers now and flinging tear gas bombs, and for the first time Barbara experienced the acrid taste of tear gas. Dominick jumped out of the car to follow Bridges, leaving Barbara sitting behind the wheel, too paralyzed with fear and horror even to attempt what her common sense told her was the only thing to do, to start the motor and get out of there before it was too late. Instead, she remained at the wheel, staring at the battle raging only a hundred feet from her — the surging mass of longshoremen and seamen, the line of police, the gunfire, and the windblown cloud of tear gas.

It ended. The last truck passed down Harrison Street, and the line of police gave back toward Harrison Street, leaving a neutral space between them and the strikers. Now Barbara could hear gunfire and shouting from the direction of the Embarcadero. It was all a dream, an insane, impossible dream.

"Lady, for Christ's sake, where the hell are those bandages?" It was Fargo, prodding her arm, shaking her back to reality, and she realized that the bloodied, hurt men being helped toward the car were part of no dream.

She forced herself into action, clenching her shaking hands, climbing out of the car and fumbling with the tailgate. "Let me do that," Fargo said. Then she crawled into the car and found the corrugated vegetable box that was packed with bandages and peroxide and iodine. Her hands were steadier now. She glanced up. A man stood in front of her, his face covered with blood. "Where the hell are the gauze pads?" Fargo shouted at her.

"None. We don't have any," she said, fighting back her tears and her desire to be sick.

"Shit! Don't none of you have an ounce of brains? O.K., cut up the wide bandage and make me pads. Where's the water?"

She was struggling with the bandage now, realizing that no one had thought to provide a pair of scissors. "Water?"

"Water! How the hell do you expect to wash wounds without water?"

"We don't have any water. Just peroxide and iodine."

"Oh, Jesus God!"

Barbara was trying to tear the heavy cotton bandage with her shaking hands and her teeth.

"Here, use this," Fargo said, taking a knife out of his pocket, opening the blade and handing it to her. "You got court plaster?"

She nodded.

"O.K. Make the pads and then have strips of court plaster ready to hold them in place." He turned to two of the longshoremen. "You two — take that can" — pointing to the milk can of coffee,

149

and saying to Barbara, "What's in it?"

"Coffee."

"Dump the coffee, and fill it with warm water."

"Where?"

"Shit! Don't ask me questions. Get the fuckin' water!"

Glancing up from the pads she was making, Barbara had a vision of the particular hell that she had been plunged into. Kneeling in the station wagon, she was looking at a mass of bleeding, battered men gathered around the tailgate, their faces covered with blood, gashed, eyes swollen and closed, one man with a bullethole in the palm of his hand, groaning with pain, another holding an obviously broken arm.

"Line up, mates," Fargo said, his voice suddenly gentle. "Worst injured first. Let me see that hand. Peroxide, Bobby."

She handed him the peroxide. She was getting the knack of stripping the bandage, piling the pads neatly in the box. "Please, don't shake so," she whispered to her hands. She began to strip the court plaster into different lengths, sticking the

150

end of each piece onto one of the ceiling struts of the station wagon. "That's the girl," Fargo said. "You're doing fine."

"There's supposed to be two doctors in the soup kitchen on Bryant Street," Barbara said.

"That's just fine. We need them in the soup kitchen. Hand me a pad. Now plaster."

"The man with the bullet wound — he ought to go there."

He had bandaged the hand. Now he was putting a pad on a head cut. "You're O.K., buddy. Take him over to Bryant Street, and if the goddamn doctors won't come back with you, get more plaster and bandages. And gauze pads. And more peroxide. And get them back here."

Now the street had almost emptied of everyone but the hurt men, yet they came, more and more of them. The battle had moved down to the Embarcadero, and Barbara could hear the shouting and the screaming and the gunfire in the distance.

"We're going to close the belt line," Fargo said.

"You mean the railroad?"

"That's right. They got their scabs and they're shipping goods. Either we stop the railroad or it's over."

The two men who had taken the milk can returned. One of them had a cut over his eye. Fargo was occupied. "Let me help you," Barbara said.

Without looking at her, Fargo said, "Get the can open. Wash it with the water. Then use iodine, carefully. We'll save the peroxide. It's half gone already."

She had stopped thinking about what she was doing, simply doing it. She washed the cut, touched it with iodine, pressed a pad on it as she had seen Fargo do, and then secured it with strips of plaster. Another man took his place. Head cuts, cheekbones laid open, a broken mouth with half the teeth gone. She recoiled from this, fighting back the tears again. "Fargo, please, I don't know what to do with this." As with a broken arm. "Hold it like this," Fargo said to her. He broke up a picket sign to make splints. Then, "More pads, Bobby. We're running out."

As she began to fold pads, she realized

that these were not just the men who had fought the police when the trucks came through Harrison Street. These were the wounded from another battle, raging down on the Embarcadero. "Buckshot wounds," Fargo said. "Where the hell are those lousy doctors?"

A longshoreman appeared with a box of gauze pads and bandages. "These are from Bryant Street."

"Where the hell are the doctors?"

"They got their hands full, Fargo. All hell has broken loose down on Steuart Street. It's like a goddamn battlefield all the way over to the Ferry Building. Maybe fifty, a hundred men lying on the street with their heads broken. Half the city is there, every cop, and they say they're calling out the National Guard. They got these fuckin' gas guns, and we're not giving ground. Jesus, I never seen anything like it."

Barbara's eyes were burning, and she had had only a taste of it, a whiff of it. The men coming up to the station wagon now were stumbling, falling, half-blinded, their hands pressed to their faces.

"Fargo, what can we do?" she asked desperately.

"Wet gauze pads on their eyes. That's all we can do, kid. Dip the pad in water, don't wring it out. Put it on their eyes wet and let them sit on the ground and hold it there until the pain eases."

Gauze pads for the eyes, clean the head wounds, pads, bandages. A police plane circled overhead. The sun was shining, the morning chill had gone, and the day had turned as gently warm and fine as only a San Francisco day can be. An apparently endless stream of the curious moved down Harrison Street, many of them filtering into 2nd Street to stand and watch. And still, in the distance, the sound of hundreds of men shouting in rage, the sound of gunfire. Time had no end. Once Barbara thought she saw a film camera directed at them, but when she looked again it was gone.

"Fargo," she said, "no more bandages, no more pads." She was very tired, but the nausea and the fear had gone away. She looked at her hands. Hadn't she seen them before? They were covered with caked blood, blood on her arms up to her elbows, blood on her blouse. The gunfire had stopped. The shouting had stopped.

"We'll send the rest to Bryant Street. No real bad ones anymore." He spread his arms. "Sorry, guys. Go up to Bryant Street. They got doctors there. We're out of everything."

Barbara was staring at what was left of the milk can of water. Blood had colored the remaining water pink. She hadn't noticed that before either. Fargo sat down on the tailgate, clasping his hands across his huge stomach. "Christ, I'm tired. What time is it, Bobby?"

She looked at her watch. "Four o'clock." She shook her head in amazement. Where had the day gone? "It's four o'clock. It's so quiet suddenly. I guess everything's over." She took a crumpled handkerchief from her purse, dipped it into the pink water in the milk can, and began to wash the blood off her hands and arms. Fargo watched her.

"You're a funny kid, Bobby," he said at last. "But you're all right. You're all right."

In the photo lab at the *Examiner,* a man named Blakely fished a wet print out of the developing solution and clipped it to the board. He stared at it for a while, and then he called over two other men in the room to have a look.

"It's all right. It's not great."

"Who's the fat guy?"

"Never mind him. Look at the girl. I seen that girl somewhere. I swear I have."

He took it to the photo editor, who glanced at it and pushed it aside. "We got too much already."

"Look at the girl. She's a beauty."

"So she's a beauty. Who is she?"

"I don't know, but I seen her somewhere."

He stared at the picture. The numbers on the license plate of the car were barely discernible. He copied them off and picked up the telephone on his desk.

A few minutes later, he dropped the photograph on the city editor's desk. "This is a lulu. Look at that girl."

"What about the girl?"

"If the car belongs to her, her name is Barbara Lavette."

"Look, this is Thursday. 'Bloody Thursday' — that name's going to stick. We got the worst war in the history of this city, two dead and God knows how many injured."

"Barbara Lavette. Her mother is Jean Lavette. Jean Lavette divorced Dan Lavette about five years ago and married John Whittier. This picture was taken on Second Street at about one o'clock today."

The city editor picked up the photo again and stared at it.

Alone in the car, Barbara drove back to Bryant Street. Fargo had taken off. She had no desire to return to the soup kitchen, no desire to do anything but get away from all this, to be by herself, to be quiet for a while; but in the car were the uneaten sandwiches, the tin cups, and the emptied milk can that Fargo had upended, a pink stream of blood and water pouring into the street.

The street in front of the soup kitchen and the alley too were crowded with men

— longshoremen, seamen, reporters. Two ambulances were in the street, backed up to the storefront. Barbara's first impulse when she saw the crowd was to keep on going; but she pushed it away and eased the station wagon into the alley, the men giving way in front of her. As she cut her motor, she saw Franco Guzie come out of the kitchen. He made his way through and stood at the car door, staring at her.

"I brought back the stuff," Barbara said. "I'm very tired. Could you have someone unload."

"Sure, kid." Still he stood there.

"What's wrong, Franco?"

"You ever get together with Dominick?" he asked unhappily. "I don't know what was with you and Dominick."

"What difference does that make?" She was tired, annoyed, every nerve in her body taut and strained.

"Dominick's dead."

"Oh, no," she whispered. "Oh, no. No." The pent-up flood of emotion released itself, and she laid her head down on the wheel and wept. A reporter worked his way down the alley and wanted to know what went on with the woman.

"Fuck off!" Guzie snarled at him. Then he opened the car door and helped Barbara out. The longshoremen in the alley pushed the reporter away and then stood there watching, grim-faced. "Come inside," Guzie said gently. "You sit down and have some coffee. You rest a little."

Irma was in the kitchen. Wet-eyed, she folded Barbara into her massive bosom. "Poor baby, poor baby."

They found a chair for her. "She needs a drink," Irma said. "One of you find her a drink." "Where?" "Jerks," Irma snapped. She took a half bottle of gin from behind the stove and poured some into a tin cup. "Drink this, baby."

Barbara swallowed the gin, choking on it. Guzie stood in front of her, watching her anxiously.

"I'm all right," she managed to say. "I don't have a handkerchief."

Guzie took a dirty, bloodstained rag out of his pocket. She wiped her face with it and handed it back to him. "I'm all right, Franco. What happened?"

"A bullet in the head. Two guys killed,

and one of them has to be Nicky."

"Has he any family? Do they know?"

"Not here. He got a mother up in Seattle."

"What happens to him? Who takes care of him?"

"The union takes care of that."

"Where is his body?" She had to ask. She had never encountered death before. She had no knowledge of the way of death.

"At the hospital. Look, kid, when the time comes, we'll tell you. You don't want to stay here. There's nothing but grief in this lousy place. You got a place to go?"

She nodded.

"Can you drive? Are you O.K.?"

"I can drive."

"All right. Just rest up a little, and then I'll clear the way and you can back out of the alley. You don't have to talk to none of them lousy reporters. We'll take care of that."

She sat there for another ten or fifteen minutes. The longshoremen who came in and out of the kitchen looked at her curiously, but no one spoke to her. They were filled with the horror of the day, and distantly, as if she were in another world, she listened to their talk of the pitched battles fought with the police and the company goons on the Embarcadero, of what had happened on Pier 20 and Pier 22 and Pier 38, of who had been clubbed and who had been gassed. Irma was cooking stew. Most of them had not eaten at all during the day, and vaguely Barbara felt she should remain and help. But she couldn't; she had to get out of there. Finally, she got up and went to the door. Guzie helped her to back out of the still-crowded alley, and then she began to drive. She just drove, with no destination in mind.

It was still early evening, a beautiful, golden California evening, the city sitting over the bay like a shining jewel, the rust-colored tower of the unfinished Bay Bridge glowing in the slanting light of the sun. Beauty and misery always go together, Barbara thought. It was all a part of the chaotic senselessness that had replaced the well-ordered serenity of her life.

She was on Franklin Street when she

realized that she had no place to go, and she pulled over to the curb and sat behind the wheel, staring glumly at the shining waters of the bay. She couldn't face another night alone at the St. Francis Hotel, not the way she felt now, and to go to the Whittier house was simply out of the question. As for another trip to Los Angeles, the very thought of the long drive turned her weariness into a nightmare. For a few minutes, she just sat there, and then, noticing a drugstore down the street, she locked the ignition and got out.

She found Sam Goldberg's number in the directory, but when she called the office, there was no answer. She should have known that; it was past six o'clock already. There were three residence numbers for three Samuel Goldbergs. The man at the counter changed a dollar for her, and she said a silent prayer. She had already ruled out her friends and her mother's friends. To face any one of them now and try to explain was patently impossible. The first number did not answer. The second number brought a familiar voice.

"Is this Sam Goldberg the attorney?" she asked.

"Yes?"

"This is Barbara Lavette. You do remember me?"

"Of course. Are you in trouble, Barbara?"

"Yes — no. Oh, I don't know. Could I see you, now?"

"Certainly. Where are you?"

"I'm at Franklin, near Clay Street. I have my car."

"I'm not far away, Barbara, at Green on the corner of Polk. A white house with yellow trim. You can park right in front."

A middle-aged black woman opened the door for her. "You're Miss Lavette? Mr. Goldberg's expecting you — right inside, dear."

It was an old Victorian house, the outside scalloped and bracketed, the inside full of framed plush pieces upholstered in olive-tinted velour. Barbara walked into a library: three walls of books and on the fourth wall an oil portrait of a pretty, delicate-featured woman. Goldberg got up out of a leather armchair and greeted her warmly.

"This is a wonderful surprise, Barbara —" He broke off, staring at her. "Is that blood on your blouse? On your neck too. Are you hurt?"

"No, I'm not hurt. I'm all right. I'm just so tired, and I had no other place to go. And please forgive me, Mr. Goldberg, but I'm so hungry. I haven't eaten all day. Could I have something, anything? A sandwich?"

Sam Goldberg sat at the dining room table with her, watching admiringly as she consumed roast chicken and mashed potatoes and string beans. "I'm eating your dinner," she protested at one point.

"Enough for both of us, dear. And for me to have company at dinner is a very special treat." He was less admiring and more dubious as he listened to her story of what had happened that day. She choked up as she told him of Dominick Salone's death.

"All right, Barbara. A man died, tragically, wastefully. It's your first encounter. You're part of the living. You accept it. Death goes with life. Sooner or later, you face that.''

"But he was so young, so alive, so cocky. I never met anyone like him before. He had no education to speak of, but he knew so much.''

"Were you in love with him?''

"No. But that only makes it worse, because he was in love with me and I didn't care about him at all, not that way. And don't you see, it's my fault?''

"No, I don't see that at all. How could it possibly be your fault? You did what you could. God knows, you did more than anyone else I know.''

"I sit here stuffing myself with food, and Nick is dead somewhere in some hospital, and Jean's my mother, and Jean's married to John Whittier.''

"And John Whittier's a monster?''

"Yes!'' she snapped.

"But suppose Whittier were a shipowner you loved instead of a shipowner you dislike intensely. As I told you, your father was also a shipowner once.''

"Daddy would never have done this!''

"I don't know." Goldberg sighed. "You know, Barbara, I saw some of it. I was on Rincon Hill at eleven o'clock, watching. That's when they were fighting on Harrison Street. I wasn't alone there on Rincon Hill. There were a thousand others, and we just stood there and watched, the way they watched the gladiators in the old days. All over the place, thousands of people watched, and they saw men clubbed and shot, the way I did, and none of us lifted a hand. You did something. You cared for people who were injured and bleeding. Now I am going to be presumptuous and didactic, so forgive me, but I must tell you something about guilt. Guilt is shared, because we belong to the human race. It is convenient to have villains like John Whittier, because it absolves the rest of us; but there's no absolution from what happens, and until we learn that, we just blunder about in the dark. Now enough of this, and certainly you have been through enough today. The question now is, where do you go from here?"

"I don't know."

"The place was swarming with newspaper men. Did any of them get your name? Or photograph?"

"Not my name. Maybe my picture. I just don't know."

"Will you go home?"

"To Whittier's place?"

"It's your home."

"No," Barbara said quietly. "I'll never go back there. I'll never set foot in that house again."

"Well, 'never' is an uneasy word. Have you seen Dan yet?"

"I was in Los Angeles yesterday. I could go back there, but I don't want to. Not now."

" 'Never,' Barbara, leaves your mother in a very difficult position. Would you like to stay here for a while? I have a comfortable guest room, and you're welcome to stay."

"For a few days? Could I?"

"Yes. Of course. Will you go back to the soup kitchen?"

"I don't know. I feel that I should, but I don't know whether I can. It's as if I did something, and now it's finished."

"The strike isn't finished. It's only begun."

"I know that. But I don't think I can go back there. It's not that I'm afraid. I was, but I got over that, and it's not that I don't feel for them. It's as if something inside of me is broken, and I have to put it together again. I know that makes no sense —"

"Perhaps it does. Now, will you let me call Whittier? Is your mother home yet?"

"No, she's still in Boston — I think. I don't want you to call John."

"Barbara, someone has to know where you are. You can't disappear. They may have already reported you missing —"

"No. I spoke to the butler. I told him mother must not be alarmed."

"But she will be. And you need clothes. I must call him. Tomorrow, I can send my secretary over to pick up some things for you to wear. Now, you must let me call him."

"You will anyway, won't you?"

"I'm afraid I must, Barbara. I'm your father's friend, and I am also an attorney."

The following day, John Whittier telephoned Jean in Boston. The conversation was unsatisfactory to both parties. Since the Boston newspapers — like the newspapers all over the country — carried accounts of what had happened in San Francisco on what was already known nationally as "Bloody Thursday," she knew more or less what had taken place. She received the news that a picture on page two of the *Examiner* had depicted her daughter in the midst of a group of injured strikers in the act of rendering first aid to one of them without comment, and when her husband angrily pressed the point, she said,

"It appears to me, John, that what she did may have been foolish and romantic, but hardly earthshaking. I'll talk to her when I return."

"When you return? I want you to start back here now, today."

"That's out of the question. I can't leave Boston today. We have things planned —"

"Jean, you don't hear one damn word I'm saying. This city is in a state of civil war. We're expecting a general strike, and that bastard Bridges and his commie pals are ready to take over. And I'm in the center of it. I'm already late for a meeting with Mayor Rossi and Governor Merriam. Can't I get through to you what's happening? There are troops on the Embarcadero, and God only knows when Bridges will decide to move against the ships. I have no time to track down your daughter and discipline her.''

"What do you mean, track her down? Isn't she at home?"

"She is not. She's apparently decided to stay with a Jew lawyer called Goldberg. I spoke to him this morning, and he sent his secretary over here for her clothes.''

"You mean Sam Goldberg?"

"I suppose so."

"All right. I suggest you forget about Barbara for the time being. You have sufficient troubles of your own. Tom and I will be back in San Francisco within the week."

"And I suggest you leave immediately. I may be able to handle this strike, but your children are more than I can cope with."

"Thank you."

"What does that mean?"

"John, this discussion is pointless. We will be home within the week. Meanwhile, try to relax and get some perspective. I don't think there is civil war in San Francisco. This will all be settled in due time."

On Sunday, two days later, Dan Lavette took the bus from Los Angeles to San Mateo. Long ago, some thirty-six years chronologically but reckoned as an eternity in California, where the land and the people still retain a sense of newness and incompleteness, a man named Anthony Cassala had lent Joseph Lavette, Dan's father, the money to buy a fishing boat. At that time, Anthony Cassala was a laborer who lent small sums of carefully hoarded money to the Italian workingmen. After the earthquake, during the few days when the city's banks were entirely inoperative, Cassala's tiny hoard of money became immensely valuable, and a few years later he obtained a license to establish the Bank of Sonoma. Together with his son, Stephan, he nurtured the bank, moved it onto Montgomery Street, and it might well have become an institution comparable to the Bank of Italy, later the Bank of America. But circumstances intervened, and after the crash of 1929, a run started that left the Cassala enterprise crippled and eventually bankrupt. Anthony Cassala died the following year, and Stephan went to work at Wells Fargo.

In their days of prosperity, the Cassalas had built a large, rambling house in San Mateo, on the Peninsula, south of San Francisco. There Cassala's widow, Maria, his son, his son's wife, Joanna, and their one child, a boy of seven named Ralph, still lived. After Dan Lavette's father and mother died in the earthquake of 1906, the Cassalas became a sort of surrogate family to him. Anthony Cassala financed his early ventures into the shipping business, and when the run on Cassala's bank took place, Dan and his partner, Mark Levy, depleted themselves of every dollar of cash they could lay their hands on in an effort to halt it. Four years had passed since Dan had seen Stephan Cassala, but he did not think that time would change anything that had existed between them. There were too many ties, too many threads that bound their lives together.

"Still," May Ling had said to him, "you must be careful what you ask. It lays a burden on them."

"I don't know that I'm going to ask for anything. I just want to see Steve and talk to him."

Then he had telephoned Stephan Cassala and asked if he might stop by and spend a few hours with him. Stephan had persuaded him to come on Sunday and stay overnight. The Sunday edition of the Los Angeles *Times* dealt in great detail with the events of "Bloody Thursday," and on page four of the main section, they reprinted the photograph of Barbara. Riding north on the bus, Dan read the story:

A curious sidelight to the events of "Bloody Thursday" still remains unexplained. The car in the above picture is registered to one Barbara Lavette, and the owner is listed as residing in a house on Pacific Heights in San Francisco. The address in Pacific Heights is the same as that of John Whittier, a prominent member of San Francisco society and the president of California Shipping, the largest operator of oceangoing vessels on the West Coast. According to a number of people who are friends or acquaintances of Miss Lavette, the woman in the photograph is Miss Lavette.

Barbara Lavette, twenty years old, is the daughter of Daniel Lavette, one-time partner in the firm of Levy and Lavette, and Jean Seldon Lavette, daughter of Thomas Seldon, and for some years after her father's death president of the Seldon Bank. The Lavettes were divorced in 1931, after which Jean Lavette married John Whittier. The car in the photograph was parked on 2nd Street in San Francisco and allegedly served as a first aid station and supply depot for the strikers. Miss Lavette could not be reached for comment.

Stephan met Dan at the bus station in San Mateo and embraced him. The four years had not wrought any great change in Cassala. Thirty-nine years old now, tall, slender, with dark moist eyes, his skin still had the pallid, yellowish tinge it had taken on after his stomach was cut to pieces by shrapnel in World War I. The same overwhelming, almost unendurable warmth and emotion greeted Dan when they reached the Cassala home. Maria, Anthony's widow, fat, shapeless, permanently encased in the black of mourning, wept over Dan and babbled away in Italian. Joanna stared and smiled at him, and then, at the table, Maria ushered in an unending river of food, pressing him to eat and eat, and still eat more.

It was almost eleven o'clock before Stephan and Dan were able to sit down alone, in Anthony's old study, and talk about what had brought him there. Stephan poured brandy. A wood fire burned in the grate.

"Like old times," Stephan said. "God, it's good to see you again, Danny. I know you been through a lot, but I swear you look ten years younger than the last time I saw you. Hard, too — no more paunch."

"Living right, and a good wife. How about you?"

"Day to day. I manage one of the branches for Crocker, but you know what banks pay. It's all right. Pop had insurance, and we keep this big barn of a place going. When I'll get a chance to pay you back what you dumped into the run — well, I just don't know —"

"Forget it."

"I haven't forgotten, Danny. But I just don't know how. I haven't the heart for the game anymore. You have to want it."

"I know." He tasted the brandy. "This is good."

"Still the old stuff, from during Prohibition. Montavitti used to make it on his place in San Martin. Pop bought twenty gallons."

"How's it going with Joanna?"

"What should I say, Danny? I live with my damn guilts. I'm a lousy husband. You know what I keep thinking? I keep thinking that if I could find a way to pay the bills, I'd enter the priesthood.''

''Hell, no. God damn it, Steve, we're alive, both of us.''

''In a world I can't make head or tail of. You know what happened in San Francisco. How? Why? Are we all going crazy? In Italy, that stupid bastard Mussolini. In Germany, Hitler. In Russia, Stalin. What's happening to the world?''

''Like always. Give it a chance, and the shit floats to the top.''

''And what about Barbara? You read the papers.''

Dan smiled. ''I know what I read, that's all. She's quite a lady, Steve. A lot like Jean in some ways, but maybe with a little of me. I thought I'd drive up to San Francisco tomorrow — you do drive, don't you?''

''I leave at seven. Sure, come with me. But what about you, Danny? What brings you up here?''

''Money.''

''God, I wish I had it to give to you. I got a few thousand. If it will help —''

"No. I don't want any money from you, Steve. Some leads, some advice. You know I've been fishing — on Pete Lomas' mackerel boat out of San Pedro. You remember Pete. He used to be my boatmaster before I teamed up with Mark. Well, in a good week, a damn good week, I bring home forty dollars. Mostly less. May Ling works in the library — thirty dollars a week. We make out, but not much more. Now Joe wants college and medical school. He's a good boy and a smart boy. May Ling's mother and father live with us, so it's tight. Well, I've been looking around. Christ, I can't go on fishing forever. There are a couple of things I know, and one of them is boats. With this rotten Depression on, there hasn't been a boat built down there in years. And they're going to need them, because the market for fish only grows. Well, there it is. I thought I'd set up a small boatyard. I might just pull it off."

"Wooden boats?"

"To start, yes. Plenty of shipwrights pleading for work, and wood is cheap. I can rent space for peanuts. And one business that isn't suffering in this Depression is films. The film people have money and they buy boats. The way I calculate, Steve, I can put together a beautiful little yawl for five hundred dollars — and undersell anything good on the market.''

''How much do you need?''

''About ten thousand to start. With less than that I'd be scrounging, and it would be pointless. Do you suppose Crocker would let me have it?''

''With what collateral, Dan?''

''We have the house — that's all.''

Stephan shook his head. ''No, I wouldn't want that. There's got to be another way. Why don't you see Sam Goldberg tomorrow. He still pulls a lot of weight around town. And he's got money.''

''I'm not going to trade on Sam's friendship.''

''Talk to him. Please. As a favor to me. We can always go to the banks.''

On the morning of the next day, Barbara awakened early and dressed herself in a plain navy blue skirt, a white blouse, and

179

a black cardigan. Goldberg's secretary had succeeded in retrieving a suitcase of sweaters, skirts, shirts, and underthings from the house on Pacific Heights. Now Barbara slipped out of the house quietly, without awakening Goldberg. She left her car parked where it had been and set out on foot for the International Longshoreman's Association's headquarters on Steuart Street. She had no desire to attract additional newspaper stories with her license plates, and anyway, it was a clear, cool, lovely morning. The blanket of fog on the bay was breaking up into rivers of creamy, golden mist, and as Barbara walked down California Street toward the Embarcadero, she felt so totally alive that she had to fix her mind willfully on the misery of the occasion. Yet that did little good, and she thought to herself that there was some deep flaw in her personality. If I had a shred of human sensibility, she reflected, I would be utterly downcast, and instead I am behaving like a perfect pig and feeling like a person going to a picnic. The thought worried her, and she sought in her mind for the source of this streak of what she could only consider as a basic lack of humanity; she finally decided that it was because she had slept well the night before and because of the weather, which was beautiful indeed.

By now, the streets were filling up with men and women on their way to work, the clanging cable cars stuffed with more crowded, clinging people than seemed possible, considering how tiny the cars were, the sidewalks bustling with properly dressed men, carrying their briefcases, as much the mark of this place as the umbrella was the mark of London's City. The stream of commuters pouring out of the Ferry Building was no different than on any other day. It shocked and startled Barbara; she was only beginning to realize how easily life and death go together.

Once on Steuart Street, it was a different matter. Here, the funeral procession would assemble. A delegation of longshoremen had visited Chief of Police Quinn on Saturday and had stated in no uncertain terms that whether he agreed or not, the funeral of the two men killed on "Bloody Thursday" would proceed along Market Street and not on some quiet side street. He agreed. Now, as she turned the corner into Steuart, Barbara became part of another San Francisco. Men, women, and children, not in their work clothes but dressed in their best, the men in old, ill-fitting suits, wearing black ties, black armbands, black hats, the women in black too, their faces grim and tired, a look that even the children shared — here they were coming by the thousands, all of Steuart Street in a slow movement that converged on the union hall. As she became a part of them, Barbara's mood changed, as if the anger and grief and hopelessness these people felt was a palpable substance that penetrated to the core of her being.

The movement slowed and stopped, and the thousands of men and women and children who packed the street stood there motionless. Slowly, the people making way for them, four flatbed trucks moved into the street and lined up in front of the union hall. An odd assortment of musicians, violins as well as horns, and two bass drummers took their place behind the trucks, and now people came out of the union hall, carrying wreaths and baskets of flowers and hundreds of bouquets, all of which they piled onto the trucks. Many of the women and children had brought flowers, most of them home-grown, roses and zinnias and marigolds picked out of gardens, which they put on the trucks; and Barbara wondered with a sudden pang why she had not thought to bring flowers. But she had not imagined that it could be anything like this. The people were still coming along the Embarcadero, and down Mission Street and Harrison Street and Bryant Street, waiting for the crush in Steuart Street to ease so that they might join the procession.

Then the pallbearers came out of the union hall, carrying the two coffins, many of them, as with so many of the crowd, still wearing head bandages and patches of gauze. Barbara recognized some of them. There was Guzie and Fargo and some others whom she had come to know at the soup kitchen. She saw Bridges among them. As they came out of the hall, the musicians began to play Beethoven's funeral dirge. The pallbearers slid the two coffins onto the flatbed truck, and then the crowd gave way for them to take their place in front of the trucks. Slowly, almost imperceptibly, the procession began to move. No one gave orders; no voice was raised other than whispered requests by a group of longshoremen that the march be ten abreast — and so the grim river of silent people turned into Market Street and began to march southwest across the city. The same group of strikers who had whispered the marching orders now spread ahead of the funeral procession, shunting the traffic off Market Street into the side streets.

Barbara fell into one of the lines and walked slowly with the procession out into Market Street. Looking back at the apparently endless stream of people coming out of Steuart Street, she realized that the procession could not consist of longshoremen and seamen alone, not even with their families. Thousands more had joined the march, and thousands of others lined Market Street to watch in silence as the procession passed. Indeed, the silence was uncanny and incredible. The little group of musicians had stopped playing. No traffic moved on Market Street, and nowhere was there a policeman to be seen. There was no other sound than the tread of thousands of slow-moving feet.

Dan Lavette, standing at California and Market, was one of the thousands who watched the procession, watched it come out of Steuart Street. He suspected that Barbara would be somewhere in that great throng, but though he looked for her, he was unable to spot her. He tried as best he could to understand what forces motivated her and what this experience meant to her, but for all their closeness now, his daughter was very much a stranger to him. He himself had never been very political. Most of his adult life had been spent climbing the path to Nob Hill, to success and wealth and power. Even as a fishing hand, he could not think of himself as a workingman. A

185

workingman was a victim by his lights, and to his own way of thinking he had never been a victim but always the manipulator, always the man who controlled his own destiny. The only time he had ever thought and acted in political terms was when he had supported Al Smith for the presidency. If Smith had won, Dan Lavette's life might have been very different, but Smith had not won.

Now, watching the mass of people passing slowly by, he could only think of the strike and of "Bloody Thursday" in terms of stupidity, stupidity on both sides, but specifically the stupidity of men like John Whittier. He didn't hate John Whittier; he simply despised him, as he had once despised Grant Whittier, the man's father. For perhaps half an hour, Dan stood and watched the funeral procession; then he turned away and walked to Sam Goldberg's office on Montgomery Street.

Goldberg received him warmly and immediately put to rest his fears about Barbara. "She's staying with me," he said, "and I hope you will too, Danny.

186

There's plenty of room in the old house."

"Have you talked to Whittier?"

"I have. It was not pleasant. He regards her as some kind of crazed kid out to destroy him. I agree with Barbara. She can't go back there."

"Did she say what she wanted to do?"

"Only that she won't go back to college. She said something about going abroad for a few years, but who knows? She's been through a profound emotional experience, and it's going to take her time to get her balance back. By the way, Jean called me from Boston. First time I've spoken to her in years. She'll be back in San Francisco on Wednesday. I think you ought to stay over and talk to her."

"Why?"

"Because your daughter's a part of both of you. And what about Tom? He's coming back with her. Don't you want to see him?"

"I'm not sure that I do."

Goldberg shook his head. "All right. We won't talk about that. We'll talk about you and May Ling and Joe."

They talked for almost an hour. For

Dan, it was a process of reliving a life he had literally wiped out of existence. Sam Goldberg had drawn up the papers when he bought his first ship, the *Oregon Queen,* and then Goldberg had walked with him every step of the way through twenty incredible years, the building of an empire and the destruction of an empire — through the divorce proceedings that put an end to that section of Dan's life. It was a long time since they had seen each other, and there was a great deal to put together. When Dan finally went into his notion of starting a small boatbuilding business in San Pedro or Wilmington, Goldberg simply spread his hands and said,

"No problem. I'll give you the money."

Dan shook his head. "That won't work. You're in a position where you have to say that. I don't want your money."

"Then whose money? I'm sixty-six years old, overweight, a rotten heart — as my doctor so cheerfully informs me every time I see him — no wife, no children, and rich. Principally as the result of having you and Mark as clients for twenty years.

Do you know what you paid me over that time?"

"I never thought much about it," Dan said.

"Did you ever collect a nickel of money you put out — as personal loans?"

"Not that I can remember. But what the hell difference does that make?"

"Look, Danny, either you go to a bank and mortgage your soul, or what is worse, May Ling's house, or you find investors. All right. I'm an investor. I'll put up twenty thousand, and we'll be partners in the deal."

"Your're crazy."

"Like a fox, Danny. You're no businessman, but you're something else. There's no word that fits it, and the time for it is over, anyway — except maybe for a few men like you. God damn, you opened Hawaii and made it a competitor of Florida. You and Mark established the first great department store on this coast. You opened the first commercial airline in California, and starting with nothing, you built one of the biggest steamship lines in the country. Now you spend your days fishing for mackerel. Why, I don't know. What in the name of God are you afraid of?''

"Myself."

"That's great. That's really beautiful. You sound like one of those psychoanalysts that this city is being plagued with."

"Nevertheless, it's true."

"True or not, I don't buy it. Now look, I'm a lot more hardheaded than you are. I'm offering you a partnership. You do the work, and we split the profits. There's only one condition."

"I'm listening."

"You stay away from the books. You create it. You manage it. Build your boats, ships — any damn thing you want to build. But leave the financial end of it to Feng Wo."

"My father-in-law? You're out of your mind."

"Why? For years, he was the best damn comptroller you ever had."

"No, no, Sam, it wouldn't work. He's an old man. He translates from the Chinese and he grows roses. I can't involve him in this."

"How old is he?"

"Almost sixty."

"Then you damn well can ask him. I swear, I just don't understand you, not one bit."

Dan sighed. "All right, Sam. If I ever understand myself, I'll lay it all out for you."

"Are we in business?"

"Let me think about it."

At dinner that night at Sam Goldberg's house on Green Street, a thoughtful, subdued Barbara asked her father quietly, "What do you think I am, daddy? Am I a fraud? Is that all I am — a fraud?"

Goldberg watched both of them with interest, this huge, dark-eyed man and the slender, bright-eyed young woman, with her clear skin and honey-colored hair, who by the wonders of genetics was his daughter. The combination of their alikeness and their unalikeness fascinated him. Both were incurable romantics; both lived their lives with zest and endless curiosity, and both of them were filled

191

with doubts and guilts and quixotic passions. Like Dan, Goldberg had been born in California, a place he was fervently dedicated to and that he often felt was the only place on earth where a Jew was not a Jew but simply another immigrant in a world of immigrants. And these two, Dan Lavette and his daughter, were unique products of California.

The three of them sat at a round, club-legged Victorian table in a fussy little Victorian dining room, untouched and unchanged since his wife had died. Dan had agreed to remain with him overnight, and Barbara had returned from the funeral late that afternoon, still in the mood of what she had experienced.

Dan took a while before he answered. "Well," he said at last, "we all are, you know. Frauds. I don't suppose we want it to be that way, but who the devil are we? If there's no way to find out, you invent your own answer." He looked at Goldberg, who shrugged.

"I'm an aging, overweight lawyer, Danny."

"I'm very rich," Barbara said suddenly.

"I mean, someday I will be."

"I suppose so," her father agreed.

"How rich?"

"Don't you know?"

"Not really. I've never thought much about it."

"Well, it depends on a lot of things. According to the terms of your grandfather's will, you and Tom were left three hundred and eighty-two thousand shares in the Seldon Bank, to be divided equally between you in nineteen forty. That will give you a hundred and ninety-one thousand shares. The stock is privately held, so there is no market price. What would you guess, Sam?"

"Hard to say. Twenty-five, thirty dollars a share. It's hard to say."

"About five million dollars. Of course, what the price will be six years from now, no one can say."

"Most likely higher."

"Then I am very rich," Barbara said.

"Comfortably so," Goldberg agreed.

"Do I have to accept it?"

"What?"

"The money, daddy."

Dan laughed. "Well, I'll be damned!" He turned to Goldberg. "There's one for you, Sam."

"Right now, Barbara," Sam Goldberg said, "you have no rights in the matter. For one thing, you're still a minor. The stock is held in trust for you. Your mother's the trustee, and she has the right to dispose of the income as she sees fit. In nineteen forty, according to the terms of the will, as I understand it, you accept the bequest. What you do with the stock after that is up to you."

"Then like it or not, I am very rich and I remain so."

"Do you find it uncomfortable?" Dan asked her.

"Yes, I do."

"Poverty can be more uncomfortable," Goldberg assured her.

"I think I know that. But I can earn my own living. No one gave anything to daddy."

"That's not really to the point," Dan said. "You've got six years to think about it. Meanwhile, I think you should go back to school."

Barbara didn't have to think about that. "No, I won't go back. That's over."

"Don't close all the doors," Goldberg said.

"I'm trying to open some."

"What will you do?" Dan asked.

"I don't know. I don't know what mother will say. I can't stay here with Mr. Goldberg. I have to think about it."

"Come back to Los Angeles with me," Dan said slowly. "We'll both sit down with Jean tomorrow or the next day. I'll talk to her. Then come back with me — if you want to."

"I think — I'd like that," Barbara said.

But it was not until three days later that Jean returned to San Francisco and Dan was able to reach her. It was the first time in almost five years that he had spoken to her, and when he heard her voice the space of time became meaningless. He found himself thinking, Only yesterday. Everything is like that, only yesterday.

"This is Dan," he said, almost casually.

195

"I'm in San Francisco, and Barbara is with me."

"Yes, Dan. I thought you might call."

"Could we sit down together, you, myself, Barbara, and Tom, and hash some things out?"

"I'd like to talk to you alone," she countered.

"No, that wouldn't be a good idea."

"Why not?"

"Because I want to talk about Barbara, and I want her there when we do."

"And if you will forgive me, I don't think that's the best idea in the world. Let's not pick up where we left off, Dan. I think we're both older and wiser."

"All right. Where shall I meet you?"

"Tomorrow? Lunch at the Fairmont?"

"At twelve-thirty," Dan agreed.

Dan was already at the table when Jean walked into the dining room, and he rose and stared at her unabashedly. She wore a Chanel suit of pale pink wool over a rose silk blouse, a shell pink felt cloche, and around her neck a double strand of pearls. His were not the only eyes that turned toward her; he could remember only too well this shift toward her that made her the center of attraction in any room she entered. It was not simply that she was a beautiful woman; she carried her beauty without self-consciousness, with an easy, erect certainty; and now, as always, Dan could not look at her without desire, without feeling that familiar longing for something that once was his yet never his.

She saw him, walked to his table, and gave him her hand, looking at him, measuring him, a slight smile and the slightest twinkle in her fine blue eyes. "Danny," she said, "you look splendid, ten years younger, thirty pounds lighter, healthy, happy — oh, I envy you." She always made the rules, specified the ground for any conversation.

"Shall I return the compliment?" he asked, moving the chair for her to be seated.

"Please."

"I have never seen you look more beautiful."

"Thank you." Her eyes took in his brown tweed suit, the white shirt and the cheap tie, without appearing to do so; but he was sensitive to her every gesture, and he said pointedly,

"The suit is eighteen dollars, Jean. I'm hard to fit, but then, I had no notion that we'd be lunching at the Fairmont."

"The suit is fine," she said with a touch of annoyance, "and I also happen to know that you don't give a damn what it cost. You never did. What have you been doing, Danny? You look as if you've been taking a miraculous health cure at some European spa, but that's hardly likely." She pulled off her white kid gloves, reached across the table, and took his hand in both of hers, smiling as she ran her fingers over his palm. "No, hardly a European spa. I do love your hands, always have. I do not like soft hands on a man."

"I'm a fisherman, Jean. I work for Pete Lomas, down in San Pedro. You remember Pete Lomas. He was fleet captain on my crabbing boats. I think you met him that first day on the wharf — back in nineteen ten. I average thirty dollars a week."

"Stop it, Danny," she said, laughing.

"It's bad taste to be so damned ostentatious about your poverty."

"Then I'm right back in form."

"No, you're not, and it's much too late to play the hard-boiled kid from the Tenderloin. Anyway, you look splendid, very healthy, very content with yourself, and I have no intention of feeling sorry for you."

"Good. We're on even ground. I have no intention of feeling sorry for you."

"I'm not sure I like that," she said slowly.

He had not intended to mention it, to speak of it at all, and then it came out. "Jesus Christ, Jean, why the hell did you marry him?"

Her face tightened. "Shall I ask why you married your Chinese mistress?"

"That wasn't called for," he said unhappily. "It's the same damn thing, Jean. Why does it always happen as soon as we start to talk? Why does it always go to pieces? When I saw you come into the room over there, I looked at you and I said to myself, Danny boy, you are wrong about most things, but not about women.

This is one hell of a woman. Do you know why I married May Ling, why I love her? Because from the first moment I saw her, she made me feel that I was a man, that I was human, that I was something of value and not misplaced dirt from the Embarcadero.''

For a long moment, Jean stared at him, then she shook her head. ''I'm sorry, Danny, very sorry. It's always too late, isn't it. I want a drink. Will you order a martini for me? And then we'll talk about Barbara and Tom.''

He ordered the drinks. They sat in silence for a little while, Jean watching him thoughtfully.

''You've changed.''

''Both of us,'' he said.

The drinks came. ''To the kids?'' she asked.

''Yes.''

''Tell me, Danny, what do you think of your daughter?''

''I like her. She's the best of both of us.''

''Then I'm not the worst mother in the world?''

''Hell, no. I'm a rotten father, but you

did something. Was John burned up about that newspaper story?"

"A perfect rage, yes. He takes it as a personal affront, something she did out of hatred for him. And of course it doesn't help his own position."

"It doesn't help hers. She can't go back there. She's John Whittier's daughter — at least in their eyes."

"I don't see why she should want to."

"For the same reason she went there in the first place."

"And what was that?"

"Guilt. Compassion. A desperate need to find out something about herself and the world she lives in."

"Not John?"

"I don't think she gives a damn about John Whittier. She doesn't like him. Does Tom like him?"

"I think so. What's more important is how Tom feels about you."

"He hates my guts."

"No, Danny, no. He doesn't know you."

"I lost him somewhere on the way. Like you said, Jean, it's always too late."

"You could try."

"Could I explain to him why I work as a boathand for thirty dollars a week?"

"I don't think you could explain that to me, Danny. How did you explain it to Barbara?"

"I never had to."

"You know, Dan, she adores you. She'll listen to you. She won't listen to me. She doesn't want to go back to college. I spoke to her this morning."

"I know."

"I think she should. I think she should heal the breach with John. This is a terrible time for John; whether you like him or not, he's facing his own moment of truth. Everyone says there'll be a general strike tomorrow."

"It looks like it."

"I can't imagine it. Everything stops — the whole world. John hasn't slept in three days; there have been endless meetings with the mayor, the governor, and heaven knows who else. If Barbara could be made to understand —"

"I think she does understand, from her point of view."

"Dan, she's not a communist. Or is she?"

"No." He grinned. "I hardly think so."

"What does she want?"

"I think she wants to get away from all of us for a while. She wants to go to Europe, to Paris. Study and work."

"And you encourage that?"

"Jean," he said gently, "I encourage nothing. I want her here as much as you do. But I won't impose anything on her. I won't even try to persuade her. You and me, my dear, we have one hell of a kid. She survived being born in a golden crib, and if she survives that, she'll survive anything. On the other hand, you're the trustee of her estate. If you cut off her money, she'll have a hard time of it."

"That's what John wants me to do."

"Will you?"

"That's a hell of a comment, Dan. I love her as much as you do. It's her money."

Dan looked at her and nodded. They ordered lunch, but hardly touched the food. They talked around things, awkwardly — Barbara's sale of her car, her horse — but the matter of their daughter was decided already. When Dan said that she would be coming to Los Angeles to stay with him until she left for Europe, Jean said almost hopelessly, "I suppose that's best. She won't come back to John's house. I'll spend the next few days with her. Don't worry about the money." Then she talked about Tom, and her tone became almost plaintive. "I never turned him against you, Danny."

"I know."

"So strange, Danny, to sit here like this, the two of us. You feel that, don't you?"

"I feel it."

"Danny, if I said to you, take a room and go upstairs and wait for me —?"

"Are you saying it?"

"Danny, I could endure anything except to have you reject me again. So I'm not saying it, really."

He reached over and took her hand. "Jeany —" He had not called her that in years. "Jeany, I have twenty-two dollars in my pocket and a return ticket on the bus, and that won't buy us a bed at the Fairmont. But thank you, I'll remember that."

"John is sure you hate me. He begged me not to see you. He actually was afraid you'd commit mayhem."

"I guess John knows as little about men as he does about women."

She made no effort to take the check, and inwardly he thanked her for that.

A few days later, the day Dan left San Francisco to return to Los Angeles, one hundred and fifteen San Francisco trade unions met in delegation and voted to call a general strike. The next day, the most feared, the almost mythical weapon of the working people came into being as the San Francisco trade unionists walked off their jobs and left the city paralyzed. Among the various devices that the employers and the so-called nabobs resorted to was the resurrection of the vigilantes, so notorious in San Francisco's past. Rumors were circulated that a communist army was already marching on San Francisco, although its point of origin was never revealed. There were other carefully circulated rumors of bomb plots and planned attacks on police headquarters and the general post office. None of the rumors was founded in any basis of reality; nevertheless, the vigilante gangs went into action, carrying out raids against the headquarters of the Marine Workers International Union, the Communist Party headquarters, the headquarters of Upton Sinclair's Epic Plan movement, and a number of other places, among them the soup kitchen on Bryant Street.

Barbara went there the day after she read the account of the raids in the *Chronicle*. She walked through a city that teemed with police, National Guardsmen, and unofficially deputized American Legionnaires. She came to Bryant Street and stood there looking at the wreckage of what had been the storefront soup kitchen. The windows had been smashed, the tables and chairs inside broken, the dishes shattered and scattered about. The destruction was maniacal, childish, and thorough.

The following day, she left for Los Angeles.

Dan did not make up his mind about Sam Goldberg's offer until after he had spoken to May Ling. He had an almost mystical regard for her good sense and wisdom. He told her all that had been discussed in Goldberg's office and then let the question hang.

"What do you really want, Danny?" she asked him.

"The money to put Joe through medical school."

"We can manage that. It's four years away. He'll go to UCLA, where the tuition's free. I have some money saved, and pop has his savings."

"I won't touch that."

"Joe will be working this summer. He'll save that money."

"Where?"

"While you were gone, I phoned Jake Levy at Higate. He offered Joe a job at the winery. Joe wants to go. So we'd manage the money."

"All right. I've had it with fishing. I'm not young anymore." He was sitting opposite her in the living room of their little house in Westwood. It was on toward eleven o'clock, the hour that was theirs alone. She sat with her hands in her lap, a small, slender ivory-skinned woman whose hair was turning gray, and he thought to himself, She's all of it — everything. Love was something he could never adequately put into words.

"You don't enjoy being poor, do you, Danny?"

"I don't give a damn about that. Only, the good years — Christ, we couldn't even walk into a decent restaurant together."

"They weren't such good years, Danny. These are the good years."

"I can't go on in that damn mackerel boat."

"Then tell Sam you accept."

"You won't mind?"

"Come to bed, Danny. You'll call Sam tomorrow."

Lying in bed with May Ling's head cradled in his arm, her naked body pressed close to him, both of them easy in the afterglow of their lovemaking, he said, "There is one thing more I should tell you about the trip."

"Oh?"

"I had lunch with Jean at the Fairmont."

"The snow lady. Yes?"

"Eleven dollars with the tip. That's half a week's wages when the fish aren't running."

"She didn't offer to take the check?"

"Come on, baby. We talked about Barbara. That's all."

"She didn't ask you to go to bed with her?"

"You know, my darling May Ling, under that satiny Oriental skin of yours lurks traces of a bitch."

"Then you've found me out. What did you say?"

"What do you mean, what did I say?"

"When she asked you to go to bed with her?"

"I said that with twenty-two dollars in my pocket, there was no way I could afford a room at the Fairmont."

"You did?"

"Yes."

"I hate you."

"I've suspected that."

She pressed closer to him, running her

hand over the hair on his body. "I like it when two bodies become one. That's the way it should be. Only, Occidental men are so hairy, apelike."

"How the hell would you know? You've never been to bed with anyone else. Or so you tell me."

"So I tell you. Would you?"

"Would I what?"

"Would you have gone to bed with the snow lady if you had had the price of a room at the Fairmont?"

"I don't know —"

"You're not very nice, Danny. But I love you."

PART TWO

The Leave-taking

Barbara met Marcel Duboise on the Champs-Élysées. It was on an afternoon in April of 1937, a cool, lovely, sun-drenched day, the kind of a day that people who love Paris will insist occurs only in Paris and only in April, although Barbara remembered many days like it in San Francisco, when the wind blew gently from the Pacific and when the sunlight danced on the water of the bay. Indeed, this kind of a day filled her with nostalgia and homesickness and led her to think that she had lived enough away, and that it was time to go home.

She had lunched out of a bag in the garden of the Tuileries, and that was when Marcel Duboise saw her. She was unaware of this until he followed her across the Place de la Concorde and up the Champs-Élysées. He quickened his pace until he was alongside her, and then he said, speaking very quickly,

"My name is Marcel Duboise. I am

honest, decent, fairly intelligent, of good character, and not a criminal or a depraved type, and I do not make a habit of speaking to strange women on the street. But what else can I do? If I don't speak to you now, you will disappear and I will never see you again. I never saw you before, so it is quite logical that I will never see you again, and then my life will be desolate and meaningless until the end of time.''

The words poured out of him with such speed that Barbara retained only a vague impression of what he had said. By now her French was adequate, but she still had some difficulty following when it was spoken very quickly, and her instinct was to ignore the man and quicken her pace. She glanced sideways at him. He was slender, tall, brown tweed jacket, gray flannel trousers, white shirt, striped tie, wide mouth bent in a pleading smile, wide jaw, brown, humorous eyes, a large, narrow nose, and a mop of unruly brown hair.

"Please, please do not ignore me."

"What on earth do you want?" she

asked him, shocked into English without thinking. "What do you want?" she repeated in French.

"Ah, you are English."

"I'm an American, if it's any affair of yours."

"So much better. Please, may I talk to you?"

She stopped, turned to face him, and stared. "Monsieur what-ever-your-name-is, you *are* talking to me. I don't know why, but you are. A mile a minute," she added in English.

"Of course. My name is Marcel Duboise. What did you say, a mile a meeneete?"

"Too fast. My French is not that good."

"Yes. Of course. Forgive me." More slowly, he asked, "Is this better?"

"Much better. Now I am sure you have mistaken me for someone else."

"Oh, no. No. Impossible. I could not."

She sighed and began to turn away.

"Please, one moment. I could not mistake you for anyone else because I have never seen you before."

"Then what on earth —?"

"I am trying to make your acquaintance," he said desperately. "Believe me, I do not make a habit of this kind of thing. I have never done it before. For ten minutes I stood there watching you eat your lunch. Then I took the plunge."

"I still don't know what you're talking about," Barbara said.

"If I try to explain, I will only sound more insane, and I'm not insane. I mean, no more than the next man. One dreams for years about a woman, and then one sees her? Well, what is one to do?"

In spite of herself, Barbara began to laugh. He appeared to be so absolutely ingenuous that for the life of her she could not be rude or coldly unapproachable.

"Only one terrible thing occurs to me," he added.

"Oh? Yes, what terrible thing?"

"That you are happily married."

She hesitated and then replied, "Neither happily nor unhappily. I'm not married."

"God be praised. Now, please, please, I introduced myself before. But now more formally. My name is Marcel Duboise. I am unmarried, twenty-nine years old. I was born in Toulouse, which accounts for my accent. I work for the newspaper *Le Monde* in a most shameful way. You see, I hold nothing back. I write a daily column about food and restaurants, and the only redemption in my work is that I am the substitute play critic. Once, twice a week, if I am lucky, I am allowed to review a play. Also films, but again as a substitute. One time, the film critic was sick for a month. That was glorious."

"That's very interesting," Barbara said, for want of anything else to say.

"Then you find me interesting. Good. Please tell me your name."

She thought about it for a while. He stood there, hopeful, earnest, not a very good-looking man, but with an undeniable charm and with a boyish openness and vulnerability that she simply did not believe could be assumed.

"My name is Barbara Lavette," she said at last.

"But that is a French name. You are not French?"

"My grandfather came from Marseille.

He was part French and part Italian.''

''Of course. The wonderful thing about Americans — they are always from somewhere else.''

She was laughing again. Common sense said to her, You do not let yourself get picked up on the street in Paris by a strange man. On the other hand, strange men do not bother to pick up a woman who wears no make-up, a brown woolen suit over a beige cashmere sweater, not to mention scuffed ghillies with heels only three quarters of an inch high. She was also lonely and homesick, and fancied the smell of the April air to be like the salty scent of the sea on a breezy day on Russian Hill.

Sensing her mood and hesitation, Marcel Duboise said, ''Mademoiselle, what harm will it do if I walk with you and we talk? If you tire of me, I will go. Surely, on the Champs-Élysées, on an April afternoon, nothing unpleasant can happen?''

''But you don't even know where I am going.''

''That's where I am going. There is

nothing in the world more important.'' A half-hour later, he was telling her the story of his grandmother, who had written her first novel — and had it published — at the age of seventy-two. ''Very risqué, very risqué, indeed.''

Barabara realized how little she had laughed in the past three years.

''But of course, you are serious,'' he said. ''There is your charm. Myself, I am a fool. So my family regards me. So the world regards me.''

''You are certainly not a fool, and as for myself, you know nothing about me. Oh, I wish my French were not so wretched.''

''Your French is very correct, and your accent is absolutely delightful.''

''Thank you. But I really must go.''

''Where? You see, you are in flight because we were not properly introduced. If an aunt of yours said, 'This is Marcel Duboise, a proper gentlemen,' then the whole thing would be so simple.''

''But my aunt is three thousand miles away, so it is impossible.''

''Miles, yes. What is that in kilometers? Oh, devil take it!'' They were at the corner of the Avenue Victor-Hugo now, and Duboise pointed to a sidewalk café. "We sit down there for one moment. I buy you a small drink. Vichy water, tea. I accept the fact that I must be neutral and harmless."

The proprietor greeted him by name. "You see, I am not a nameless thug," he reassured her.

"All right." She dropped into a chair. "You are Marcel Duboise. I am Barbara Lavette. We have met. It is absolutely formal now. For a half-hour, you have been introducing yourself to me."

"And you have not driven me off."

"True. Could I have a beer?"

He ordered two beers and stared at her in delight.

"Monsieur, you must not stare at me like that."

"But certainly. Forgive me. I have told you who I am, what I do, what my father did, what my grandfather did. You have told me nothing."

"How could I? Do you always talk nonstop?"

"Oh, no. Certainly not. I was fighting

time and tradition. I was talking for my life — really, truly. Now tell me about yourself, Barbara Lavette.''

''You are rather nice —''

''Thank you. Bless you.''

''And I am entirely able to take care of myself. But when a stranger tries to pick you up in Paris —''

''Not to pick you up. Only to keep you from walking out of his life.''

''That's just it. Would I select a man and accost him on the street because I was attracted by his face? It stinks a bit, doesn't it? That's an American expression,'' she explained. ''It doesn't work when I put it in French.''

''I get it. My face? Never. But it wasn't only your face, but yourself, all of you.''

''And still you know nothing about me.''

''Not so. It's true, you have told me nothing. But just wait. The suit is Molyneux? Am I right?''

''Heavens, no. I bought it in San Francisco.''

''Well, so much for clothes. I know this: you are kind, gentle, sure of yourself, intelligent and — all right, I say it. I think you are one of the most attractive women I have ever seen. So I have sinned. And your French is excellent, so you have lived here for some time.''

''I wish that were true.'' Barbara sighed. ''I had four years of French at secondary school, two years at college. Six years. So I would be a perfect donkey if I couldn't get along with it. I've been here for almost three years.''

''With your family?''

''No, alone. I came first to study at the Sorbonne, which is the rationalization of so many Americans who come here, but I just don't have the character of a student. I stuck it out for a year and a half. I was almost ready to give up and go home when I ran into a piece of luck. I met Frank Bradley, who is editor of *Manhattan Magazine*. Do you know it?''

''Yes, of course. My English isn't good enough for me to enjoy reading it, but I love the cartoons.''

''So do I. Well, you know, it's a weekly, and every other week they publish a 'Letter from Paris,' a sort of grab bag — some politics, fashion, the arts and letters, and whatever gossip might strike a chord back in the States. Well, Bradley and I got to talking, and then I showed him some pieces I had written. He liked them, and he let me try the "Letter from Paris." They liked what I did and I got the job — I guess for want of anyone else at the moment — and I've been doing it ever since."

"Then we're both writers. Do you see how sound my instinct is?"

She nodded, smiling, and he ordered another round of beer.

Ten years after the turn of the century, the leading citizens of Los Angeles, already suffering from a sense of inferiority imposed by San Francisco, which was arising like a phoenix out of its ashes, realized that they needed a harbor. History had bequeathed them a city twenty miles from the sea, and they felt that as an inland city in a semidesert, their future was far from bright. Long, long ago, ancient Athens had faced the same problem, and the Athenians, a vigorous and intelligent people, decided to build a pair of walls, each four miles long, to connect their city with Piraeus, their seaport. On the Pacific coast, in the vicinity of Los Angeles, there was unfortuntely no harbor worthy of the name, but there was an ocean; and, never daunted, Los Angeles incorporated into itself a strip of land a mile wide and sixteen miles long, stretching from the westernmost edge of the city to two coastal fishing villages, San Pedro and Wilmington, two sleepy villages that fronted on a great mud flat called Terminal Island. The citizens of San Pedro and Wilmington, facing sudden absorption, were of mixed feelings, but the City of Los Angeles undertook a public relations campaign calculated to convince these people that their destiny and future were much brighter within Los Angeles than outside of it. In August of 1909, elections were held in San Pedro and Wilmington, and when the results had been counted, Los Angeles was at long last a seaport. Eventually a stone breakwater, miles long, threw a great circle around San Pedro, Wilmington, and the neighboring port of Long Beach, providing Los Angeles not only with a seaport but with a large, safe harbor.

Within this enormous breakwater were enclosed the mud flats of Terminal Island, which was transformed into a busy hive of shipbuilding during the years of World War I and in the early nineteen twenties, employing literally thousands of men. With the onset of the Depression, the shipyards of Terminal Island closed down, succumbing one by one to the economic malaise that gripped America, until only a hardy handful were left to try to survive and dream of better times.

One of the companies that failed to survive and ended up in the hands of local banks was Occidental Marine, a medium-size shipbuilder that had specialized in the construction of wooden minesweepers during the war. It had twenty acres of land, shops, cradles, groundways — even a small drydock that had fallen into disuse and disrepair. The whole enterprise was offered to Dan Lavette for a hundred thousand dollars, but, hoarding his tiny store of capital, he delayed, bargained, and finally took over the place for a total price of sixty-five thousand dollars, the bank taking back a mortgage of sixty thousand dollars at four percent interest, and considering itself fortunate in the deal. Dan was less fortunate in his plan to make enough money to send Joe through medical school. During the next three years, he built seven boats, only managing to keep his head above water, to pay his bills, and to meet the payroll for the five men he had hired — and to make them understand the situation when he had to lay them off. The first boat was ordered by Pete Lomas, whose converted mine sweeper-turned-mackerel-boat was beginning to come apart at the seams. There were two other fishing boats, one of which saw its owner go out of business. The remaining four vessels were small sailing craft, pleasure boats. The bank, which dreaded the possiblity of another bankruptcy and the possession of worthless property, forgave him a year of interest payment, and somehow or other Dan forced his enterprise to survive.

One day in the early spring of 1937, Pete

Lomas walked into Dan's office on Terminal Island and offered him a pure Havana cigar. The office, where Dan was the only occupant — the little bookkeeping he required was done by Feng Wo at home — consisted of six rooms in the main shop building, all but one deserted. The room that Dan occupied had a desk, a swivel chair, a row of empty filing cabinets, and a splendid walnut architect's chest, whose many shallow drawers were filled with old Occidental blueprints of boats Dan would never build. There was also a table and five captain's chairs, obviously for meetings to discuss the plans.

Pete Lomas dropped into one of the chairs while Dan examined the cigar and admired it.

"Courtesy of Alex Hargasey."

"Thank him. Who the hell is he?"

"Oh, nobody. Nobody. Only the most important director in Hollywood."

"Yeah. And that's why you're sitting here in white ducks and a white shirt and that silly captain's hat of yours instead of being out fishing."

"Exactly."

Dan bit off the end of the cigar, and Lomas leaned over to light it for him.

"Go on," Dan said.

"You be nice to me, Danny," Lomas said. "You be very god damn nice to me because I am going to blow your ass sky-high. You want to know why I'm not out fishing? Because Paramount Pictures — you heard me, Paramount Pictures — is paying me fifty dollars a day, seven days a week, and all expenses and the crew's wages for the use of my boat. They're making a film about a fisherman, and they're using my boat. Only today they're not shooting on location, which is my boat, so I'm a gentleman of leisure. You got anything to say about that?"

"It couldn't happen to a nicer guy. But it doesn't blow my ass sky high."

"Be patient." He reached into his pocket, took out his wallet, and extracted a folded check. "Five hundred." He handed it to Dan. "Last payment on my boat. Took two years, but it's done."

"It helps. Believe me, it helps."

"Now, listen to me Danny. This Hargasey, he's a Hungarian, very emotional, blows up, yells, screams, but he's a nice guy. Since they start this film, he becomes absolutely crazy over the sea. He says it's because there's no ocean anywhere near Hungary. Well, he wants a yacht. He's got this girl, Lorna Belle — you heard of her?''

"I heard of her.''

"She's the star in the film, and I guess they're shacked up, not married or anything, but that ain't too important with them, it seems. Well, she's just as nuts as he is on this business of a yacht. Hargasey is in love with my boat, and when I tell him that you built it, nothing else but you got to build him a yacht.''

"What?''

"Hold on, Danny. Not just a yacht. He wants a hundred-foot Diesel with eight bedroom suites.''

"Is he crazy?''

"Have I blown your ass sky high or not?''

"Pete,'' Dan said, "you can pick up yachts all up and down this coast — and for a damn sight less than it costs to build one. You know that. He must know it. And who has enough money for a hundred-foot Diesel? It could run to a quarter of a million — more.''

''Danny, they got nothing but money. There's no Depression in the movies. Anyway, he wants to meet you, and I said I'd arrange it. One deal like this could turn this white elephant of yours into a paying proposition. You phone him at Paramount Pictures and arrange to meet him. And bring some stuff with you — plans, blueprints, photographs.''

''I can do that,'' Dan agreed. ''I got a beautiful set of Sparkman and Stephens blueprints and drawings that I inherited with the place. But, god damn it, how much does a movie director earn?''

''The hell with that! Go out there and sell him the job. Let him worry about paying for it.''

Three days later, Dan drove his 1930 Ford from Westwood to Hollywood, turned off Melrose Avenue into Marathon Street, and faced the imposing gates of the Paramount studio. The guard at the gate regarded his car dubiously, checked his name, then passed him through and directed him where to park and how to find Alex Hargasey. It was the first time he had ever been inside a film studio, and after he had parked his car, he walked past the huge sound stages and the bungalow-like office buildings and dressing rooms with the gawking curiosity of any tourist, thinking that this was certainly an intriguing, childlike world, the great factories of make-believe drenched in the morning sun, men and women hurrying past in the colorful costumes of cowboys and Indians and maidens and knights of the Middle Ages. He found the half-timbered building that housed Hargasey's office, fake English between fake modern and fake Spanish, and was directed upstairs to a suite of offices. There he sat for fifteen minutes, leafing through a copy of the Hollywood *Reporter,* an object of interest to the peroxide-blond receptionist who sat behind her desk and studied him unabashedly.

Finally Hargasey emerged, an enormous, fat, bald man with a bulletlike head, his stomach pressed tightly behind a broad leather belt that encircled whipcord riding breeches. "Ah, boat-builder!" he boomed. "You are this Lavette. I am Hargasey. Come on in." He studied Dan as they entered his office: a white rug that Dan felt was enveloping him like quicksand, white overstuffed chairs, a great black desk. "Son of bitch!" Hargasey exclaimed. "You are damn sight more photogenic than stupid star I got to work with. Maybe I forget about boat and I make you star? What do you say, Lavette? No. Joke. I got idiot sense of humor. Sit down. I got half-hour to tell you what I want. Then you make it for me."

That night at dinner in the cottage in Westwood, May Ling, her son, her mother and father, listened fascinated as Dan described his experience at the studio. "It makes no sense," he said. "The country's going down the drain, starving, dying, and this man tells me to spare no expense. Mahogany woodwork, silver-plated fixtures, teak decks. I told him it might run to three hundred thousand. He just grinned at me and said, 'Good, good.'"

"Then you'll build it," May Ling said calmly, "if you can."

"I can build it. I can build anything he wants."

Watching his father thoughtfully, Joe finally said, "You don't want to build it, do you, pop?"

"I guess I don't."

"I know," May Ling agreed. "But what difference does it make, Danny? It means work for a lot of men. If you don't build it, someone else will."

"If I don't build it," Dan said, "then I close down. It's the end of the road. So I guess I'll build it."

When Marcel Duboise came into Barbara's apartment on the Quai de Passy for the first time, he looked around him and then shook his head and sighed hopelessly. "You lied to me," he told her. "You said you were a journalist. No journalist lives like this. No journalist lives on the Quai de Passy."

"What on earth are you talking about?"

He prowled through the place. "Bedroom, sitting room, kitchen, bathroom, shower, tub, bidet — you're an heiress.''

''All right. Then you've found me out. I am. You thought I was a plain *fleur de l'asphalt,* since you did pick me up, and here I am an heiress.''

''Don't be silly.'' Still, he kept turning and staring. ''A place like this — at least a thousand francs a month.''

''Eight hundred.'' She smiled at him. ''Do you like it? I adore it myself. It's my first real home, can you imagine? And you never have to meet the man who pays the rent. He comes only one evening a week —''

''Don't talk like that!'' he snapped at her. ''I've known you for two weeks and you've never talked like that before. I don't like it.''

''There you are, my dear Marcel. Every Frenchman is a moralist. They pretend otherwise. Oh, stop being so pompous and sit down.'' He sank into the chair, fingering the upholstery. In her mind, Barbara could see him calculating the price. It irritated her. So much that was French irritated her, and yet so much enchanted her. "I'm an heiress," she said deliberately. "I should have told you that at the beginning, but at the beginning I was sure I'd never see you again, and anyway, it's a cliché for an American girl in Paris to be an heiress. I'm very rich — oh, not at this moment. Don't be so alarmed. I don't come into the money for another three years, and anyway, how do you think I feel about it with my country in the middle of this rotten Depression?"

He just sat there and stared at her. Then he asked, "Why did you never let me take you home before?"

"Oh, you ass!" she exclaimed. "You think I'm a *putain*. You do, don't you? A classy whore. You don't believe a word I said."

"Should I? After all the lies?"

"What lies? I told you I'm a correspondent. I am!" She walked over to a pile of magazines, picked up a handful, and flung them at him. "Read it, if you can read English. That's the work I do, and I'm damn proud of it." She stared at him, shaking her head. "Oh, what's the use! You'd better go."

"No!"

"Then stay there and let your thoughts rot in that stupid bourgeois mind of yours."

"So I'm bourgeois? Me?" he cried indignantly.

"Yes. And now, excuse me." She went into the bathroom, washed her face with cold water, stared at the angry face in the mirror, and then began to laugh. Her lips were still twitching with a smile she fought to control as she returned to the sitting room. Marcel stood facing her.

"I love you," he said desperately.

She burst out laughing.

"And you laugh at me, you heartless bitch!"

"Who do you love, Marcel, the *putain* or the heiress?"

"Stop that!" He grabbed her, started to shake her, and then embraced her. She stopped laughing. She met his lips and closed her eyes and felt the tears start. Then she pulled back and stared into his dark eyes.

"Why are you crying?" he whispered. "Did I hurt you?"

236

"You're such a strange Frenchman. I've seen you eight times and you never made a pass. I could have been your sister. Oh, I know you were being careful. And now, when you decide that I am a kept woman —"

"No!"

"That's not why I'm crying. Don't you see? I love you so much."

In a way, she told herself, she had never been made love to before — remembering the clumsy pawing on college dates, remembering the argumentation and pleading of those who did it vocally, remembering what was almost a knock-down, drag-out fight on a Princeton football weekend, remembering and then remembering nothing, only lying naked and alive with a man whose hands and lips worshipped her body, and who told her over and over again, in a language so well made for it, how very beautiful she was.

"Marcel," she said.

"Yes, my love?"

"When it happens, don't be alarmed."

"Alarmed? My God, alarmed?"

"Oh, I hate to have to tell you this, but

I'm a virgin."

He raised himself from where he lay beside her, stared at her, reached out, and touched her cheek. "Oh, no."

"God's truth," she said in English.

"You're twenty-three years old. You've been in Paris almost three years."

"I know. I don't know what else to say. I'm so ashamed." She was giggling.

"Darling, lovely Barbara," he begged her. "Don't laugh. You cannot make love and laugh at the same time."

Later, hours later, lying side by side, smoking, watching the tendrils of smoke drift and twist, too languorously surfeited even to dress, Marcel said, "Being an heiress makes it difficult. It would have been easier the other way."

"What other way?"

"A kept woman. We could have worked that out. But an heiress — I don't have two francs. What I earn, I spend."

"Then we'll both be poor."

"And what about the fortune?"

"I'll probably give it away," Barbara said indifferently.

Late at night, on the twenty-seventh of May, 1937, Thomas Lavette knocked at the door of his mother's room. There was no response, and he opened the door gently. Jean sat at her dressing table, and as he opened the door, she turned to face him.

"It's me, mother. Is it all right?"

She picked up a handkerchief and wiped her eyes.

"You've been crying?" He had never seen his mother in tears before.

"Not really. Tears, but not really crying, Tom. Just a long day and too much emotion."

"May I come in?"

"Please."

"It's past midnight."

"Come in, come in."

"John's asleep?"

Jean nodded. She pointed to a chair and then dropped into a chaise lounge. "Sit there, Tommy. Let me look at you. I haven't seen you for days."

"Not my fault, mother. You've been so wrapped up in the bridge. How did it go today?"

"You don't want to know about the tears?"

It embarrassed him. "I don't want to pry."

"I wish you would pry. I wish we both could pry at each other enough to break through. Well, I was crying. Today, just before the ceremonies began, Mr. Strauss came to me —"

"Mr. Strauss?"

"You don't know, do you, Tom. The name doesn't even ring a bell."

"That's not fair, mother. He had something to do with the bridge."

"A little. He and Clifford Paine built the bridge, the Golden Gate Bridge that we dedicated today. I first met him six years ago —"

Tom half-rose. "Mother," he said, "it's very late."

"No. I'm in a very singular mood, Thomas. I wish you would just sit there and listen to me. I intend to talk to my son, perhaps because I have no one else to talk to. So if you will — please."

"If you wish."

"I do. It's very late, but I am not a bit

240

tired. I want to talk about Joe Strauss, a small, not terribly impressive, Jewish man. At least I think he's Jewish. Perhaps not. When I was your age, I had all the normal — no, not entirely normal — prejudices against Jews. Your father's partner, Mark Levy, was Jewish, and I could barely tolerate him. So you see, I have a very clear understanding of what growing up rich on Nob Hill does to one. It happens quickly. My grandfather panned gold. My father was Thomas Seldon —"

"You're going to lecture me again," Tom said.

"Again? No. I think this is the first time."

"Have it your way."

"I intend to, this once. You see, there never would have been a bridge without Joe Strauss. It was his demonic compulsion. Everyone said that it was impossible — oh, mostly the geologists. They knew it was impossible. But Joe decided to build the bridge or die in the attempt, and I think he did both."

"He died?"

"No, my dear. Please don't ask me to

explain. But, you see, once he fought it all through — the legalities, the politics, the plans, the concepts — once he did all of that, he still required the money, and there all the wise and practical people decided that they had him stopped cold. He needed twenty-seven million dollars. Six years ago, he walked into my office at the bank and introduced himself. Oh, I knew who he was, but we had never met. He told me that he was putting out a bond issue. The banks had laughed him out of their offices until he went to Giannini. Giannini didn't laugh. He told Joe that his bank, the Bank of America, would take the bonds. But there was still an overage, some six million. So Joe Strauss came to me. I asked him why, and he said, 'You're a woman, Mrs. Lavette. You know about men, the kind of men who remain children and dream the dream that kids dream.' Or something like that. I don't remember exactly.''

''That was a damn strange thing for him to say.''

''Not really. He knew about your father, and I did something to your father once

242

that he never hated me for, so perhaps I knew less about men than Mr. Strauss thought. Anyway, I took the bonds, and I bullied my board of directors into accepting my position. That was how I came to know Joe, and today the bridge was finished and opened and dedicated, all nine thousand feet of it, all twenty-seven thousand strands of wire — and that's why I was crying. Now, please go to bed."

Tom started to say something, to tell her that he had come into her room to talk about his job and money. Then he shook his head and sighed. "All right. Goodnight, mother." He walked over to her and kissed her dutifully, then he left the room, and Jean sat there, staring at the door, disliking herself for being obtuse and unreasonable with him.

Lately, it was getting to be a habit for her to dislike herself. Tom was no worse, perhaps a little better, than most of the young men in his set. He tended to his work at the bank as an assistant vice president in charge of loans, and in view of her own obsession with the building of the bridge, it was quite natural that he

243

should block out Strauss's name, natural even if it were simply a pretense to irritate her. She irritated him, and she certainly irritated her husband, John Whittier. Why on earth she should have started out, a few minutes before, to tell Tom of all people what Joe Strauss had said to her before the ceremony, she simply did not know. Of course, Strauss was in an unusual condition, keyed up, filled with the wonder of the miracle that they had wrought there in San Francisco, yet depressed too. He took her hand in both of his and said, "Dear Jean, I will tell you what it's like today, the way it must feel to a man who knows you and loves you — when the love is returned. So the bridge is built and done. There's no other way I can say it."

Her husband overheard this, and Whittier said to her afterward, "Now what the devil did he mean by that? Is the silly ass in love with you? Or have you —"

He stopped short. She was staring at the bridge, at the great, incredible red-orange monster of steel and wire, as delicate and graceful as a glowing spider's web in the sunshine, so proper and immediate a signature for this strange people who had settled the Pacific edge and, oblivious to desert and earthquake, built there the one American city that was like a dream. She was staring at it, a part of it, until Whittier spoke; and then she turned and glanced at him as if she had never seen him before.

And now she wept. Her tears were her own. She had never shared them before, and it provoked her to have to share them with her son. She felt strongly that if you are alone in the world, utterly, totally alone, you use that loneliness as your comfort and your strength.

Barbara gave a party for Marcel's friends. She felt that since neither of them had any family available, friends were the next best thing, and the occasion, though unannounced, would be to celebrate the fact that someday, in the distant or not too distant future, they would be married. Two of her own friends, the only close friends she had in Paris, were included: Susan Clark, a Philadelphia girl who was a student at the Sorbonne, and Betty Greenberg, a junior correspondent for the New York *Times*. Marcel invited his three best friends, Jean Brissard and Maurice Jouvelle, both of them staff writers on *Le Monde,* and Claude Limoget and his wife, Camille. Limoget, Marcel explained, was a reporter for *Humanité,* the Communist Party daily, which meant that sooner or later the evening would explode into a wild argument, but then, as he said, "What else makes a good evening?"

"Food, for one thing, and I'm a rotten cook. But this Claude Limoget, he's a real, live communist, in the flesh?"

"Why not?"

"Because I've never met one."

"After all you told me about the strike in San Francisco? What about that man who was killed, Dominick Salone?"

"I never asked him. You don't ask anyone in the States."

"Why? It's not Germany."

"We'll go into that another time. Meanwhile, what ever am I to cook? I can't cook for Frenchmen. It would be grotesque."

"We'll do it together."

"Marcel," she exclaimed in delight, "can you cook?"

"This and that. Not really. But I do know how to prepare a *cassoulet,* a huge pot of beans and sausage and pork. That's all we need — and good bread and good wine."

The *cassoulet* turned out to be delicious. The fresh, golden spears of bread were like no other bread in the world, and the inexpensive table wine was as good as any Barbara had ever tasted. Marcel's friends were charming, full of praise for everything — the apartment, the food, and the three "absolutely delightful" American girls. They were all in their late twenties: Brissard stout, jolly, a sort of French G. K. Chesterton in appearance, at least to Barbara; Marcel had described him as Balzacian. Jouvelle and Limoget were small and slender and filled with energy, and Camille Limoget was petite and pretty, causing Barbara to feel oversized and gross. Thank heavens, she told herself, that Marcel was taller than she. The two American girls were both in the five-foot-two or -three range, attractive and unconcerned over their execrable French. Barbara rarely gave much thought to her height — she had grown up in a city where tall women were not uncommon — but now she whispered to Marcel that she felt utterly grotesque. He in turn assured her that she was the loveliest and most desirable grotesque in the City of Paris.

They ate the food and drank the wine and talked at first about America, San Francisco, Roosevelt, the New Deal, the sit-down strike in Flint, Michigan, the CIO, and the ravings of Father Coughlin. Barbara answered questions when they were put to her, but otherwise she listened in silence. She was amazed at their knowledge of what went on in her own country. They were all newspapermen, but still and all, they were far better informed than she was. Also, it was the first time in her life that she had ever been at a dinner party where the discussion was totally political. Not even at college had anything like this ever taken place, and she found herself concentrating fiercely to follow their rapid French.

Then the conversation turned to Spain and the Spanish Civil War, which had been going on for almost a year now. Camille Limoget had a brother in the French Battalion of the Internationals, fighting on the Republican side and against Franco, and she spoke bitterly of the embargo of munitions.

"I put Roosevelt with Hitler," she said. "One is no worse than the other."

"Why not with Hitler and Stalin?" Brissard said lightly.

"Of course, of course," Claude Limoget said sarcastically. "What is the difference? Only that Hitler fights on the side of Franco and Stalin for the Republic. But how can that make any difference?"

"They are both practicing, testing arms, testing airplanes. You are going to tell me that Stalin gives two damns for the Republic? Each has theories. They work them out in Spain."

Until now, Barbara had sat in silence. She started to say something, but Limoget broke in with, "Ah, that is splendid! How I love a cynic. He is absolved from responsibility. A plague on both your houses. Isn't that Mr. Roosevelt's phrase?"

"If you mean —" Barbara began.

"What I love," said Jouvelle, "is the way you cannot be wrong. You cannot be open to argument. No discussion. When Zinoviev and Kamenev were beaten and tortured into submission and forced to confess and then executed like dogs, you knew. Oh, yes, you knew they were guilty. Of what? But you knew they were guilty, even before they knew it themselves."

"Who were Zinoviev and Kamenev?" Barbara whispered to Marcel.

"Two loyal old Bolsheviks. Stalin accused them of treason and executed them."

"Tell her the whole story," Camille snapped.

"That would take all evening. How many were there — sixteen in the first trial, seventeen this past January, Marshal Tukhachevski and his whole general staff — it is simply too dismal.''

''Absolutely,'' Limoget agreed. ''Dismal. You see,'' he said to Barbara, ''this never angers me. I don't hear Marcel. I hear *Le Monde*. Who speaks? The whore or the pimp? The driver or the horse?''

Barbara expected Marcel and his two friends to react in rage, but instead they exploded with laughter. Evidently they had been through all this before.

''You were trying to say something before,'' Marcel said to her. ''Talk quickly, or you'll never get a word in here.''

''I can't in French, truly,'' she told them. ''Only you were blaming Roosevelt for the embargo. It was an act of Congress, you know.''

To her amazement, all four of them turned on her. Only Marcel forbore to attack.

''Your Congress!''

''Running dogs of the bourgeoisie!''

''Running dogs of Roosevelt!''

''Who is the lead dog of the bourgeosie!''

"You abuse the child. The child is innocent."

Through all this, Betty Greenberg and Susan Clark had sat as silent as Barbara. Now, Betty came to her defense, saying, "You really don't know all that much about the States. It was a joint resolution of Congress on January sixth. I am sure that if Mr. Roosevelt had made the decision —"

"He did!" Limoget snapped. "You Americans are children when it comes to politics. He leads your Congress by the nose."

"It hurts me to agree with Claude," Jouvelle said placatingly. "But, mademoiselle, it is a fact. Roosevelt could have blocked that resolution. He did not. Thereby, he practically condemns the Spanish Republic to death. Where will they find arms? Franco gets all he needs from Hitler and Mussolini."

"Then why not from Russia?" Susan Clark demanded.

"Because Stalin is very careful about offending Hitler," Marcel said.

"Nonsense! Everything the Republic

gets is from Russia."

"But your own Léon Blum is a socialist," Barbara protested. "It's easy to blame Roosevelt three thousand miles away, but why does Blum do nothing?"

"Why indeed?"

"Because a French socialist," snapped Camille Limoget, "is a French pig. No difference. Frauds, cheats, liars —"

"Oh, come on, come on," Jouvelle said.

It continued. It went on and on until midnight. They consumed every drop of wine, and never paused from talking, shouting, waving their arms, and insulting each other. After the first exchange, Barbara and the two other American women retreated into silence; at last, when everyone had left, Barbara sighed in relief and said, "Thank heavens. No blood spilled."

"But they are dear friends," Marcel protested.

"And they always do that?"

"When you have communists, a socialist government, a war in Spain, Hitler, Mussolini — oh, yes, they argue. I suppose it might be thought of as a sort of intellectual exercise.''

''I've never heard anything like it before.''

''Then, my darling Barbara, you've been in the company of dullards.''

''Perhaps. But the things you say to each other —''

''Better said than unsaid. You know, you Yankees pretend to be so different from the British, but you share their fear of passion. It is the same word in English as in French, no?''

Barbara nodded.

''Only I think it goes further in our language. Did it ever occur to you, my dear Barbara, that our whole world is coming to an end?''

''You are being very serious, and I have to think about that. Mostly, you are only serious when you make love to me.''

''And you refuse to be serious.''

''It's so late. And do you know, Marcel, in spite of all the sound and fury of your friends, I had a wonderful evening, and since Jouvelle and Brissard took the girls home — well, who knows, I may have done my good deed for the day. And it's

254

impossible for me to consider that the world is coming to an end. I'm much too pleased with you."

"Not the world. That goes on. Our world. I cannot understand communists, I cannot agree with them, but damnit, they see what is happening in Spain, and if the lights go out in Spain, as in Germany and Italy —"

"But not tonight. Tonight, only the lights in this apartment. After which —"

"For a good, innocent American heiress, you have the strangest single-track mind."

"One of these days," Barbara decided, "we will examine that entire question. Probably we will discover that the white Protestant American schoolgirl has the most explosively repressed sexual urge of anyone on earth. And in French, that is a mouthful for me. But not tonight. Tonight, let's just curl up in bed and let the world take care of itself."

Alex Hargasey was fascinated with Dan Lavette and with the yacht that Dan was building for him. On Dan's part, he had never before come in contact with this particular type of man-child-idiot-artist, all of which described Hargasey and none of which described him adequately. He appeared to know his business of making films, but emotionally he was infantile. At the age of fifty years, he was alternately enraged, gentle, wild, or demonic. He was paid enormous fees, tolerated, kowtowed to; and he in turn abased himself before the stars in his film. He would not be crossed. When he demanded Dan's presence, Dan had to appear or endure his threats to break his contract for the yacht; and he in turn spent hours at the shipyard, watching the work in progress, asking endless questions.

At first indignant, angry, ready to tell him to go to the devil and take his damned contract with him, Dan came to realize that Hargasey and the people around him lived in a world totally separated from reality. Their work was the substance of dreams. They admitted no other responsibility than that to the film they were making, and like overindulged children of overindulgent parents, they simply accepted the fact that rules contrived for others did not apply to them.

When Hargasey informed Dan that he was giving a party at his home to celebrate the completion of his sea film — a wrap party, he called it — the information included a royal summons. Dan was to appear, with his wife, if he had a wife and desired to bring her, without her if he so desired — there would be single girls in plenty — or with anyone else he cared to bring. Informed of this, May Ling's immediate reaction was, "No, I can't go, Danny. You go without me."

"Why can't you go? My word, honey, I would think that just out of curiosity you'd want to. He tells me that Garbo will be there, and Joan Crawford and Spencer Tracy and Marlene Dietrich and a lot of other names that I can't even remember — and it's the kind of thing we'd never get to see if not for that crazy yacht of his. Come on, come with me."

"Danny, darling, how can I go? I'm a middle-aged librarian, a very plain Chinese lady."

"Like hell you are!"

"I have nothing to wear. Danny, we haven't been to a party in years."

"Then it's high time, isn't it? Whatever you say about Hargasey, he's ended our condition of being broke. He's spending money on that yacht like it's going out of style. So just you go out and buy any dress you think is right for it."

"What about you?" she asked forlornly.

"I'll rent a tux. I got no choice. This is a crazy man. If I don't show up there, he'll go out of his mind."

Many years before, when Dan Lavette was still married to Jean, he had made a trip to Hawaii to open negotiations for building a hotel on Waikiki Beach. He had taken May Ling with him, and at a party given by their hosts, she had worn a dress of thick black silk decorated with dragons in gold thread. The dress had been a gift from her father, and she had worn it only once, on that single occasion. Now she took it out of the chest where it had been all these years, carefully wrapped in layers of tissue, and tried it on. It still fit perfectly, a very simple dress, ankle length, split on the sides to above the

258

knee. Anyway, her figure had not changed.

The night of the Hargasey party, she remained in the bathroom, making up her face, until after Dan had dressed and gone downstairs. She felt like a silly young girl and giggled at her reflection in the mirror — it was so long since she had used make-up. Her skin was still smooth and unflawed. She sighed when powder failed to conceal the tiny wrinkles about her eyes. How awful it was to feel that the perfectly natural process of aging was your enemy! She had never cut her hair, but since she was a Chinese lady they would make allowances for that, just as they would for her curious dress. But what if Dan were to be disappointed? After all, he had urged her to buy a new dress; but a new dress for one single occasion made no sense whatsoever, and anyway, it was too late. She drew her hair into a heavy bun at the back of her neck, pinning it in place with two gold combs that Dan had given her. When? She tried to remember. It was the first anniversary of the night he had taken her to bed with him. And the evening slippers had come with the dress, of the same black silk and same gold thread. Dressed, her hair finally set, she stood there lost in thought, remembering how Feng Wo, after five years of working for Lavette, had finally gathered up the courage to ask Dan whether he and his wife would come to partake of a Chinese dinner at their home. Jean, as Dan told her afterward, had reacted in horror. Dan came alone, and that was the beginning, the first time he had seen her. But she was already in love with him before he ever set foot in her father's house, in love with the image of this strange, huge, unruly man who had defied all mores of San Francisco prejudice to hire a Chinese to run his business. And then, the second time, he had turned up at the library where she worked, the temporary library that had been put together after the earthquake, fumbling, uneasy, like a small boy avowedly doing wrong, asking her whether he, a married man, could take her to dinner.

His booming voice broke in on her reverie. "May Ling, we're going to be the last ones there!''

She came downstairs slowly, very
tentatively. They were all waiting there to
review her — Dan in his rented tuxedo,
Joe, Feng Wo, and So-toy. No one said
anything as she appeared. They just
stared at her speechlessly, and Dan's
thoughts, like hers, leaped back to that
evening in Hawaii, when, with her hand on
his arm, they had come out onto the lawn,
under the light of the Japanese lanterns,
and every face in the great crowd of
people at the luau had turned toward her.
It seemed to him that nothing had
changed, and now he said, almost
reverently, ''My word, you are one hell of
a woman!''

Marcel's English left more to be desired
than Barbara's French; but then, she had
been living in France for almost three
years, while his English was simply the
product of school and two weeks in
London. The letter she proposed to read to
him would, she insisted, help him
practice.

''But I don't need practice,'' he said. ''I

261

live in France."

"Now. Conceivably, someday, you might desire to live somewhere else."

"Why? You know what the Frenchman said when asked why his was a nation of nontravelers?"

"I don't. Tell me."

"He said, 'Monsieur, why should I travel? I am already in Paris.' "

"That's not arrogant, it's only modest and reassuring. This letter is from Dan's wife. She's Chinese."

"The letter is in Chinese?"

"You know it isn't. She's a lovely, cultured woman, a librarian, and her name is May Ling. It's a very romantic thing, although when I was a kid I thought it quite horrible. He met her a few years after he married my mother, and then for years she was his mistress and lived in a little house on Willow Street in San Francisco, which he bought for her —"

"It sounds very French."

"I suppose so. She had a child, who is my half brother, Joe, but that was before they were married, and it wasn't very romantic, I guess, but pretty terrible, and then she couldn't stand it anymore, and she and Joe and her mother and father left San Francisco and went to Los Angeles, and then finally my father divorced my mother and followed her there."

"If you hadn't told me this before, there's no way in the world I could follow what you're saying. Must you read me the letter in English?"

"Yes. You'll meet her someday. She's dear and sweet and very clever, and she looks like one of those porcelain ladies out of an old Chinese print."

"Porcelain ladies out of a print?" Marcel asked dubiously.

"You know what I mean."

"Then read slowly, please." He kicked off his shoes, sat cross-legged on her couch, lit a cigarette, and prepared himself to listen. Barbara stared at him thoughtfully until finally he said, "Well, go on. Begin."

"I was just thinking — I do love you. You're very kind and very gentle and very patient, nothing like my notion of a Frenchman. No, that's not exactly what I mean."

"Of course it is. Don't go on with this. Just read your Chinese letter, very slowly."

"Dear Barbara," she read, "I have allowed too much to accumulate, which is the punishment of a very bad letter writer, so this will have to go on and on. I have the whole evening, because Dan drank too much last night, and he's not a good drinker, so here it is nine o'clock, and he's sound asleep. And the reason he drank so much is that we went to one of those Hollywood glamour parties that you read about in the newspapers, except that it was in Beverly Hills and not in Hollywood —"

"I don't understand that," Marcel interrupted.

"They live in Los Angeles, and it's very confusing. If you are in the movie business, they call it Hollywood, but there are lots of small towns in Los Angeles, and Beverly Hills is in Los Angeles. It's kind of a city inside of a city, and very posh —"

"That's enough," Marcel protested. "Just read the letter, but slowly."

"— not in Hollywood," she read, "but in one of those fantastic pink stucco palaces that these people live in, and it all happened because Dan is building a yacht for a Hungarian film director by the name of Alex Hargasey. You know about the old boatyard that Dan and Sam Goldberg took over on Terminal Island. The whole venture wasn't going well at all until Hargasey hired Pete Lomas's mackerel boat for a film he was making, and then Pete brought Hargasey to Dan, and now Dan is building him this huge, expensive yacht that will cost enough money to keep the boatyard going another year.

"Well, Hargasey is absolutely intrigued by your father, and he insisted that we come to this party, which was held to celebrate the completion of the film, which will be called *The Angry Sea*. Can you imagine, a middle-aged Chinese lady among all those movie stars and glamorous people! At first I absolutely refused to go, but then Dan and Joe insisted that I must, and I put together a sort of Chinese costume, and Dan rented a tuxedo, and there we were. Barbara, your father was wonderful. Not only was he the most impressive and handsome man there, but all these beautiful, celluloid women were practically climbing all over him. But Hargasey, who is about fifty and paunchy and has the most incredible accent, attached himself to me, and presently informed me that he had conceived a great passion for me and that we must have what he called a 'liaison.' Isn't that a wonderful word? They are absolutely the strangest people I have ever known. When I told Dan about it, I expected him to be furious and prepared myself to calm him down, but he laughed himself silly. I think he's becoming much too sure of himself. We were introduced to Greta Garbo and Bette Davis and Spencer Tracy, only I think it was not Spencer Tracy but his twin brother, who goes places instead, and it was all absolutely unbelievable. And the strangest part of it is that my father, who is such a serious old Chinese gentleman, insisted that I go into every detail of who I saw and met — such is the power of the movie industry.''

"Your grandfather is Chinese?" Marcel said in awe.

"No, no, no. How many times must I explain to you? Feng Wo is Joe's grandfather, a very scholarly and dignified gentleman who translates Chinese philosophy and who has had a book published by the University of California Press. He also managed my father's business for years and years."

"No, please, don't explain anymore. Is the letter over?"

"Not quite. I'll read slowly. Joe — I'm reading now —"

"I can see that. Your brother, Joe."

"Joe is starting his second year at college. He spent the summer in the Napa Valley, at Higate, working for Jake and Clair Levy. You never met the Levys, but you will soon. They're taking a trip to Europe and they'll be in Paris, and I took the liberty of giving them your address and telephone number. They'll arrive, I think, about three weeks after you get this letter. I know that it was a liberty, but they're dear, good people. Jake's father, Mark, was Dan's partner for twenty years, from nineteen ten to nineteen thirty. Clair's father was Dan's first captain. He died when the *Oceanic* was torpedoed in nineteen seventeen, and after that Clair lived with the Levys until she and Jake were married. Jake had some bad experiences overseas during the war, and he wanted no part of his father's money. Very idealistic. He felt the money was tainted, since Dan and Mark built their empire out of war shipping, and he and Clair took whatever savings they had and bought an old winery for a song during Prohibition. It's quite a place now, and part of the reason for their trip to Europe is Jake's plan to put their wine on the French market. Can you imagine Frenchmen buying California wine?

''And if it were not sufficiently complicated with Joe being half Chinese and one quarter French and one quarter Italian, Sally, Jake Levy's youngest child, has fallen madly in love with him. Since she's not yet thirteen, no one is taking it very seriously, but the combination, at some future date, would be absolutely fascinating, since Jake is Jewish and Clair is a mixture of Irish, English, and German. Sally is a strange and lovely child, wild as a hare and smart as a whip and as unlike Joe as anything you could imagine, skinny, long legs, and the same pale blue eyes and straw-colored hair that her grandmother, Sarah, once had. She is convinced that she is ugly and undesirable, and she confessed to me in utter misery that her breasts were too small, her legs too long and skinny, her skin too freckled, and her hair no better than straw. Can you imagine? From a thirteen-year-old. She is much too liberated for her age, and she told Joe that if he ever looked at another girl, she would kill him. I think he is flattered.

"Anyway, there is a little of our life back here. Please, do be kind to the Levys. But I know you will. I don't think you could be unkind to anyone. Dan sends all his love, and I do keep after him to write, but to him a letter is a monumental task. Joe misses you, as we all do. When will you come home?"

"Zat, dear one, is zi question," Marcel said in English.

"Very good."

"The question or my English?"

"Your English."

"Thank you. But if we were married, it would make for problems."

"Are you asking me? It's an odd way to propose."

"I'm afraid to ask."

Barbara, staring at him thoughtfully, said nothing.

Joe Lavette could not get her out of his mind. The University of California campus did not lack beautiful girls. There was a long-limbed, tawny-skinned breed that California seemed to produce, robust, good-looking women whose eyes followed and admired the young student. With good reason. Twenty-one years old, Joe Lavette stood six-foot-two, slightly taller than his father; he had Dan's broad shoulders without the thickness, without the heavy overlay of muscle; his features were more delicate, the nose smaller, the dark eyes with a slight Oriental cast, the black hair straight and cropped short. He was not simply a handsome young man, but different, unusual, race and breed titillating the curiosity of everyone who noticed him. Warm, emotional, perhaps overly sentimental, he found that he fell in and out of love all too easily. His problem, which he recognized, was to remain unattached until he finished medical school and his subsequent internship. It had been a miracle to him that he had been accepted at all, and to resist making a permanent alliance with one of the number of blond, blue-eyed women who welcomed his affection required all his will power.

Sally Levy helped. At least to the extent that once the summer at Higate was over, he found himself thinking about her constantly. "I am not in love with her," he assured himself. "I am not stupid or romantic enough to be in love with a demented thirteen-year-old kid." He had had affairs with four girls, successively, and had convinced himself that he was sincerely in love with all four of them, also successively. But when he fixed any one of them in his mind as candidates for marriage, the image was always blocked by the memory of Sally Levy, her oversized hands scratched from the grape picking, her fingers stained with grape juice, her face covered with freckles, her straw-colored hair an unwashed tangle, and her eyes filled with a foolish, cowlike worship. She followed him everywhere, made an ultimate nuisance of herself, and then finally said to him, one evening,

"You might as well know about it. I love you."

"You're crazy," he told her.

"Sure, that's a fine thing to say."

"Jesus, you're thirteen years old."

"I didn't have anything to do with that. Anyway, it's no reason why you can't be nice to me."

"I am nice to you."

"You are like hell. You don't even know that I exist. You pay more attention to the damn dogs."

"Why don't you stop trying to talk tough?" he asked her gently.

"Maybe it's just the way I am."

"Maybe."

"How do you feel about me?" she demanded.

"What do you mean, how do I feel about you. I like you all right. We're sort of related, aren't we?"

"No. How could we be related? You're Chinese. But that doesn't bother me."

"Thank you."

"Because I'm in love with you."

"Yes, you said that before."

"In a few weeks you'll be going back to Los Angeles. You'll forget all about me."

"Not very likely."

"You don't even say that nice. You think I'm just a crazy kid, don't you?"

Joe shook his head hopelessly.

"Well, I'm not. I started to menstruate."

He stared at her, unable to think of an appropriate comment.

"Well, if you're going to medical school, that shouldn't shock you."

"It doesn't shock me. It's just a funny thing for a kid to say."

"Why don't you stop calling me a kid? Why can't you take me seriously? If you did, you'd at least come up here sometime to see me. I can't go down to Los Angeles. What do you think my mother would say if

I told her that I was in love with you and I have all kinds of crazy dreams about you making love to me?"

"I can imagine what she'd say."

"So you won't come to see me, not even once?"

"How can I, Sally? I'll be in medical school. Do you know what medical school is like? They work you twenty-four hours a day."

"And in between, you sleep with the nurses."

"God Almighty, where do you get your ideas?"

"I read a lot."

"I bet you do."

"Anyway, you can be sure of one thing. If you marry anyone else, I'll just kill you."

"Just like that?"

"You bet."

"Well," he said, "you don't have to kill me, because I don't intend to marry anyone."

Thinking about it now, months later, her image remained with him, vivid, alive. Whoever he was with paled into dullness against that memory.

It was a year since Barbara had met Marcel Duboise, and to celebrate the occasion, she prepared dinner for the two of them in her apartment on the Quai de Passy. She had been reading French cookbooks, practicing assiduously, and for the occasion she decided on a *boeuf en croûte*. She had to finish her piece for the magazine, and that took the morning. Then she skipped lunch, contenting herself with a cup of coffee and a cigarette, and went to work on the *boeuf*, wondering meanwhile, as she had so often before, how it was that a nation of superb cooks built apartments with such wretched kitchens. Hers was no better than a large closet. The dish was a challenge; for herself, she considered *haute cuisine* to be an utter waste of time and rather silly in the bargain, but since she happened to be in love with a Frenchman, she was determined to conquer it. She had done her shopping in the early morning, in the best local tradition. Beef fillet. She trimmed it carefully, tied it up, giggling at her careful effort, rubbed it with pepper, and then browned it in fresh sweet butter, all the while feeling that she was working out a puzzle rather than preparing food. Ten minutes in a hot oven. While it was cooling, she read over her piece for the magazine: the new spring fashions, a smattering of politics that she had picked up from *Le Monde* — she was still on uneasy ground with politics — the three new best-selling novels, particularly Aragon's new book, and the opening of a new loan exhibit of the Impressionists. She was on firm ground there; at least that much her mother had given her, and after reading it, she decided that Jean would like it. Jean read every piece she wrote, and discussed her pieces in the letters they exchanged. It was in her last letter that Jean had observed that her daughter was becoming a "damned competent and professional writer." It was high praise.

The meat had cooled by now. Slice the mushrooms, sauté in butter, chop the mixed herbs with the parsley, add that, cool again. Now to make the puff pastry, so absolutely foolish and so absolutely complex. She had pinned up the recipe on the wall in front of her. Roll out the pastry and divide in two. Mixture of mushrooms and spices on the larger piece. Place the beef on top of it, fold pastry up and around, second piece of pastry over the top. The egg glaze. She had forgotten that entirely. Then into a hot oven for forty minutes. It left her only enough time to shower and dress. When she took the dish out of the oven, brown and beautiful, filling the house with its good smell, Marcel was at the door.

He brought a bottle of champagne and another of red wine, and under his arm was a long loaf of fresh bread. "A double celebration," he announced, after Barbara had taken the packages and kissed him.

"Double?"

"Our anniversary and my promotion. I am no longer a contemptible critic."

"Oh, wonderful! But you never were a contemptible critic, never a contemptible anything."

"All critics are contemptible. Who was

it, Shaw or some other very wise man, who said the critic is like the eunuch in the harem? He watches the trick turned every night, but knows he could never do it himself."

"Yes, very clever. Now please tell me what happened," Barbara begged him.

"Ah. So you wish to know?"

"Yes, I wish to know."

"Very well. My estimable editor, I hear he is looking for someone on special assignment in Spain. True, we have three men there already, but this is very special. So I go to him, I plead, I threaten, I entreat, I become a veritable Cyrano of persuasion — and finally he melts, he agrees. Whereby, I am going to Spain."

"What kind of special assignment?" Barbara asked slowly, quietly.

"Ah, come, come." He started to kiss her again, but she pushed him away.

"What kind of special assignment?"

"What is that marvelous, enchanting smell?"

"Stop it! Don't be cute now. I want to know what you are going to do in Spain."

"All right. You have heard of the

Fifteenth Brigade, the Internationals. It includes an American Brigade of volunteers, which they call the Abraham Lincoln Brigade. My editor wants a series of pieces on them. They are very brave, very gallant, and we have printed very little about them. You see, I speak English, thanks to you.''

''You told him you speak English?'' she asked coldly.

''But I do, Barbara.''

''I suppose you do, in a manner of speaking, if you call it English. I think the whole thing stinks.''

''Just like that?''

''How else? Shall I tie it up in a rose-colored ribbon? You know how I feel about war, about this insanity of men killing each other for their filthy causes, for their noble aims.''

''We never talked about it.''

''You've been living with me and sleeping with me for almost a year. You don't know me? Must I spell everything out — this is how Barbara feels about this and this is how Barbara feels about that?''

''You're right. There's a lot I don't know

about you. I've never seen you in such a royal rage before."

"Then it's time."

"Baby, baby," he said, "we can't have a fight. We never had a fight. Please, please try to understand what this means to me, a by-line assignment as a special foreign correspondent. I don't have to argue the cause of the Spanish Republic. You know it as well as I do, and you know what that butcher Franco has done. I'm not enlisting. I'm not a volunteer. I am simply going as a writer, as a journalist, to put down what I see and hear."

"So you can say, thank God for a war."

"No, that's not fair."

"What is fair? For me to fall in love with a man who goes off to get shot at in this stupid game? I told you about the kid in San Francisco, his poor wasted life. He was in love with me. I was selfishly spared, because there was no way I could love him. But I do love you, and I will not have this happen to me again. I will not. I know I live in a world of maniacs, but I thought that you and I —"

"Would be spared?" he asked gently.

"No one is spared, Barbara, dear love, no one. And this is something I have to do, believe me. It's not forever. Only six weeks, and then I'll be back, whole and safe and sound, I promise you."

She dropped into a chair and began to weep.

"No, no tears, please." He knelt beside her, kissing her hand, first on the back and then on the palm, a gesture so French, so unexpected, that she began to giggle through her tears.

"May I open the champagne?" he asked her.

"Yes."

"And will you tell me what the marvelous smell is?"

"Boeuf en croûte."

"Am I not the most fortunate of all men? Am I not?"

Later that evening, her emotions under control, Barbara tried to be both practical and helpful. "Remember," she said to Marcel, "you are an observer. You have no obligation to put yourself in a dangerous situation. That would be stupid and wasteful. Your job is to see things and write about them."

"Yes, my dear," he agreed.

"You're not listening."

"But I am. Every word."

"By the way, I do know someone in that unit. Well, no, I don't really know him, but the Levys do. You remember? I told you about them."

"Yes. Of course."

"It seems that this boy worked for them at the winery. His name is Bernie Cohen. Can you remember that?"

"I will try. What is he doing in Spain?"

"Well, he's Jewish and he's a Zionist or something of that sort, and he intends to go to Palestine. From what my brother wrote to me, he enlisted in the Lincoln Brigade to get experience in fighting — which is perfectly insane, but I don't know what part of this is not insane. But Joe met him at Higate, and he says he is competent and reliable, so at least that would be one person you would know."

"Barbara, I don't really have to know anyone. I'll be with the press. You simply must not worry about me. I'll be all right."

"You don't have to go. You can still tell them that you don't want this wretched assignment."

"I can't. You know that."

"All right. I won't speak of it again. You know how I feel. Just think about it."

"Not only that, but I'll do the dishes."

"To hell with the dishes. Take me to bed, and we'll pretend there are only two of us in a very beautiful, uncomplicated world."

Marcel left for Spain the day before the Levys arrived in Paris, and the evening of the day they arrived, they telephoned Barbara and asked her to dine with them the following day. On her father's side, Barbara had no blood relations. Daniel Lavette, the child of two immigrant parents, had been left an orphan at the age of seventeen. Since she was a child, Barbara had known of his close attachment to the Cassala family in San Mateo and the Levy family in Sausalito, and she had also known of her mother's distaste for both families. They were a part of her father's life. She had never met any of them, but through the years she had heard a great deal about them. For most Californians, the wine business wears a halo of romance, and Barbara was intrigued with the notion of two young people buying an abandoned winery during Prohibition and turning it into a prosperous enterprise — and now the thought of selling California wine in France delighted her. In any case, they would fill some of the empty hours that faced her during Marcel's absence. Until he left, she had not realized how totally she had come to depend on him, and when she looked back at her years in Paris before she had met him, they appeared to be lonely and barren beyond belief.

There were no tears after her initial outburst. She had gone with Marcel to the Gare de Lyon, and while waiting for his train, they lunched at one of the stands in the station, agreeing that the ham, sandwiched in small loaves of fresh bread, and the mugs of cold beer were as good as anything they had ever tasted. They laughed a good deal, and she expunged the scene that had taken place in her apartment by assuring him that she would steal from his pieces in *Le Monde* without conscience, incorporating what she stole into her own 'Letter from Paris.' They were self-consciously gay and young and delighted with themselves until it was train time, and then she clung to him, whispering, "You bastard, I'll never forgive you for going away." But then, when the train began to move and he had poked his head out of his compartment, she ran alongside and shouted, "I've forgiven you, but only for six weeks. One day more and I'll cut your heart out."

Two days later, getting out of a cab at the Hôtel de la Trémoille, where the Levys were staying, she felt that she had worked out her period of being alone and that six weeks was by no means the eternity she had imagined. Jake and Clair Levy were waiting for her in the lobby. Barbara recognized them; she knew that Clair Levy was a redhead, but she was unprepared for the striking, unusual look of the woman, almost as tall as her husband, who was well over six feet, long-limbed, almost raw-boned, a high, full bust, and a strong-featured freckled face under a mop of flaming red hair. She was quite beautiful, yet Barbara felt that to think of her simply as a beautiful woman diminished her. Jake Levy was a burly heavyset man, with dark hair turning gray, a prominent nose, pale blue eyes, his heavy shoulders tight in his clothes, like a farmer in city dress.

Barbara walked over to them and said, "I know you because daddy told me so much. I'm Barbara Lavette."

Their greeting waited on a moment of amazement and delight; then Clair Levy folded Barbara in her arms, kissed her, and then stepped back to look at her. "Oh, great! You're just what you should be!"

Barbara kissed Jake. He stood there grinning at her. "We're such old friends," Barbara said. "We mustn't pretend that we've just met. I knew you both the moment I came into the hotel. Daddy always spoke of the green eyes and the red hair."

"You see," Clair told her husband, "being a bit freakish has its advantages."

"Oh, no!" Barbara cried. "I think

you're the most stunning woman I've ever seen."

"So do I," Jake said comfortably. "We're so glad to finally meet you, Barbara. I saw you once, when you were two or three years old. Danny sneaked you out to Sausalito. You remember, Clair?"

"I certainly do. You've changed, darling."

"I'm sure I have."

"We didn't make any dinner arrangements," Jake explained. "This is my first time back since the war, and the first for Clair, and I've forgotten what little French I picked up then. I thought you'd know where the food is good, since you're practically a native."

"One of the delicious things about Paris is that the food is good practically everywhere. There's a little restaurant on the Left Bank called Lapérouse where I know the proprietor. We're sure to get a table, and the food is good. We can take a cab."

They listened with the awe that Americans hold toward anyone fluent in a foreign language as she gave directions to the cab driver and then to her conversation with the owner of the restaurant, to whom she introduced them as members of her family.

"Your French is amazing," Jake said as they were seated.

"It should be. My goodness, I had four years of it in private school and then two more years at college, and I've been living here almost four years. I even think in French now, and do you know, I dream in French."

"Don't go on." Clair sighed. "I don't have two words."

"She speaks Spanish like a native," Jake said.

"Oh, come on, Jake. Don't be defensive. We have Chicanos working at the winery, and I can tell them what to do. That's about it."

At Jake's urging, Barbara ordered dinner while he pored over the wine list. He selected three chateau Burgundies, each a different label and a different year.

"Are you sure?" Barbara asked him. "We'll never finish three bottles."

"We don't have to. We've been tasting

Burgundies at every meal on the ship coming over.''

''It's a practically demonic compulsion with Jake,'' Clair explained. ''They talk of carrying coals to Newcastle. We come carrying wine to France. Every grower we know says we are totally out of our minds — even for dreaming that America could sell wine to France. But I guess Jake and I have been out of our minds since we got into wine, and do you know, Barbara, I do think that all wine makers are a little crazy. It comes from breathing fumes day and night.''

''That's nonsense,'' Jake said. ''If we're crazy, we're crazy like foxes. I'm the kind of jingoistic American who thinks we can do anything better than anyone else, and that includes wine. Are we boring you with all this talk of wine?''

''No, no, please. I'm fascinated,'' Barbara assured him.

''All right. I'll try to explain. Up in the Napa Valley and the Sonoma Valley, where wine is like a religion, the growers with very few exceptions have decided that our Cabernet Sauvignon is the great red wine of California and thereby of America. Oh, it's good all right, and when it's well made, really well made, it can compare with some of the fine French Médocs. Essentially, it's a claret. Also, it's a wine that can stand aging, and if you can afford to lay it away and let it sit for ten years, you have a wine as good as anything in the world. But we can't put away our wine for ten years; we just don't have the money or the reserves, and as for a young Cabernet — well, it has a little too much tannin for my taste."

"That's the stuff in wine that makes the cheeks pucker," Clair said. "It's also rather sharp."

"So we broke with the crowd," Jake said, "and decided to experiment with Pinot Noir. That's a Burgundy. The first of our vines came from France, but California soil and California sunshine change it — improve the grape, to my taste. Pinot Noir is a beautiful wine, soft and smooth as velvet when it's well made, and with much less of the tannic taste. But the decisive fact is that while it is also a red that needs aging, two years of laying it away will produce as fine an aged wine as eight or ten years with the claret. Now ours is a varietal, which means wine made out of a single type of grape. The French tend to blend their Burgundies. By now, Clair and I have tasted at least forty Pinots and Burgundies, and we still think we're sitting on top of the lot."

"That's to *our* taste," Clair said. "We're by no means great wine tasters. We know a little, much less than Jake likes to think we know, and the wine is as much an excuse for this trip as a business venture. We shipped ten cases over here, not so much for France as for Holland and Denmark, where we think there might be a market. Just for tasting. Not for selling. Germany would be ideal, but we wouldn't set foot in that hateful place. Anyway, American wine might just be a novelty. What do you think of the notion?"

"I think it's great," Barbara said. "Just great. And I think I could be of some help. I know people on *Le Monde,* which is one of the most prestigious papers in Paris, and I think I could arrange for an interview. They're Marcel's dear friends, and I do think it's newsworthy. I'll write about your visit myself, but I'm afraid publicity in New York won't help you much."

"Marcel?" Clair asked.

Barbara smiled. "There goes the cat out of the bag. You're the first to know. I haven't told mother or daddy, but I simply must tell someone. Marcel Duboise is a French journalist whom I love very much. Someday, I suppose, we'll be married. He's thirty years old, dark, skinny, kind of funny-looking, and very kind and very smart."

"I'm so glad. He sounds wonderful," Clair said. "Will we meet him?"

"Only if you can stay six weeks. He left two days ago for Spain." Then she went on to tell them about Marcel — who he was, what he did, and how they had met. She found herself talking to Jake and Clair as if she had known them all her life, in part because she was so hungry for some part of home, of California, and in part because they were warm and open and easy to talk to.

The food came and the wine came. The

wine was tasted, judged, discussed. Barbara knew very little about wine. She and Marcel were quite content with *vin ordinaire,* a liter of which could be bought for a franc, and she was quite in awe of the manner in which Clair and Jake discussed the virtues of the three Burgundies. Then they told her how they had gotten into making wine, with old Rabbi Blum coming to them with the proposal that they make the sacramental wine for the Orthodox synagogues of San Francisco. "He's been dead these past five years, rest his soul," Clair said. "But would you believe it, we just about built Higate on sacramental wine. We sold to the Jews, the Catholics, the Episcopalians — sweet, horrible stuff. Yes, we still make a good deal of it."

A whole past came alive for Barbara that evening. They told her the story of how Dan Lavette and Mark Levy bought their first iron ship, the *Oregon Queen,* from an old Swede called Swenson. Clair's father, Jack Harvey, was the captain of the *Oregon Queen,* and Clair, then ten years old, had her first mad crush on Dan.

"He was always my hero," Clair said. "That never changed. Martha — poor child, she's dead. She was Jake's sister — Martha and I both worshipped the ground Dan walked on —"

Jake, uncomfortable, changed the subject. They had scheduled ten days in Paris and then would be off to Amsterdam. Would it be possible for Barbara to spend some time with them, perhaps show them some of the sights? She said she would love it, and with Marcel away, it was the best thing that could have happened to her. They talked on and on, and suddenly they discovered that it was midnight, and that they were the last ones in the restaurant.

Before she left them, Barbara said, "By the way, Joe wrote to me that there was a man named Cohen who had once worked at Higate and who's now with the Lincoln Battalion."

"Bernie. Of course," Clair said.

"He's quite a guy," Jake added. "A little mad, but then, who isn't?"

"A little mad?"

"He has this obsession about a Jewish

294

homeland in Palestine. He learned farming, and now it's fighting. That's a hell of a reason to enlist in a war, but it takes all kinds."

Barbara waited — for a by-line dispatch in *Le Monde* or for a letter. With the Levys, she wore an air of relaxed gaity. Her anxieties were none of theirs; they had planned this trip and looked forward to it for years, and she felt a proprietary responsibility for their time in a city she knew so well and loved so much. Jake and Clair were almost childlike in their delight with what they saw. They put themselves wholly in her hands, and when she told them that they must have an entire day for the Ile de la Cité, they accepted the assignment willingly. Barbara's first hour in Westminster in London had left her in tears; her first hour in Notre-Dame had left her in a state of exultation, and when she came there now with Jake and Clair, she tried to recapture the feeling, to feel that in the Europe of 1938, God was in His heaven and all was right with the world. It was not there, and she slipped away to be by herself and let her tears wash out her eyes. When she joined them again, Clair said, "You've been crying. Why? What's wrong?" And Barbara assured her that she was simply an overemotional person. "I cry at the drop of a hat. This place is haunted, you know. Let's go to the flower market. This little island has the most marvelous flower market in the world." But then she changed her mind, as if she had betrayed her new friends, and insisted that they climb to the top and see the breathtaking view. They stood there entranced, all the hazy, misty beauty of Paris spread out beneath them.

It was almost midnight when they dropped Barbara at her apartment, and in spite of her vow to be both patient and calm, she telephoned Marcel's friend Jean Brissard, awakened him, and then begged him to forgive her. "But there's been nothing," she said, "nothing in the paper and no letter."

"Barbara, he's only been gone five days."

"But the paper must be in touch with him."

"Barbara, don't you understand about Spain? He had to go over the Pyrenees. The lines are very fluid. He might have to hole up for days. Also, he's not there as a regular correspondent. He's not required to file a dispatch every day. He's doing a background piece on the Americans. He might not file it for two weeks. As for the mail, it goes by sea. It could take a week for a letter to reach Paris. So just be patient and don't worry."

It was reassuring, and Barbara, exhausted after her day as a tour guide, slept well. The Levys had a wine-tasting appointment the following afternoon at the offices of Lebouche & Dume, one of the largest wine wholesalers in Paris, and Barbara had agreed to go along as interpreter. The Levys had been assured that English would be spoken, but Barbara explained to them that such assurance meant very little in France. She assigned the morning to the regular American tourist routine, up the funicular to the heights of Montmartre, or the

Butte, as she called it, apologizing for the cheap, touristy gimmicks that had invaded it, but also repeating Marcel's story of the bloody battle that had raged there during the time of the Paris Commune. They lunched at a little restaurant in the shadow of the Sacré-Coeur, where they were plagued by the vendors of so-called Paris postcards.

"But this is a part of it," Barbara explained. "How could you go home and tell them you were not at Montmartre?"

"I love it," Jake said. "Don't apologize."

"Tomorrow we will begin with the Medicis fountain in the Luxembourg Gardens, and that will take the taste of this away."

With Clair carefully cradling two bottles of Pinot Noir in a canvas bag, they made their way to the Faubourg - St.-Honoré, where Lebouche & Dume had their offices in an old town house that rented space to an antique dealer on the main floor. They passed through an archway and went up a lift and then into a splendidly furnished set of rooms. An ancient, gilded wine press was the only indication of the business conducted there. The waiting room contained an assortment of lovely pieces from the time of Louis XIV and XV that caused Barbara to exclaim in delight. A door opening momentarily revealed another room where half a dozen clerks labored at desks, but no sign or sound of commerce was permitted in the waiting room or in the office of Monsieur Lebouche, into which a stout, middle-aged receptionist conducted them and where they were received by Lebouche himself, a bearded gentleman in his seventies, dressed in striped trousers and a morning coat, pink-cheeked and white-haired. He greeted them graciously, obviously amused at the notion of American wine being sold in France.

"Monsieur Dume is indisposed," he explained. "Otherwise, we would both be here, no? He is only sixty-two, a young man, but he abuses his body. You are Mr. and Mrs. Levy, of California. But this enchanting young lady?"

Barbara explained her position and the Levys' lack of ease with the

French language.

"They do not speak French?" Monsieur Lebouche asked in amazement. "They make wine and they do not speak French?"

Barbara apologized profusely. California was very far away. It occurred to her to mention that they both spoke Spanish.

"Excellent. We will converse in Spanish."

Jake sighed and resigned himself to silence. Clair unpacked the two bottles of wine, explaining that it was a varietal out of an ancestry of Burgundian vines. Lebouche could not keep his eyes off Clair. She was at least four inches taller than the wine merchant, and the interesting combination of green eyes and red hair obviously fascinated him. "Ah, what a splendid woman!" he said to Barbara in French. "If Monsieur Dume were here, he would be quite out of his mind. An extraordinary woman."

Clair was holding forth in Spanish about California soil and sunshine. Barbara whispered to Jake in English that

Monsieur Lebouche considered Clair to be an extraordinary woman.

"So do I," Jake said. "This is a damn peculiar way they do business here."

Lebouche found a corkscrew and opened the bottles. Then he took two beautiful crystal decanters out of a cabinet. "We decant it now," he explained to Clair. The others no longer mattered. "We let it breathe a little. Then we taste." He selected two wine goblets. Obviously, he and Clair were to be the tasters. "Madame," he said to her, "you ennoble the art of wine-making."

"You haven't tasted it yet," Clair replied, smiling.

"I refer to you, not to the wine. Now we taste."

He poured two glasses of wine. "You must drink with me," he said to Clair. The others watched and waited, Barbara utterly entranced by the old man, his manner and ritual, Jake trying to maintain a calm face and repress a desire to burst out laughing. Clair accepted the ritual gravely and calmly. No toast. She followed the old man's motion as he

raised the glass to his lips and tasted. He
rolled his head, rolling the wine around in
his mouth, and she did likewise. Then he
swallowed. Then he held the glass to his
nostrils, sniffing the aroma.

"Pinot Noir?"

Clair nodded.

"How long is it aged?"

"Two years."

"In what wood?"

"Our cooperage is German oak."

"How long in the bottle?"

"Four months."

"We'll taste again." He lifted the glass
to his lips. Again the ritual. "You've
tasted our Burgundies?"

"A good many of them," Clair replied.

"This is quite different. Is it warm in
your Napa Valley?"

"The summers are hot, yes."

"Very strange. Hot weather spoils the
Pinot Noir, but this — very excellent. And
different. A most unusual wine, befitting a
most unusual woman. If I were ten years
younger, I'd challenge that great ox of a
husband of yours, I would, the woman and
the wine. He doesn't know what I'm

saying, does he?"

"I'm afraid his Spanish is not up to it," Clair said sweetly. "I am sure that if you were ten years younger, Monsieur Lebouche, we would welcome the challenge. Will you take the wine?"

"Can I refuse you so small a thing. But only as a novelty. France is France. What will you charge me for two hundred cases?"

"What the devil's going on?" Jake demanded.

"But you speak Spanish, dear."

"Plain Spanish, not this."

"He says he'll take two hundred cases to start. He feels it will be simply a novelty, but he's interested. He wants to know the price. Oh, yes, he approves of the wine."

Outside again, Clair asked Barbara whether she had followed the conversation inside.

"No, I don't have two words of Spanish. But you were wonderful, I could see that."

"Enlighten me," Jake said.

"He liked the wine. He said that if he were ten years younger, he would have both, myself and the wine. Isn't that perfectly wonderful, Jake? I'm almost forty years old. France is one hell of a place, don't you think?''

"That old goat. I'll be damned."

Six days later, the Levys departed for Holland, and on the same day, Barbara received a letter from Marcel, the first letter. He told her how much he loved her, assured her that all was going well, explained that since he did not care to have the letter censored he would go into no details, and promised to write again very soon. It was not, to Barbara's way of thinking, a very satisfactory letter, but it relieved her anxiety. He also mentioned that he had met her fellow Californian, Bernie Cohen, and that he liked him immensely.

Dr. Kaplan had never treated a Chinese before — there were few Chinese families in Westwood — and now he appeared troubled and uncertain as the frail Chinese gentleman dressed himself. Feng Wo sensed this, and directed the conversation very matter-of-factly. "It is cancer, isn't it?"

Kaplan was a young man, in his early thirties, and he had come to Los Angeles from New York and set himself up in practice only a short time before. Feng Wo had chosen him almost at random, looking for a physician who would have no possible connection with his family. He suspected that it might well be Dr. Kaplan's first terminal case.

"It's not operable, is it?"

"Both lungs," Dr. Kaplan said miserably.

"You're quite sure?"

Strange, a small Oriental gentleman who spoke perfect English, who appeared to be undisturbed by a sentence of death. Dr. Kaplan nodded. "I mean, there's no reason why you shouldn't have another opinion, but it's not something that is easily mistaken. If you'd like me to recommend an internist?"

"No, that won't be necessary. How long do I have?"

"A few months, perhaps a little more."

"I understand."

"I'd like you to see me again, perhaps in

a week or two."

"Yes, most likely."

It was almost noon when Feng Wo arrived at the boatyard in San Pedro, and during the trip down there, he examined himself, his being, and the fact of his impending death. He was only sixty-three years old; he had not yet begun to think of himself as an old man; and once again he was managing the affairs of Dan Lavette. From the moment his son-in-law had asked him to come in and take charge of the books and finances of the new enterprise, he had felt youthful and renewed. Years before, when Dan Lavette's great empire had washed out in the debris of the Depression, his daughter, May Ling, had arranged for him to make a translation of the writings of the Chinese philosopher Lao Tzu. At that time, he had paid tribute to her skill in putting together a situation where he was commissioned to do the work for the University of California Press. His scholarship left something to be desired, yet somehow he had managed the translation, plodding through the work more as an effort to please his daughter than himself. It was only a temporary stopgap in the process of dying from lack of purpose and a feeling of utter uselessness. Now he was dying in fact, from a malignant disease for which there was no cure.

He went into the office that he now occupied at the shipyard and sat down at his desk, just sitting there and staring through the window at the mud flats and the still water of the bay. Then the door swung open and Dan Lavette entered, his voice booming with energy and excitement.

"Feng Wo, where the hell have you been? It's starting again, and I don't know whether to start climbing that lousy shitpile of success or to kick the whole thing into the mud."

Feng Wo turned to face him, his wrinkled face as impassive as ever. "What happened, Mr. Lavette?" he asked calmly.

"You won't believe this. Hargasey comes down this morning to look at his yacht. He's like a kid. He can't stay away from it, and this time he brings Samuel

Carlwin with him. Carlwin's the owner of the studio where Hargasey's slated to make his next picture, and I suppose he has more money than God. I lead them around the boat and explain things, and Carlwin never says a word. Then, when we climb down from the cribbing, Carlwin takes me aside. Lavette, he says to me, I want you to build me a yacht. Just like that. I say, sure, I'll be happy to build him a yacht. Then he says to me, I want it to be twice as big as the one you're building for that sonofabitch Hungarian gypsy.

"Can you imagine? I try to calm him down. I try to explain to him that a ship that size would be damn near an ocean liner, that it would cost him over a million dollars. But he doesn't want to listen. All he wants to know is what I need to get the job started. I tell him I need fifty thousand to draw up the plans and start ordering the material, and so help me God if he doesn't take out his checkbook and write out a check on the spot. Here it is." He took the check out of his pocket and handed it to Feng Wo, who looked at it, smiling slightly.

"Well, what about it, old man? What do we do?"

"We build the ship," Feng Wo said calmly. "In this strange and unreasonable world, nothing should surprise you, Mr. Lavette."

"I'll draw up a letter agreement, and I'll telephone Sam Goldberg to put together a contract. Meanwhile, get the check to the bank before he changes his mind, and then we'll get to work on costs. I don't know any more about what he wants than he does, but we'll figure something out. Twice the size of the one out there. Can you imagine?"

A week later, on his way home from San Pedro, Dan stopped to pick up May Ling at the library. She was waiting for him at the entrance. She took his arm and said, "Leave your car parked for a while, Danny, and we'll walk on the campus. I want to talk — here, not at home."

"You sound damn serious."

"I am, Danny. Very damn serious."

They began to walk. He didn't press the point. May Ling would tell him what she had to tell him in her own good time.

Anyway, it was a good evening for a walk, the sun dropping into a lacework of clouds, the air sharp and cool.

"It's about my father, Danny," she said at last.

"He's not feeling too well, is he?"

"Then you noticed."

"Do you know what's wrong with him?"

"He's dying, Danny."

"No! Good God, what are you saying?"

She nodded miserably.

"How do you know? That's crazy. He was down at the shop today. All right, he's tired. He doesn't have to work that hard. I don't push him."

"Danny, Danny, listen to me. Joe noticed that something was wrong, and he asked me if I could get papa to go down to USC with him, where they could do some tests. Papa got very annoyed at me. Joe insisted that I try to find out something, so I called five local doctors. The fifth was a Dr. Kaplan, and when I told him who I was, he admitted that papa had seen him twice. I went to see Dr. Kaplan. Papa has cancer of the lung. It's inoperable. He hasn't very long to live."

"My God," Dan whispered. "Are you sure? Who is this Kaplan? We don't have to let it rest there. We'll get the best doctors in California. There must be something we can do."

"Danny, dear, there's nothing we can do. Joe spoke to Dr. Kaplan. He took the X rays down to the medical school at USC. It's too late. Nothing can be done."

"Oh, Christ, what a lousy, rotten deal." They walked on. After a few minutes of silence, he asked her, "Does your mother know?"

"I'm sure she doesn't. I can't tell her. It has to come from papa. Danny, I want you to do this for me. Don't treat him differently, please, and don't let on that you know. Just let him work on as before. Dr. Kaplan said that in a few more weeks, he won't be able to work, but until then, he must decide."

It was an empty evening. Barbara had tried all day to begin her "Letter from Paris," but the words wouldn't come. Her contributions to *Manhattan Magazine* had achieved a reputation for their air of

311

gaity, for their lightness and gossipy quality, but all this day her heart had been heavy as lead. The single letter from Marcel had been her only word from him; then, day after day with nothing, no word in *Le Monde,* and nothing in the mail. She had gone to the newspaper and had been assured that they knew no more than she did. Then she waited, while all the joy and exuberance drained out of her life and the wonder-city of Paris became a bleak and lonely and strange place. She had never experienced anything like this before — days utterly empty, time moving like thick, reluctant oil. April became May. Susan Clark returned to America. Betty Greenberg went to London to cover an economic conference. And Barbara felt utterly abandoned and forsaken.

Then, a little after six o'clock, her doorbell rang. It was Jean Brissard, and before she could even ask what he was doing there, he said to her, "He's alive. He's all right, and I have a fat letter for you right here in my pocket. So may I come in?"

She threw her arms around him and

burst into tears. "You darling, sweet man!"

"Actually, I had hoped he would never show up. Then I could have you for myself."

"I don't believe that. Come in. Come on in." She ran into the bathroom to throw cold water on her face and wipe away the tears. Then, a moment later, she said, "I must get over crying about everything. I never do it when I'm alone."

"We were worried," Brissard admitted.

"Where is he? When will he come back?"

"First question. He's in Toulouse, in a hospital."

"Oh, no!"

"He's all right. I told you that. He was wounded in two places, a shell fragment in his right arm and a bullet wound in the leg. But he's all right."

"Are you sure?"

"Decide for yourself. Here's a letter to you." He handed her a thick envelope. "It's dictated. He found someone down there to take his dictation, and he's charged the paper the two hundred and

313

eighty francs he paid her. But he sent us one hell of a story, believe me. It's on the front page tomorrow.''

''What hospital?''

''The Sacred Heart.''

''Could I get a train to Toulouse tonight?''

''I doubt it. Look, Barbara, he's all right. You can telephone the hospital, if you wish. You can't speak to him because there's no telephone in his room. Go down there by all means, if you wish. But wait until tomorrow —''

She was tearing open the letter, her hands shaking.

''I'm going to run along,'' Brissard said. ''I'll be at the paper if you want to talk to me.''

She hardly realized that he had gone. She began to read:

''My darling Barbara, I am dictating this letter because my right arm is unfortunately not functioning. The lady taking the dictation, Madame Clouet, is, we think, some sort of a distant relative. She has five children, and she is an excellent stenographer and typist. You

314

know that my father and mother still live in Toulouse, so in a way I have finally come home to them, a bit battered, but otherwise in fine fettle. As for the story, I think it's good. As for my English, no more snide remarks from you and no more innuendos. I have been communicating in English — or American, if you will — believe it or not. My God, how I love you! How I adore you! Now Madame Clouet is regarding me very strangely. She is very proper. She says that for a writer, I am diffuse. She reads Balzac. I tell her to read Proust. She says she has no time for Proust, and that he bores her."

Laughing and crying all at once, Barbara paused to dry her eyes with the towel she had brought from the bathroom. "Not at all true that I don't cry when I am alone," she whispered to herself. "Not at all true." She turned back to the letter.

"Very well, where have I been? You will read my story in the paper, but it's a newspaper story. I have to tell it to you differently. To get here, they had to carry me part of the way over the passes in a litter, and in my rational moments I debated with myself whether to tell you what happened. Then I decided that I must, since neither of us has ever held anything back. So I begin with the group I joined, the 58th Lincoln Battalion, Americans. It is, or was, part of the 15th International Brigade, and when I joined them they had about three hundred men. Very young, most of them younger than we are. I wore my old service uniform, with a correspondent's patch and a tricolor. Not much of anything, but most of the kids in the 58th wore old pants and what you Americans call sweat shirts. They were volunteers from every part of the States, lots of them from New York City, and a good many from your place, California, and I felt that those were particularly wonderful, since they shared a place of origin with someone I love so much. Have you predisposed me toward America? I think I fell in love with those kids. They didn't look like soldiers. They carried bolt-action Springfield rifles, most of them, and they didn't even have cartridge belts. They stuffed their pockets full of cartridges and hand grenades. But my God, they are something.

"I had heard rumors when I joined them that the Republican front was breaking up and that soon there might be a general retreat across the Ebro, but they didn't know anything about this. I was with them two days, mostly experimenting with my English and trying to get some background stories, when orders came for the 58th Battalion to advance and to keep advancing until the orders were countermanded. There were six other correspondents there at their bivouac, three of them Americans. We had a meeting, and the correspondents decided that, in the light of the rumors they all had heard, the best thing would be to head back toward Barcelona for the time being. But I had just arrived. My lovely darling, I am not a brave man, and I know how you feel about 'heroes,' which is why I put it in quotation marks, but I had just arrived, and where was my story? Believe me, I had a vision of a lifetime of cursing out bad restaurants in print and reviewing second-rate plays, and I could not face it.

So I decided to move along with the 58th and see what happened. I had made some slight acquaintance with the two officers in command, one by the name of Dave Doran and the other by the name of Bob Merryman. Merryman was from California. Poor boys, they both died. I also met your Bernie Cohen, but more of that later.

"At first, they said flatly that I couldn't go along, but when I explained that I would be doing a special feature for *Le Monde* and that, since I was French, I had done my army service and that if it came to the worst, I could take care of myself, they relented and agreed I could move with them.

"The 58th began to advance. No opposition. It was hot and dry and bleak. Our water gave out, and we lost our liaison. We didn't know it then, but the Republican army had already broken, and the whole line was in retreat. The 58th had simply cut loose, and there we were, three hundred men advancing against the whole fascist army. About noontime, we spotted a fascist water truck. The men guarding it gave up without a fight, and everyone's mood changed. We had plenty of water, and the little victory over the truck gave us confidence. We tied up the three rebel soldiers, left them there, and continued our advance. But Merryman was nervous about the silence all around us, and he cut out on our flank to try to effect some kind of liaison.

"It was very hot. About three o'clock in the afternoon, we decided to rest, and we sprawled in the shade under a grove of olive trees. We waited there for Merryman to return. It was very strange, just the American battalion, all alone, a few goats in the distance, not a living soul otherwise, the hot Spanish sun sinking slowly toward the west, and silence. Where were the armies? Where was the war? Then Merryman returned and told us that the 58th had advanced deep into fascist territory, while behind us the whole Republican army was in retreat. Also, he had met a Republican soldier who told him that the way back behind us was closed.

"Doran gave the orders to march, and

we headed back, not quite the way we had come but through some rough country. We marched very quickly, and it was quite exhausting. Then we came to an elevation where we could look down into a little Spanish town — I think it was called Gondese or something of the sort. That's where the line of battle was, behind us now. We were behind the fascists, and we could see them driving their attack through the streets of the town, while the Spanish soldiers were trying to hold the little clay houses. Merryman and Doran decided that the only thing to do was to break through and join up with the Spaniards. It was getting on to twilight now. They detached a patrol of twenty-five men, and ordered them to fight their way through the fascist lines, join up with the Spaniards, and then we would mount an attack and drive the fascists out of the town. I thought it was very poor tactics to send out twenty-five men with no support, but I was in no position to comment. Well, we watched it happen. The whole patrol was wiped out. My God, those boys were so brave and so senseless! They were caught in a crossfire, attacking against machine guns with their old Springfields, and we watched it happen. There was nothing we could do.

"Then the Spaniards gave up the town and retreated to a hill beyond it, and there we were, holding our hill with the Republican soldiers on the other hill, and the fascists between us. We tried to dig in, but there weren't enough trenching tools. Then, in the last light of day, the fascists sent a regiment of calvary charging up the hill against us. Would you believe it, men in shining cuirasses waving their swords? I guess that with the Republican army retreating everywhere, the fascists felt that any show of force would carry the day. We stopped that charge and took a heavy toll of the cavalry. Night came, and we were joined by a few hundred Spaniard soldiers who had been cut off. But by then the fascists had brought up their artillery. For two hours they shelled us. It wasn't good. Eight more Americans died there, and that was where I got the piece of shrapnel in my arm. It wasn't too bad at first. But we knew that if we stayed there, it would be the end.

"We set out in the dark, and we walked all the rest of the night. By some miracle, we were not intercepted by the fascists who had been shelling us. Then, toward dawn, we ran smack into what may have been a German Nazi outfit. It was as if all the devils in hell had broken loose, as if their machine guns were set up and waiting for us. The Americans, instead of turning and getting out of there, attacked, and they were just cut to pieces. Afterward I heard that Merryman and Doran were both killed there, and I don't think that even a hundred of the Americans survived that battle. Anyway, it was the end of the 58th Battalion. I was shot in the leg, and the same Bernie Cohen I spoke of before dragged me out of it, and then it was over, with only the crying and moaning of the wounded, and I got out of it somehow, hanging on to Cohen, and we found a little shed, which we crawled into. We couldn't see what was happening from where we were, but we heard German voices all around us, and we were sure that sooner or later they would find us, and Cohen said that if they did, they'd shoot us on the spot, that the Germans didn't take prisoners. Whether or not this is true, I don't know, but I heard the same thing from others. Cohen was very strong and competent. He made splints out of some old wood in the shed and bound up my leg. I was in great pain, and after that, the events are somewhat vague.

"We stayed in the shed all day, and when night came, we left the shed, Cohen carrying me on his back. We were close to the Ebro. He asked me if I could swim, and I said I thought I could, and somehow or other we got across the river. It's all like a sort of nightmare. Then, to compound it, an Italian division of Black Shirts was encamped on the other side. With Cohen dragging me, on our hands and knees, we crawled through a whole sleeping Italian division, believe it or not. They didn't even have a single guard posted. Then Cohen carried me on his back, and toward morning we were picked up by an English ambulance that was searching for wounded in the area between the fascists and the retreating

Republican army.

"So there is the whole story, my dear love, a confused, tragic little bit of an obscene and heartbreaking war. I wait now and count the hours before I see you again."

The nature of the immigrant is the state of being alone. Even if he goes to where he goes with a wife and family, he leaves behind him the whole intricate structure of the extended family that is hundreds of years in the making. So it was that when Feng Wo was laid away in the ground in the bleak, interdenominational cemetery in Los Angeles, six thousand miles from the land of his ancestors, in another land that designated him an outsider, a yellow man, a Chinese man, there were only six people present to hear the dirt fall on his coffin, Dan and May Ling, Joseph, So-toy, bent, withered, drying up from her tears, and Sam Goldberg and Sarah Levy, both of them down from San Francisco for the funeral.

They all returned to the little house in Westwood after the burial. It was the first time since she had been married, in the year 1895, that So-toy had not prepared the evening meal — with the exception of those days when there was no food at all to put on the table. She sat in a corner in the kitchen, a tiny, withered woman, as if the death that had claimed her husband had mistakenly passed her by, waiting now to be taken.

Sarah and May Ling prepared food, and May Ling explained to Sarah, "You see, she never learned English. She speaks a dialect called Shanghainese. So who will talk to her? That's the most terrible part of it."

Joe had returned to school. Dan sat in the living room with Sam Goldberg, who was recalling the day they bought the *Oregon Queen,* that first almost mythical, iron ship on which the empire of Levy and Lavette was built. Feng Wo had brought his abacus with him then, and when Swenson, the owner of the *Oregon Queen,* proposed that they buy his two garbage scows along with the iron lumber freighter, the abacus became as active as a modern computer. Goldberg remembered how the kids had gathered around to watch with awe as Feng Wo added, subtracted, and multiplied on what Dan had called his "Chinee harp."

"They were all there, weren't they," Goldberg said, "Steve Cassala and his kid sister — what was her name?"

"Rosa."

"Right, and Clair Harvey and Jake Levy and Martha Levy, all the kids."

"I remember," Dan said.

"Well, it's gone. God Almighty, the world changes. Only thirty-two years since the big earthquake, and the whole world's different. Do you think we'll have a war, Danny?"

"I've thought of it. You know, it was the last war that made us millionaires. Christ, when I think of it, it sours my gut. Still and all, that Nazi bastard won't be satisfied. Sooner or later, he'll want the whole hog."

"You don't want any part of it, do you, Danny?"

"None."

"Still, if we couldn't stay out of it, where would they find the ships?"

"That's not my worry."

"What do you hear from Barbara?"

"We got a long letter. Jake and Clair were over there, and that let the cat out of the bag." He smiled ruefully. "She's in love, or so she writes, with a French journalist. She says she intends to marry him."

"And live in France?"

"God knows. I hope not. I miss her. On a day like this — Christ, it eats my heart out the way I miss her."

May Ling came into the room, leaned over Dan, and kissed him gently. "I've been meaning to say this since papa died. I'm in your debt for a great deal, my husband."

"For what, May Ling? For all the years of grief?"

"For all the years of love. But something else — for what you gave papa. You gave him his manhood. Without that, life is wasted, the way thousands of Chinese here live wasted lives. His life wasn't wasted. And I thank you for that."

She went back into the kitchen. Dan said slowly, "You know, Sam, she's Chinese.

She's the second generation in this country, and she's still Chinese."

"She's also a very remarkable woman."

"She is. She certainly is."

The earliest train to Toulouse was a sleeper, which arrived there the following morning. Barbara was thankful to have had the compartment to herself, with no one to intrude on her thoughts except a solicitous Wagon Lits conductor, a London cockney who assumed that every American or British girl traveling alone on the Continent was in constant and mortal danger. She read Marcel's letter again and again. The end of it troubled her. An ambulance had picked him up, and then he was in the hospital in Toulouse. Even with a bullet wound in the leg, he should have been able to limp — unless it struck the bone. She had read somewhere that a bullet striking the bone in the leg makes the most devastating type of wound. What had happened at the end of the letter? Was he simply tired of reliving the experience?

She compared his letter with the story

in *Le Monde*. The headline read: LE MONDE CORRESPONDENT WITNESSES THE GALLANT FORAY OF AN AMERICAN BATTALION. The story was longer than the letter and it went into more detail, and *Le Monde* provided background material on both Doran and Merryman. The facts of the battle with the German detachment were more explicit, as was the story of their progress through the Italian division. And there it ended. She read and reread both pieces until she could repeat most of it by heart. She had telephoned the hospital last night, but only a night nurse was on duty, and she could give out no sensible information. Now she regretted that she hadn't called again before she rushed off to catch the train. The train was impossible, slow, tortuous, stopping again and again. How much of her life had been spent on trains! They were lonely places that trapped her and forced her to examine the innermost recesses of her being. And she had brought nothing to read, nothing but the letter and the copy of *Le Monde*. Anyway, she did not want to read or divert herself. She wanted to be with the man she loved, and she wanted to recreate him lovingly in her mind, each part of him — the way he thought, the way he smiled, the way he touched her, the thin wrinkles that curled around either side of his mouth, the way he spoke English, mangling words and sentences, the time he bought a straw boater to do an imitation of Maurice Chevalier, their endless walks through the streets of Paris, the time they charmed a barge captain on the St.-Martin Canal and then drifted through an afternoon on that incredible, dreamily improbable waterway — all the days and weeks that they had been with each other, examining each other, finding each other. They were both so far from home, so free, so uninhibited in their giving.

She fell asleep. The Wagon Lits man awakened her to make up her bed. Didn't she care for dinner? The thought of food was impossible. "I am certainly the most overemotional, neurotic woman in the world," she told herself. Then she forced herself to go into the dining car and order dinner. A diaper salesman sat opposite her, a fat, jolly man as pink as a baby himself. What an extraordinary way to earn a living, she thought, listening to him pour out the tales of his trade. He chattered through the whole meal, and she was relieved to have something to divert her thoughts.

She slept poorly that night, awakening each time the train stopped, and then lying awake, listening to the sound of the wheels. She was up and dressed with the first light of dawn, waiting eagerly with her single small suitcase as the train pulled into Toulouse. A taxi took her to the Hospital of the Sacred Heart, a cream-colored stucco building on the edge of the city, and, still carrying her suitcase, she told the nurse at the admissions desk that she wished to see Marcel Duboise. The woman regarded Barbara dubiously and then stared at the suitcase.

"I've just come from the Paris train. I didn't want to stop at a hotel. Can I put this somewhere?"

"It will be safe enough right here. Are you Monsieur Duboise's wife?"

"I will be — when we marry."

Again the woman stared at her. In sympathy or annoyance? "What is your name?" she asked.

"Barbara Lavette."

"Mademoiselle Lavette, the visits are restricted to members of Monsieur Duboise's family. He's a very sick man. Those are the doctor's orders."

"I am as close as any member of his family," Barbara said, her voice hardening. "I want to see him now."

The woman regarded her thoughtfully, then nodded. "Very well. Try not to tire him. The sister will take you there." She motioned to another nurse who stood nearby. "Take her to Monsieur Duboise."

Barbara followed the nurse down a corridor, up a staircase, and along another corridor. She had never been in a French hospital before. This place was cloisterlike in its stark white severity.

"His father and mother are here," the sister told Barbara.

"Oh? Where are they? With him?"

"There is a sitting room at the end of this corridor. I saw them there before.

Shall I tell them you're here?''

"I suppose so.''

"What is your name, Mademoiselle?''

"Barbara Lavette.''

"Here.'' She opened the door for her.

Barbara went into the room, white, white counterpane on the bed, an arched window with sunlight trickling through the slats of the blind, making a pattern on the bed; and Marcel lying there, very still, his eyes closed, his face drawn, his skin white.

She walked softly to the bed. Could such a change take place in a matter of weeks? His hands lay on the counterpane, thin, fleshless.

Then he opened his eyes and saw her, closed his eyes again, opened them, and whispered, "I have been feverish. This is a hallucination?''

"No, my dear darling.'' She bent and kissed his lips.

"Barbara?''

"Yes, Barbara.''

He reached up to touch her face. "You're real. I am not delirious.''

"Very real, my darling.''

"You never were before."

"Always. Always real."

"Thank God. Everything is proper now."

"Everything."

"You won't go away?"

"From you? Never." She laid her hand on his cheek. It was hot to her touch.

"When did you get here?"

"This morning, on the train from Paris."

"We'll go to Hermès and I'll pick out a purse for you. You never let me buy you things."

"Yes."

"After lunch. First, lunch. Then we take the afternoon off and cheat the monsters of *Le Monde*. That's good, isn't it? The monsters of the world."

"Marcel," she whispered, "Marcel."

"We'll find a new place and charge the paper. I'll review them. The soufflé is noble but the traffic, the traffic —" He closed his eyes, and his voice dropped to a mumble of meaningless sound. The door opened. A small, bald man with a pince-nez entered the room, tapped Barbara on the shoulder, and nodded toward the door. She followed him out into the corridor, her heart sinking.

"I am Dr. Lazaire," he said to her. "And you are Barbara Lavette."

"Yes."

"I hope you are not a hysterical young woman."

"Not when it matters."

"This matters. I know all about you. He has told me, and his mother and father have told me. Now listen to what I have to say. Your young man had the bone in his leg, the femur, splintered by a bullet. A very serious wound, and not properly attended to before he arrived here. He is suffering from what we call 'spreading gangrene.' Under the best conditions, such a wound is very serious, but in that ghastly situation in Spain, their medical services are primitive. Now, understand me. His leg must be amputated. It should have been done five days ago, immediately when he came here, but he refused permission. Now you must understand clearly. This is not an amputation at the knee but at the thigh. It may already be too late. I am not the surgeon but the Duboise family doctor. I brought this young man into the world, so it means something to me. If another night passes without the operation, he will almost certainly die, and even if we operate immediately, I can guarantee nothing. He is very weak, and he may not survive the amputation. He says he will not live in that condition, and we cannot amputate without his consent. His mother and father have pleaded with him, but to no avail. Now you are his beloved and pledged to him. I must ask you this. If the amputation takes place, will you still marry him?"

Moments went by before Barbara could reply. She felt a hollow sickness, a hopelessness such as she had never known before. Curiously, she did not weep. She tried to make an image in her mind of the man without the leg.

"That's not the question," she blurted out. "The operation must take place. You must not let him die."

"That is the question. You must know the answer and he must know it."

336

"I love him. The answer is yes. Yes!"

"Good. Now go back into the room. Don't be tender with him. Part of the delirium is a matter of will. He can slide into it as a retreat from reality. I want you to shock him. Don't be afraid to shout, to become angry, to make him angry. You will be fighting for his life. Can you do that?"

"Yes."

"Go ahead then. His mother and father want to meet you, but that can wait. This is more important."

Barbara went back into the room. Marcel lay there with his eyes closed. "Marcel!" she said. He opened his eyes and stared at her. "Marcel, we must talk."

He shook his head and closed his eyes.

"Marcel!" She sat on the edge of the bed and laid her hand on his hot cheek. "Marcel, listen to me! When I say I love you, I am repeating an old cliché. But those are the only words I have. You are my flesh and my blood. You are the first man I ever loved, the only man. We know each other. You knew me before you ever spoke to me. Now if you die, a part of me

337

dies. I don't give a damn about your leg. I don't love your leg. I love you."

"Who told you?"

"Well, who do you think told me? Dr. Lazaire told me. And I want you to do it, now!"

"No."

"Don't say no to me. What gives you the right to say no?"

He closed his eyes and shook his head tiredly.

"No! Don't go away from me! Damnit, we are going to talk about this. You've wasted enough time dreaming."

"All right. We'll talk. Do you know what they want to do? They want to take my leg off at the thigh. Is that what you want — a monster with half a body?"

"Yes, that's what I want."

He was alive now, aware of her. "Then think about it! Reach down for my penis to fondle me and think about what you'll find there. Think of what it will look like. You'll look at it every day of your life. You'll watch me crawl around, like some rotten beetle."

"Is that it?" she snapped. "Is that

338

your whole case?"

"Don't you understand that I love you?"

"No. Such love is worthless, because you're putting yourself in my place, and you can't stand the thought of looking at me with one of my legs gone."

"No, no," he whimpered. "No."

"Yes. Don't deny it. It's not my love that frightens you. It's yours. And because your love can't stand the test, you're ready to die. What a rotten, lousy thing that is!"

"Oh, God, no. You don't understand."

"I understand only too well."

"It's because I love you. Barbara, believe me. How can I come to you with half of me gone? How can I ask you to give your life to a worthless, helpless cripple?"

"You don't have to ask me. Nothing you can do would stop me. I intend to marry you, and I intend to marry a man who is alive, not a corpse."

"No."

"Stop saying no like a broken record. What do you expect me to do, to agree with you, to kneel down and weep with you and say that you're better off dead? We're not living some stupid, romantic story. We're two people of flesh and blood who love each other and who are tied together with that love. What have I ever asked of you? Now I'm asking for your life. How can you refuse me?''

''Because I love you,'' he said weakly.

''Damnit, I will not accept that. We are beyond words. Words are for those who have nothing to give and nothing to lose. You have a life to give me, and I have a life to lose — and I will not accept no for an answer!''

His face slowly breaking into a smile, he raised himself on one elbow, stared at her for a long moment, and then said, ''You are splendid. I am so proud, so proud.''

''Then you'll do it?''

''No.''

Her control collapsed. She stood up, moved back from the bed, sat down in a chair, and began to cry.

''Barbara.''

''Leave me alone, damn you!'' She leaped to her feet suddenly and shouted at him, "You're killing the only thing I love, you bastard!"

"Barbara, please, please —"

"No!" she shouted. "No, damn you. If you say you love me again —"

He began to laugh, shaking with laughter and wincing with the pain of it.

"What are you laughing at?"

"You. My God, I adore you. You are quite magnificent. I love you so, I'm not afraid of anything, even of death."

"Bullshit!" she snapped, using the English word. "You're not afraid of death. Only of life."

He stopped laughing and stared at her. Then he sighed, closed his eyes, and fell back onto his pillow. Used up, Barbara sat and waited. Two, three minutes passed. Then Marcel said softly, "Over there, dear love, on the chest of drawers, is the form they want me to sign. There is a pen there too. Give it to me and help me sit up, and I'll sign it, and then you can give it to Dr. Lazaire, who, I'm sure, is waiting outside the door. You win, God help us both."

It was an hour and a half since the operation had begun. Barbara sat in the little waiting room with Monsieur and Madame Duboise. As with so many French parents of that generation, their single child was born in their later years. Duboise was well past sixty, his wife in her mid-fifties. Duboise, a pharmacist, was very much like his son, slender and tall, but stooped and bald, with a fringe of gray hair around his head. His wife was a tiny, pretty woman with prematurely white hair, very neatly and correctly dressed, very prissy, even in her grief, out of a lifetime habit. Evidently Marcel had written to them in detail over the past year, for they knew a good deal about Barbara. Under other circumstances, they might have been distant and difficult, regarding her with the peculiar suspicion the French reserve for all foreigners and for Americans in particular. But in this case, she came to them as a sort of savior. What chance their son had for life was due to Barbara's intercession. They embraced her and poured out their hearts to her. That their son should return to them this way, after so long; that he should have to endure this mutilation — that was almost too much. Yet at least they would have him for a while, and with him this lovely young American.

Thus they sat for an hour and a half, while the day outside turned bleak and dark, the rain beginning, sometimes in silence, again with Barbara as the object of their attention and solicitude, Madame Duboise recalling some incident of Marcel's childhood, clinging to his childhood now, or with Monsieur Duboise gravely questioning Barbara about life and family in that half-mythical place called San Francisco. It came out that Marcel had written to them of the possiblity of himself and Barbara making their life in the United States, testing himself as well as his parents; and they questioned Barbara about America. Was there any place on earth as beautiful, as civilized, as France? Of course they could not expect Marcel to live in Toulouse; it was much too provincial a place. But was there anything that could not be found in Paris?

It was a dream, all of it — all the fears, all the hopes: Barbara knew this the moment Dr. Lazaire entered the waiting room. His face spelled it out.

"I'm so sorry," he said. "But it was too late. The infection had taken over his body. Gangrene is a monster. Even yesterday it would have been too late."

"What is he saying?" Madame Duboise whispered.

Her husband put his arm around her. "He is telling us that Marcel is dead."

"Is that what he's telling us? That can't be what he's telling us."

Barbara rose and walked out, past the doctor, down the long white corridor, down the stairs, and out into the rain.

PART THREE

Into Egypt

In April of 1939, late in the afternoon, the doorbell rang in Barbara's apartment in Paris. She had been expecting no one, and she opened the door to find the hall filled with an enormous hulk of a man, at least six feet two inches in height, broad, sloping shoulders, thick hair, a round, moonlike face, large nose, and pale blue eyes. He wore a leather jacket over a turtleneck sweater and shapeless corduroy trousers. He smiled at her tentatively and wanted to know whether she was Miss Barbara Lavette.

"Yes?"

"Good. I'm glad to meet you finally, miss. My name is Bernie Cohen."

"You?" She was astonished, speechless, dislocated in time and space. A year that had begun in misery and hopelessness backed up and jarred her mind, and then she grasped one of his oversized hands and pulled him into the apartment. "Forgive me, please, but my mind wouldn't work.

It's yesterday and it's also an eternity ago. But you're blessed in my memory, believe me. Come in, please.''

"Yes, ma'am, I can understand the way you feel. It's been one hell of a year, hasn't it? It's all over in Spain, all done and finished. I'm just passing through, and I thought I owed it to Marcel to just stop by and at least have a word with you."

"More than a word. Oh, I'm so glad to see you. Sit down, please. I'll get some wine."

He eased his bulk into a chair while Barbara brought wine and glasses.

"You know about Marcel?" she asked him.

"I stopped in at *Le Monde*. They told me. They gave me your address. I'm sorry, believe me. I liked him."

"You saved his life."

"I wish I could have saved his life. It was a lousy, rotten bloodbath. So many good boys died there, and for what? To be sold down the river by those bastards in England and here."

"Still, you saved his life. You sent him

348

back to me — at least for the little time I had with him. I'm so grateful. How many times I said to myself, I'll meet you one day and tell you how truly grateful I am."

Obviously embarrassed, he raised his glass. "What shall we drink to, Miss Lavette?"

"We'll drink to peace, and a little human decency. And call me Barbara. We're old friends."

"O.K., Barbara. A little human decency. Only, I don't look for it in my time."

"When did you leave Spain?"

"Two weeks ago, after Madrid fell to the fascists. It was all over then. Most of the Internationals had left already. I walked over the Pyrenees, same way I came in. Funny thing, I'm pretty big, but I was never hit, never even scratched. Ah, it was a nightmare, first to last. But I don't know why I'm talking to you about Spain —"

"Please, do, yes."

"Well, what's to say? Now the Nazis have it their own way. France will be next. I hope to God you get out of here."

"The magazine wants me to stay, but I don't think I can. I'm homesick and lonely, and without Marcel, Paris is empty. Suddenly, I look at it and it's a city without a soul. And my mother and father give me no peace. They're very upset at what is happening in Europe."

"They should be."

"Then you think there'll be war?"

"There'll be war, no doubt about it. Spain, Czechoslovakia, Poland next — and then England and France, maybe America."

"I hope not. I hope you're wrong," Barbara said earnestly. "It's such madness, such insanity, a whole world gone insane and thinking of nothing else but to kill."

"Or be killed."

"That's such an ancient excuse, isn't it? Thank God I'm a woman."

"I can say amen to that."

They sat and drank and talked and finished a bottle of wine between them. Cohen was an easy man to talk to. He was from San Francisco; they had common ground. Barbara was overcome with nostalgia. How good it was to talk in her own tongue! Cohen told her how he had worked at Higate when the Levys were filling their first order for sacramental wine. The federal agents had staged a raid, and he, Cohen, had faced them with an old, rusty shotgun.

"Real stupid," he said. "They could have shot me. Life was so damn simple then. No Hitler, no Nazis, no war, just the feds to cuss out and hate. I was just a kid then. First time I ever held a gun in my hands. And now —"

"What now, Bernie?" Barbara was a little drunk, warm, almost content, her eyes wet with the memory of a lost love, not with tears, only moist with the remembering.

"Marcel said you were beautiful — but damnit, I think you're the most beautiful woman I've ever seen."

"You're a little tight, Bernie. So am I. Let's go out and eat."

"Well, I don't know."

"If you have a dinner date?"

"Date?" He began to laugh. "Funny thing is, I was going to tell you that. Hell, look at me. I haven't had a bath in two weeks. I just can't imagine what I smell like. I came out of Spain without a dime. When I got to Ceret in France, I sold my rifle and a German Lügar to a Rumanian who had an arrangement with the border guards, a small-time munitions dealer. He gave me two hundred francs. I have four francs left. That won't buy us dinner.''

"Then let me buy you dinner.''

"No!''

"Oh, great! I just love men who are proud. The whole world is bleeding and ready to die from the pride and stupidity of men, and now you're too proud to let me buy us dinner.''

"Hey, don't get angry at me!''

"Why not?'' Barbara demanded. "You won't accept repayment. You're too proud for that. You saved the life of a man I loved more than anything on earth, but I can't buy you dinner.''

"All right. O.K. I'm half-starved. If you're not ashamed to be seen with me, buy me dinner. But I warn you — I eat a lot.''

"I'm not ashamed,'' she said.

They went to Allard's; it was the first time she had been there since Marcel died, her first evening out with a man. It seemed incredible to her that she could have been alone so long. Her mourning had been like a death of her own. Her American friends had left Paris. There had been days and weeks when she had sat in her apartment, did nothing, and saw no one. Then one day she left her apartment and walked for hours in the rain, "As if the rain had never stopped after that day in Toulouse," she told Bernie Cohen. "And then the rain stopped and the sun came out. Suddenly, it was all right for me to be alive. As if I had paid a debt. Do you understand?"

"I know the feeling, after they die," he agreed. "I felt that way. Like I'm the murderer, not the fascists."

"I'm all right now. I'll never let go of Marcel, but I'm all right now."

"I know."

"Good. Dessert?"

"Sure. Why not. I've eaten like a pig. I might as well finish like a pig."

"You're a big man. You need food. You

353

remind me of my father."

"I don't want to remind you of your father."

"O.K. You remind me of Jake Levy. How does that sit with you?"

"Better. I like him. It's a damn small world, isn't it? Here we are, you and me, and we got a link that goes way back. I used to hear a lot about your father. Everyone in San Francisco knew about him. There was a kid in the Battalion from Palo Alto, and it turns out that his father worked on one of Dan Lavette's ships during the World War, he was a mate or something. So who knows, maybe there are only a hundred people in the world and they're all connected."

"And what about you?" Barbara asked. "Where are you connected? Where are your mother and father and sisters and brothers?"

"I draw a blank. I grew up in the Hebrew orphanage — no mother, no father, nothing. Old Rabbi Blum sort of adopted me, and I did odd jobs for him, and then after I got out of high school I worked for the Levys for two years, and then I got into school at Berkeley, where I majored in agriculture. I worked all over the place — Sonoma, Napa, Fresno — a strong back and not too much brains to bother me. I'm a kind of crackpot Jew, and ever since I was a kid I had one goal, to settle in Palestine. There were two things I had to learn about, agriculture and guns. I got the first in California and I joined the Lincoln Brigade for the second. At first, they wouldn't have me. They claimed I had no ideological commitment. I had none to communism, but I hated the Nazis with the best of them. I got on a ship to France as a deck hand, and then I got to Spain and joined up with the Fifty-eighth Battalion there. Their casualties were heavy, so they didn't bother about commitment. Well, I lived through it, and I learned what I had to learn."

Barbara shook her head. "I don't understand that. You're warm and kind and gentle, and you join an army to learn the trade of killing. If you believed fervently in the Spanish cause, if you felt that the Republic had to survive, that might make some sense, but just to learn how to kill —"

"I killed fascists and Nazis. You know what's happening in Germany."

"I do know, and still I don't understand it. A bullet makes no judgment. Marcel died because men play a lunatic game, but it was meaningless and senseless."

"You don't hate, do you?"

"No, I find it too hard," Barbara said.

"You're a strange, sweet woman. Can I ask how old you are?"

"Twenty-five."

"I guess Marcel was the luckiest man on earth."

"To die the way he did?"

"I didn't mean that. I meant to have your love, to be loved by you."

She shook her head, tears welling into her eyes. "No, Marcel was not lucky."

"I'm sorry I said that."

"It's all right. Only, it reminds me of myself. At least you have a goal and a drive. I don't. I'll go home, but not because it makes any great sense. What will you do, Bernie?"

"I was thinking I'd head south tomorrow. Hitch my way down to

356

Marseille. Get a job as a deck hand there on something heading east. That's not hard, I'm told. Then I'll jump ship at Suez or Beirut, and then to Palestine. That's all the plans I have."

"And it doesn't worry you — being broke? Eating? Sleeping?"

"I've always been broke. It's normal for me."

"What about tonight? Where will you stay?"

He shrugged. "I'll make out, kid. Believe me."

"Come home with me. Sleep on the couch. No, you won't fit. We'll pile some cushions on the floor."

"You're sure you want me to?"

"I'm sure."

"I'm rank. The place will smell like a barracks."

"I have a real shower, a real, North American shower. Oh, come on, don't be silly about it."

She didn't want him to leave, to walk off into the night. The taste of home was on her lips, the salty smell of the fog as it rolled into the bay, the remembrance of the treeless, rolling hills, the singing hum of the cable cars. Suddenly, she was alone and dreadfully lonely in this strange place. Her time of mourning had been virgin and aseptic; she had clutched death in a dying place, and by now she had had enough of the taste of death. There had been no men in her life since Marcel died, and now here she was, mellow with wine and food and with the open ingenuousness of the man who sat with her, a huge, heavy, round-faced man — she could understand how he had lifted Marcel to his back and carried him for miles — with a boyish, diffident smile and pale, baby blue eyes that worshipped her unequivocally. He was right about his smell, a strong male body odor that Barbara did not find particularly unpleasant; but where does one bathe in France when one is penniless? His attitude was full of respect and diffidence and admiration, but he had not even reached out to touch her hand. He had crossed the Ebro River, bearing with him the broken body of the man she loved, and again her eyes filled with tears, remembering a childhood picture of Saint

Christopher wading through a rushing stream with the Christ child on his back.

"Don't cry, please," he said to her.

They walked back to her apartment. It was a calm, lovely evening, just two years from the time Marcel had intercepted her on the Champs-Elysees, pouring out his plea that she not disappear from his life. Was that always to be her fate, to step in and out of the lives of others?

At the apartment, she gave Bernie Cohen a robe that Marcel had kept there, and while he showered, she scrubbed his shirt and underthings, wrung them out, and hung them to dry. He came out of the bathroom grinning, the robe, so small on him, pulled tightly around him. He looked at the couch and shook his head. "The floor's better. I can sleep anywhere."

"Come to bed with me," Barbara said simply. Her whole body ached with desire. She could not face the thought of seducing or of being seduced.

His smile went away and he stared at her thoughtfully. "You're sure you want that?"

"Yes, I'm sure."

"You're not in love with me?"

"No."

"I think I love you. Not that it can mean anything to you. I know who I am. I know who you are. So maybe it would be better if —"

"I asked you to come to bed with me. Don't you want to?"

"My god, Barbara, what do you think?"

"Then come to bed and don't talk about it anymore."

After they had made love, she fell asleep in his arms, easily and trustingly. For hours he lay awake, afraid to move for fear he would disturb her. Then he slept. It was just dawn when he opened his eyes. She was asleep next to him, and for a while he lay there quietly, wondering whether he should wake her. He knew he had to go, and he knew she would not let him go without pressing money on him, and because he was quite sure of that, he slipped out of bed silently, moving with ease and grace for so large a man. He found his clothes in the kitchen, not quite dry but clean. He dressed, found pen and paper on her desk, wrote a note, and then left, closing the door gently behind him.

An hour later, Barbara saw the note and read it: "My darling, lovely woman: I am leaving like this because there is no way I can say goodby. If things were otherwise, if I had anything to offer you, I might stay and fight it through. I don't think I fell in love with you yesterday; I think I fell in love with you just listening to Marcel talk about you. Well, there it is. I don't know what else to say. Half of being a proper guest is knowing when to leave. This is the time."

Jean telephoned Dan at his home in Los Angeles. May Ling answered the phone, turned to her husband, and said uncertainly, "It's Jean. She wants to talk to you." She handed him the phone gingerly, as if it were something unsavory, and then walked out of the room.

"Dan," Jean said, "I want to talk to you about Barbara."

"Sure. Go ahead."

"Not on the telephone. I want to see you. I want you to come up here."

361

"That's impossible. Not for the next ten days, I couldn't. Why can't we talk about it now?"

"Because I won't discuss this on the phone. If you can't come to San Francisco, I'll fly down to Los Angeles."

"If you wish."

"Can you lunch with me tomorrow at the Biltmore?"

"All right. I'll see you there at twelve-thirty."

He walked into the kitchen, where May Ling sat with her mother, the old woman silent, obscure, still living with her grief. "I behave so badly," May Ling said. "I was never that way. I'm getting old and ugly."

"I think you're very young and very beautiful, and the hell with it! Do I stop loving you because we pass forty?"

"I'm forty-three, Danny."

"She wants to talk to me about Barbara."

"Oh, no. Nothing happened?"

"No. She wants the kid back. So do I."

"Are you going to San Francisco?"

"No, she's coming here. I'm having

lunch with her at the Biltmore tomorrow."

"Why at the Biltmore?" May Ling asked. "Why doesn't she come here?"

"Do you really want her to come here?"

"No! But she's so damn beautiful —"

"You never used to swear."

"Damn isn't swearing. The way you talk, that's swearing."

"How do you know she's still beautiful?"

"Because you told me so."

So-Toy said something to May Ling in Chinese.

"What's that?" Dan asked.

"She said I must not challenge the opinion of a man so good and wise as my husband."

"She's right."

"Danny?"

"Yes?"

She rose, took him by the arm, and led him into the living room. "My mother understands more than she admits to. I want to talk very seriously."

He pulled her down on the couch next to him, curled an arm around her, and drew her to him. "Go on. Talk seriously."

"I used to be very strong, Danny. No, I can't talk when you do this to me." She pulled away and faced him. "I knew how to be alone. Now I've had you for eight years. I don't know how to be alone anymore. What if you fall in love with her all over again?"

"What if I do?"

"I couldn't stand that, Danny."

"Well, I'd have to stop loving you first, wouldn't I?"

"That's just talk, Danny. You never got Jean out of your blood."

"I was never in love with Jean, not the way I love you. You know that."

"You wanted her and you never really had her, and that's worse."

"Chinese thinking."

"What?"

"That's Chinese thinking. Jean's married."

"Oh, sometimes, Danny — Chinese thinking! What a dumb thing to say. You told me who Jean married. You despise him."

"But she doesn't."

364

"How do you know she doesn't?"

He didn't know, and he didn't want to talk about it. They went to bed, May Ling pleading softly, "Make love to me, Danny, make love to me. Make me feel that I am not drying up, withering away. Make me alive." But he was asleep almost immediately, and she lay there with her eyes open, looking into the darkness and remembering the single time she had seen Jean Lavette. How strange it was, knowing Dan Lavette, knowing about him at least since she had been fourteen, falling in love with him when she was eighteen, and never really being apart from him, at least in her heart, in all the twenty-five years since then, yet seeing his first wife only once. It was before she actually met Dan. She was seventeen at the time, applying for a job in the Oriental section of the San Francisco Public Library, and there were some papers her father had to sign. She met him on the Embarcadero, in front of the Levy and Lavette warehouse, and as she stood there, the "snow lady" swept by, in a white silk dress under a white woolen

365

coat, a piled mass of honey-colored hair, and the bright blue eyes that were for May Ling so much a symbol of the Caucasian. She had caught just that single glimpse of her, yet the image was printed on her mind and remained there, clear, beautiful, untouched by time, of a translucent, enviable creature that had haunted her all through the years. If she herself, May Ling, had aged and changed through the years, the illusion persisted that Jean had remained untouched by time.

The following day, in the dining room of the Biltmore in downtown Los Angeles, the same notion occurred to Dan. Five years had passed since he had met Jean in San Francisco. Time was kind to her. A little more make-up, more careful grooming, perhaps a few tiny wrinkles around the eyes, but the totality of her beauty remained untouched. Perhaps she dyed her hair. He himself was almost entirely gray, but not a gray hair showed on Jean's head. He tried to remember how old she was. He had just passed fifty; she would be forty-nine then. More than she had been five years ago, she was now a stranger, a woman he had known once and only in fragments — or had he ever known her at all?

Yet there was a difference, and he sensed it almost immediately. The certainty was lacking, the almost unconscious arrogance, the built-in, magnificent confidence of the very rich and the very beautiful, as a gift of birth and never requiring cultivation. There was both fear and uncertainty — in the way she greeted him, in her petulant criticism of the place, the unlikely pretentiousness of the Biltmore.

"It's ridiculous in this wretched city. How can you live here, Dan?"

"You get used to it. Los Angeles has its points."

"I haven't noticed. I heard you're doing very well."

"Well enough. I build yachts for millionaire movie moguls."

"And what happened to all your vows of poverty?"

He looked at her thoughtfully. "That's a damn funny thing for you to say. Anyway, how did you know that I was doing well?''

''I had lunch with Sam Goldberg. You know, he's Barbara's lawyer, so we talk occasionally.''

''You don't approve of him.''

''He's old, Dan. He's past seventy.''

''And he's also Jewish.''

''That's not fair. You never forget, do you? You never forgive, either.''

''I told you once that there was nothing to forgive.'' He grinned at her. ''No fights, Jean. I'm glad to see you, I swear I am.''

''When you smile like that — well, it's like long, long ago. All right, Danny. I'm worried about Barbara. I want her to come home. Europe is boiling and it's going to explode.''

''Have you asked her to come back?''

''Pleaded with her in my letters.''

''Well, she's coming back. We had a letter from her yesterday.''

''When?''

''Soon. She said she had one more thing to do, and then she comes back.''

''What thing?''

''She didn't say. You know, she's had a bad time of it. She was in love with a

French boy. They were going to be married. He was wounded in the Spanish war, and he died. That was about a year ago."

"Oh, no. I never knew a thing about that. Why didn't she tell me?"

"Maybe she didn't want to upset you. Barbara's not the kind who likes to share grief. She locks it inside herself."

"Danny, I've lost her," Jean said, her voice full of anguish. "I love her so much, and I've lost her."

"We've neither of us lost her, Jean. Give it time. She'll be back."

"I've run out of time, Danny. How much time does anyone have? I lost you — and now my daughter."

"No, you never wanted me. Don't make a world of illusions now. It doesn't help."

"You're a damn fool, Danny."

"Thank you."

"Did it ever occur to you to wonder why I wouldn't give you a divorce all those years?"

"It occurred to me. You told me once that Seldons didn't divorce."

"What's the use?" Jean sighed. "I'm

making a fool of myself, and I don't enjoy that. I came here to talk about Barbara. What shall we do?"

"She's a grown woman."

"I thought of going over there and talking to her."

"That's not smart. She has to make her own decisions. And Europe's no place to visit now. Jean," he said gently, "I think she'll be back soon. She had to get over what happened to her, and she chose to stay there until she got over it. I think she's over it now, and I think she'll come back."

"Who was the boy? She told you, not me. Do you know how that hurts?"

"A writer. He worked on the newspaper *Le Monde.*"

"What was he like?"

"She sent us a picture. I thought you'd like to see it." He took the picture out of his pocket and handed it to her, and he watched her as she stared at the smiling face in the photograph.

"It's a nice face," she said wanly. "Poor Barbara, how she must have suffered."

Dan reached across the table and took her hand. It was a new sensation for him. He had never pitied Jean before.

The following day's edition of the San Francisco *Examiner* carried the titillating tidbit that Jean Whittier had "flown to Los Angeles for a rendezvous with her ex-husband, Daniel Lavette, where they were seen lunching at the Hotel Biltmore." It said no more than that, but it was suggestive and sufficiently embarrassing to John Whittier for him to bring it up the first time he saw Jean, which was at dinner that day. Tom was at the table with them.

"I think we should discuss this another time," Jean said coolly.

"This is a very appropriate time. At least you're here. I see little enough of you these days."

"I prefer our squabbles to be private."

"If Tom wants to leave, he can leave."

"I'm having my dinner," Tom said. "I'll take it elsewhere if you wish."

"No, you might as well remain," Jean said. And then to Whittier, "You want to know how it got into the papers? I can't tell you that. Someone must have recognized us at the Biltmore. Certainly I had nothing to do with that.''

"This is the second time you've seen him — as far as I know.''

"In five years! You're tiresome.'' Jean sighed. "I don't enjoy this. I see whom I please when I please.''

"Yes, you can do as you damn well please, but don't involve me in any scandal.''

"Do you ever listen to yourself?'' Jean asked gently, and when Whittier stared at her, she added, "You tend to be pompous and quite boring. I saw Dan to discuss my daughter, Barbara. That's it. We'll drop the subject.''

Flushed, Whittier rose, his cheeks puffed out, his face red. He swallowed, contained himself, and then said coldly, "I'll have my dinner elsewhere.'' He turned on his heel and left the room.

Jean and Tom sat in silence. The butler entered with the roast and looked at Whittier's place. "He won't be dining with us,'' Jean said. "He was called away.''

Tom remained silent. The butler served them and left.

Tom took a few bites of his food, then bit his lower lip and shook his head. "It gets worse."

"Yes, my dear," Jean said. "But it's my problem, not yours."

"If you felt this way, why the devil did you marry him?"

"Because, Thomas, I did not feel this way at the time."

Now in his twenty-seventh year, Thomas Lavette was tall, slender, and still unmarried. His face had fixed into a rather controlled, handsome mask. He had the refined, almost plastic good looks of a film star or a men's clothes model, light brown hair that he parted on the side and that fell gracefully over his brow, blue eyes, and a wide, slightly petulant mouth. As the years passed, he had retreated behind his face and figure, rarely permitting himself to exhibit either pleasure or disappointment. Women found him attractive, clever within limitations, and coldly closed to any specific designs on their part. He had remained as part of the Whittier household, showing no desire to move out or to establish a place of his own. He had joined Whittier's city club through the sponsorship of Whittier, he was a member of the San Francisco Golf Club, and he kept a small boat at the wharf, although he rarely sailed. He had moderated his drinking, and he smoked an occasional cigarette. He lit one now and said to his mother, "What do you intend to do?"

"Nothing. Anyway, I don't see that it concerns you, Tom."

"It does."

"Might I ask how?"

"I like John."

"That's very nice."

"Do you intend to divorce him?"

"What is your sudden interest in my intentions?"

"I simply think that another divorce would do you no good. I think it would be a mistake."

Jean smiled coldly. "So now you advise me on my conduct."

"Someone has to."

"You're insolent and rather nasty. I

have no desire to discuss this with you."

"I'm sorry. I didn't mean to be insolent. I just don't want you to leave John."

"Why?"

"Can I talk to you, mother?"

"You've been talking to me. Quite outrageously, I think."

"I apologized for that. Can I talk to you, straight off the cuff?"

"Go ahead."

"All right. In a few months, your trusteeship will expire. At that time, Barbara and I will have not only the ownership but the voting rights to our Seldon Bank stock, which will amount to about twenty million dollars apiece. John and I have discussed this at some length. I will control the bank. A combination with the Whittier interests would constitute the largest and most powerful financial block on the West Coast. John has been to Washington, and he has it from the best authority there that the arms embargo will be repealed before the year is out. You can see what that would mean to the Whittier shipping interests. I must say that the idea of a combine of interest

375

came from John, and I think it's very decent of him. He doesn't need us as much as we need him."

For a long moment, Jean just stared at her son. "You amaze me," she said at last.

"Why?"

"Never mind why. That can wait. Tell me, why do we, as you put it, need John Whittier?"

"Because without him we are just a bank, a large bank, but still just a bank. With him — well, damnit, mother, you must see the power in such a combination."

"And that's what you want? The power?"

"Frankly, yes."

"You're a strange boy, Tom," she said, thinking to herself that "stranger" would be a better word, a stranger who was her son and whom she knew so little.

"What else should I want?" he demanded. "Money? I've always had enough money. My job at the bank? It's piddling nonsense. I have my own dreams, mother. Is that so strange?"

"And if I were to divorce John, it would endanger all this?"

"It would make it very awkward."

"And what about Barbara? You've left her out of your plans. She gets half the stock."

"I think I can handle Barbara."

"Do you? That's interesting."

"I mean, why shouldn't she do what's best for the family?"

"Are you sure you know what's best for the family? Barbara might have other ideas — or she might decide to do what she feels is best for Barbara."

"I still think I can convince her. The first problem is to get her out of the hands of that Jew lawyer of hers."

"God help us both," Jean whispered.

"Just what do you mean by that ?"

Jean did not reply, only looked at her son, feeling that she was going to scream, to burst out in rage, yet realizing that she was entitled to neither reaction.

"Don't tell me you're shocked, and don't accuse me of anti-Semitism," Tom said. "I had dinner last night at the club with Arthur Schwartz, and he's about as

377

Jewish as you can get. It's just that Sam Goldberg is Dan's partner. You know that."

"I'm sure that some of your best friends are Jewish," Jean said.

"You're right."

"And Dan happens to be your father."

"He happens to be."

Jean sighed hopelessly.

"I'm sorry, mother," Tom said. "If I offended you in any way, I'm sorry."

"I don't deserve sympathy, my dear. I have a son who is enormously rich and has no sense of humor, and I deserve both. It took me half a century to grow up, and it's too late to weep over that."

"I think I have as much of a sense of humor as the next person. But damned if I see what's so funny about all this."

"No, I don't suppose you do," Jean said.

In mid-May of 1939, two weeks before Barbara planned to leave Paris for Cherbourg, where she would board the *Queen Mary* for the journey back to America, Marcel's old friend Claude Limoget telephoned her and asked whether he and his wife could drop by to see her. Barbara was working on her last "Letter from Paris," and she hoped that by late afternoon most of it would be out of the way. She was not particularly eager to see Claude and Camille, but they were friends of Marcel, and even didactic company was better than no company at all. And they were didactic. They were well-meaning enough; they had come by half a dozen times in the year since Marcel's death, and she had been to their home for dinner on two occasions, but one always paid a price of instruction. They lectured her on Spain, on fascism, on Nazism, on the new world that was being wrought in the Soviet Union, on the weakness of Chamberlain, on the wickedness of Deladier, on the spinelessness of the Czechs, on the betrayals — of Spain and Czechoslovakia — by Roosevelt, and on other kindred subjects.

Since Barbara disliked argument and had a deep-seated conviction that little was gained and no one really convinced by it, she was more inclined to listen and swallow her various disagreements than to attempt to prove her point. In her own way, very slowly and thoughtfully over a period of years, she was crystallizing her own point of view. She had possessed an almost instinctive repugnance for suffering inflicted on anyone, for cruelty, for the act of inflicting pain and for the ultimate act of killing. Five years ago, she had left Sarah Lawrence College possessed of a gentle and comprehensive innocence, which, as a very sophisticated student in a very sophisticated college, she would have denied completely. Since then, she had learned a great deal, coped with the situation of a young woman alone in a foreign country, found a job as a correspondent, and proved to herself and others that she could do her work in a professional manner. In a sense, she had formed herself in terms of ideas and beliefs, and she saw no need for inflicting these ideas and beliefs on others.

She had listened to the arguments and persuasions of the Limogets as she had listened to the arguments and persuasions of others. If at times she was bored, boredom was something she had learned to cope with. This time, however, she was not bored.

Claude and Camille Limoget arrived at precisely five o'clock, which they had learned was the proper American cocktail hour. They brought a bottle of wine, downed a glass apiece, munched on Barbara's crackers and cheese, made the proper inquiries about her health and state of mind, and then came directly to the point.

"We understand," Claude said, "that you plan to return to America in two weeks."

"Yes. I've overstayed my leave."

"Of course. Yet Paris has been a happy as well as an unhappy experience."

"That's true, Claude. Some of each."

"Barbara," he said very seriously, "we are coming to you to ask you to change your plans. We would like you to put off your departure to America and go to Berlin instead."

She smiled. "You can't be serious."

"Very serious. Let me explain the reasons for this request."

"No," Barbara said firmly. "Whatever you have in mind, I don't want to hear about it. I regard what is happening in Germany, in Berlin, with loathing and with horror and disgust. Nothing you have to say could persuade me to go there, now or ever."

"Will you only listen?"

"No. I am going home. I have been away almost five years. I am totally heartsick for home. You're French. You ought to understand that."

"We do understand it," Camille said. "But isn't it unreasonable to refuse to listen? You're not a person of weak character. We've spent too many hours trying to convince you of things you absolutely refuse to accept, and I'm sure we haven't convinced you. But at least you listened."

Barbara sighed. "Very well, I'll listen."

"That's all we're asking," Camille said. "I insisted on that with Claude. We would simply put the facts to you, and then you could say yes or no."

"You know we're communists," Claude said. "We've made no secret of that."

"Indeed you haven't." Barbara was forced to smile. There were times when she almost liked the Limogets.

"All right. Now, over the past few years, there have been many discussions in Party circles concerning the question of Nazi Germany. In the beginning, German comrades participated in these discussions — comrades who had escaped from Germany, a few others who moved back and forth. These few became fewer, and finally all our contacts with Germany were broken. At this moment, we don't even know whether the Party exists in Germany, and the way events are moving, it is desperately necessary that we know, not only for ourselves but for the whole world —"

"Oh, no," Barbara interrupted. "You can stop right there. I am not a communist. I don't think I am even a communist sympathizer."

"You said you'd hear us out," Camille reminded her.

"All right. Go on."

"I want to say right here that we have no intention of placing you in a position of danger. Other measures are being undertaken to make contact in Germany. This is a singular case, for which you are ideally suited. No, please wait" — as Barbara began to stop him — "please, listen to me. There is a Professor Wolfgang Schmidt, who teaches philosophy at Friedrich Wilhelm University in Berlin. He is one of those who espoused the Nazi theories of the master race. He has published two books on the subject, and his writing has been warmly received by the Hitler gang. Nevertheless, we have reason to believe that this man, who was once secretly a Party member, still remains a communist and uses his present role as a cover. If that is the case, he may have contacts, there may be some sort of organization that can be reached and helped."

Barbara shook her head hopelessly. "You are quite mad."

"I don't think we are. Barbara, we are not asking you to try to establish that contact; others will do that. We only ask that you see this Professor Schmidt, that you talk to him as what you are, an

American correspondent, that you get a sense of the man and of what his deepest beliefs are. This is something you can do quite legitimately — and if you are able to give us a sound estimate, then the next man we send will not be going to his death. He won't be walking into a trap."

"You mean I am to spring the trap for him."

Camille Limoget's round, pretty little face took on an expression of pain, as if Barbara's remark had cut to her soul. Her wide blue eyes became moist, and Barbara reflected that she was indeed the most unlikely communist.

"We loved Marcel," she whispered. "We love you. What a thing to say!"

"I'm sorry," Barbara apologized. "I shouldn't have said that. But I am not going to Berlin. You know, you and Claude and your friends — you've told me a dozen times how you feel about everything that's happening today. But you never asked me how I feel. Of course, I understand that American women are not supposed to have much sense —"

"That's not fair," Camille protested.

"We never stopped you from speaking. You were always quiet, listening."

"True," she responded, not feeling that this was the best moment to remind Camille that to get a word in during one of their discussions was virtually impossible. "Then it's my fault. Let me tell you what I feel, in just a few words. I feel that men who fight wars share a common insanity, and that men who kill, for whatever reason, for whatever justification, are also insane. I have listened to the theories and rationalizations and accusations for hours, but I still feel just that way. I loved a man who was like a part of me, and he died senselessly, for no reason and no cause." She sought for more words, and then felt that what she had said encompassed the whole matter. "That's the way I feel," she said.

Camille bit her lower lip and pouted. Claude studied Barbara thoughtfully, and for a little while the three of them sat there in silence.

Finally, Claude said, "Marcel was my friend. I don't like to parade my emotions, but I sat down and cried when I heard that he was dead.''

Barbara nodded.

''It wasn't an accident. The Nazis killed him. They have killed thousands, and they will kill thousands more.''

''And Stalin?'' Barbara asked tiredly. ''He kills no one?''

''It doesn't change what happened in Spain and what is happening in Germany.''

''And will I change that if I go to Germany? Can anyone change it?''

''I don't know,'' Claude said quietly. ''We try. If we don't try, there's not much worth living for, is there?''

Again they sat in silence, and at last Claude said, ''I don't blame you if you're afraid. I'd be afraid.''

Barbara didn't deny it. There was a cold knot in the pit of her stomach when mentally she placed herself in Germany. Her strength and independence did not come from a lack of sensitivity. For years now, day after day, she had read the newspaper reports of life in Nazi Germany, not to mention the books on the subject that filled the French bookstalls.

In her mind, it had become the place of ultimate horror, a gigantic and grotesque nightmare that had grown like a fetid mushroom out of the heart of Europe.

"But, you see," Claude went on softly, "there is really no one but yourself we could turn to. You are not political. You never have been. You have no organizational connections, yet we trust you. When I told you Professor Schmidt's name, I put his life in your hands. We know you."

"And you know a hundred others," Barbara said unhappily.

"Not really. Consider. You're an American, and the Nazis are cultivating America with every bit of sleazy propaganda they can contrive. You are a correspondent, so you have a legitimate reason to go there and to interview. There is nothing on you in the Gestapo files. You are also the daughter of one of the great, wealthy families of America. You can't imagine what kind of clout that will give you there. Barbara, I would die before I would ask you to step into a dangerous game. This isn't dangerous. Nasty,

388

perhaps. Any sewer is nasty and stinks to hell. On the other hand, you're a writer, and this can be an experience well worth having. There's profit along with the loss. And you might just be saving the lives of a good many decent people.''

''I think I'd like a cup of coffee,'' Barbara said. ''Will you join me?''

They shook their heads and sat in silence while she brewed the coffee. She had stopped thinking, stopped building protests within herself. She felt a dead, heavy weight inside of her, a kind of hopelessness. She was like a boat without a rudder, without an anchor. Everything and everyone went in and out of her life — her father, her mother, her brother, Dominick Salone, Marcel Duboise, Bernie Cohen. She suddenly felt an intense longing for the big, slow-moving, slow-speaking man, for his judgment, for his advice.

She drank the coffee strong and black. ''It's American coffee,'' she explained. ''I'm an addict. It comes of living alone. You turn either to drink or coffee.''

''I grew up with chicory,'' Camille said,

smiling. "You lose your taste for the real thing." She was relaxed, gentle. The argument was over. Barbara had never particularly liked her before. She liked her now.

"If I were to go," Barbara said, "and I am not committing myself to anything — but if I were crazy enough to do this, what makes you think that I could find out anything worth finding out about this Professor Schmidt? I'm no great judge of character. I can't ask him outright."

Claude shrugged. "I have faith in you."

"I wish I did."

"Can we take you to dinner?" Camille asked.

"No. No, I want to think about this whole thing. I have to think it through, and it's better if I'm by myself."

There were no more arguments, no more persuasion, and awhile later, Camille and Claude left. Barbara took the wineglasses and her cup and saucer into the kitchen, washed them, and then decided that the floor of the kitchen was quite dirty. Why hadn't she noticed that before? She got a pail of suds and a brush and scrubbed the kitchen floor, obtaining a good deal of satisfaction out of the physical act of doing something. Then she took a bath, luxuriating in the steaming hot water. It was nine o'clock by the time she dried herself, combed her hair, and slipped into a robe, and now she felt ravenously hungry. She had a piece of *chèvre* and some bread that she warmed in the oven, and she sat in the kitchen, stuffing herself with cheese and hot, golden-crusted bread and drinking what was left of the coffee. Afterward, she would recall that there were no interior discussions with herself during this time, no profound thoughts to weigh, one against the other. At half past nine, with the last crust of bread in her hand, she picked up the telephone and asked for the overseas operator. She then put through a person-to-person call to Frank Bradley, the editor of *Manhattan Magazine.*

It was well after ten when the telephone rang and the operator informed her that she had her party in New York. It was a good connection. Bradley's voice boomed out at her.

"I hear you quite well, Frank. You don't have to shout."

"Girl, you've become famous and you're deserting us. When are you arriving? Why didn't you call me collect?"

"Because I'm rich, and I'm not arriving. I've decided to look the beast in the eyes. What would you say to a few 'Letters from Berlin'?"

"I love you."

"You know they censor everything. I'm no great political commentator."

"Just write about the weather, the women, the food — anything you want. Or make notes and write the stuff in Paris."

"How many words?"

"As many as you want. I love you."

"I know that. You said it before."

"How long will you stay?"

"I have no idea, Frank."

"Now don't get into trouble. Three publishers have been bugging me about doing your letters in a book. But I'm holding off until you get back. So just don't get mixed up in anything and write me something immortal."

"What publishers?"

"That can wait. Now look, Barbara, I don't want you to stick your neck out, and I know how you feel about those bastards, but if you could get an interview with Hitler or Ribbentrop or Himmler, or any one of those lice, it would be worth its weight in gold."

"Frank, you're crazy."

"Like a fox, I am. You're a beautiful woman, and that counts. Look, if it comes your way, grab it. If it doesn't, I still love you."

Dan observed his son Joseph occasionally with awe, frequently with admiration, and always with wonder that this tall, long-limbed creature, with the strange mixture of the Occident and the Orient written on his snub-nosed, serious face, could be a product of his loins. A few months past, a chain lift had snapped at the boatyard, and the raw link had gashed Dan's arm from elbow to shoulder, not deeply, but nevertheless leaving a long, painful cut. They had bandaged it crudely out of a first aid kit, but when Dan got home, Joe —

there on a day off — regarded it with disgust, removed the bandage, cleaned the wound, put it together with what he called plaster butterflies, and then rebandaged it. Half a year in medical school had not made him a doctor, but in Dan's mind he was a repository of medical knowledge.

So-toy's sight was failing, and Joe with the aid of a medical flashlight diagnosed the condition as cataracts, which was later confirmed by the ophthalmologist to whom May Ling brought her mother. Joe explained the required operation in great detail to his mother and father, thereby increasing Dan's awe, and to the amazement of May Ling, he spelled out some of the facts to So-toy in Shanghainese.

"Where on earth did you learn to speak Shanghainese?" his mother asked him.

"I picked it up from granny."

"You picked it up? I've been around her all my life and I don't know much more than a hundred words."

"Well, that's the way it goes. Anyway, mom, you know more than a hundred words. I like her. You can't like someone

394

and not want to talk. You know," he added, "it's funny, but I'm picking up some Cantonese. Whenever they get a Chinese patient in the ward and they can't get through, they send for me. Mostly, it's Cantonese."

When May Ling told Dan about this, he said, "You know, it puts me in a hell of a spot. His school will wind up in a couple of weeks, and he's got to earn some money this summer. I can put him on as a laborer and justify paying him twenty-five a week, but hell, I can't."

"Why can't you?"

"He's a doctor. How the hell can I ask him to work in a boatyard as a laborer?"

"Just ask him. That's all."

"Ah, no. I can't."

"Well, you won't have to. He wrote to Jake Levy up at Higate, and Jake offered him a job for the time between semesters."

"What? What kind of a job?"

"The same thing you're afraid to offer him, digging irrigation ditches, picking, pruning — goodness, I don't know. Whatever a hand does at a winery."

"What is Jake willing to pay him?"

"You know," May Ling said gently, touching Dan's hand and smiling at him, "your son isn't a doctor. He's just a medical student. And if he appears to be very bright to you, it's perfectly natural, because he has a very intelligent father."

"Come on, I'm a boob and a roughneck. That's all I've ever been."

"I suppose so, but you're an unusual boob and a remarkable roughneck, and that's what counts."

"Thank you. What's Jake paying him?"

"Forty a month and keep. That's what Jake pays, and Joe wouldn't have him show any favoritism because he's your son. Anyway, Joe says it's ten dollars a month more than most of the growers pay."

"He's got to be crazy!" Dan exploded. "I can pay him twice that!"

"Calm down, Danny. He wants to go to Higate."

"Why?"

"You don't notice things. Sally Levy's been writing to him every week through the winter. I think he wants to be around her, that's all."

"Sally Levy? Jake's kid? God Almighty, she can't be more than ten years old!"

"Will you calm down. She's almost fourteen."

"Joe's twenty-one. What in hell does he want with a kid of fourteen?"

"When you were twenty-five, I was only eighteen."

"That's different."

"Why? You're seven years older than I. Joe's eight years older than Sally."

"You were eighteen. Fourteen! God Almighty, that's jailbait, and with Jake's kid it stinks."

"You are a hoodlum," she said, smiling sadly. "You'll never be civilized."

"You call that civilized? A fourteen-year-old kid."

"I just don't want you to talk to Joe about this. His head is on right. Leave him alone. You remember what you said about Barbara. She had to be left alone. That goes for Joe too."

"All right. All right. But I still don't see it."

He was not the only one. His son was

almost equally confused about his own motives for going to Higate. He was not in love with Sally Levy, who was not yet fourteen years old. He was confident that he knew all about love, having found time during his first year in medical school to conceive a passion for two more girls, both of them as blond and blue-eyed as his college infatuations. But both passions were short-lived, coming to earth in two frantic bouts of lovemaking: once at night on the beach at Santa Monica, when it was so cold and wet that his true love shivered and shook all through it, begging him to get it over with so that she could put on her clothes and not freeze to death; and with the second girl, unconsummated when her parents came home early and informed her, in his presence, in very high decibels, that if they found this "Chink" in their house again, they'd call the cops. He took the insult philosophically, deciding that it was all a question of time. Romance required time. As a college student, he had had all the time in the world, whereby his success. As a medical student, regardless of the depth of his passion, there simply was no time to make love properly. As a college student, he had been content to be mistaken for an American Indian, although their lot in Los Angeles was little better than the lot of the Chinese; in medical school, he affirmed his identity as a Chinese. For some reason, the eighteen-hour day of a medical student, instead of stultifying his sexual drive, increased it to a fever pitch. There were three middle-aged, cooperative nurses at the teaching hospital, but like a good many medical students, Joe had fallen prey to what was called "first-year hypochondria," and having learned all the symptoms and details of venereal disease, he avoided promiscuous women like the plague.

All this went through his mind as he drove his father's ancient Ford north from Los Angeles to the Napa Valley. Dan had given the Ford to Joe — the very first Model A, 1929 vintage — and had replaced it with a secondhand 1935 Buick. Joe treasured the tiny car and its apparent ability to run forever, the odometer having given up at a hundred and ten thousand miles. He drove it without haste, and the long trip gave him time to ask himself just why he was going back to Higate and exactly what he felt for Sally Levy. It was not an easy question for him to answer; he only knew that he wanted to see her again, an admission that he modified with the arguments that he loved Northern California and that he wanted desperately to get away from home for a time.

Sally had written to him as regular as clockwork, every week, apologizing for the wretched scrawl of her handwriting with the excuse that she had been born left-handed and then forced in school to write with her right hand — a situation that her mother had attempted to reverse recently, but too late, since the scrawl from her left hand was even worse than that from the right.

Joe had discussed the matter with one of his professors, who admitted that so little was known about the alteration of a left-handed person into a right-handed person that no firm conclusion could be drawn, and then he asked whether the

400

child in question was strange?

"Pretty strange," Joe confessed, and the professor said, "Well, there you are."

"Strange" was a rather generic term. Some of the letters Sally had written were very detailed, sensitive, and often quite beautiful. Once she had written two lines: "It's all over, and I think you stink for not writing to me." Another time she sent him two beautiful sonnets, which she claimed she had written, one of which began, "Unlike are we, unlike, o princely heart! Unlike our uses and our destinies." Joe was so impressed with the language and the flight of fancy that he showed them to his mother. May Ling read them through, sighed, and studied her son thoughtfully.

"They're great, don't you think?" Joe asked her.

"Oh, indeed they are. I could never interest you in poetry. If I had, you would know that both these lovely poems were written a hundred years ago by Elizabeth Barrett Browning. They were copied faithfully from her *Sonnets from the Portuguese*. That's an unusual little girl, your Sally."

"No. Why would she lie?"

"To impress you."

"That dumb kid!"

"Not at all. At least she read the poems. That's more than you can say."

He wrote back to her, annoyed and accusing, and she replied, "So what! I could write poems just as good if I was her age."

He came to wait for her letters, to read them eagerly. For his part, he replied about once a month, generally when she had become angry and threatened to stop writing.

Now, driving north, he decided to dismiss her from his thoughts. She was an interesting kid, a little crazy. He had no intention of allowing her to tag around after him as she had done the summer before. But when finally, late in the evening, almost at sundown, he arrived at Higate, having driven with just a few stops for fourteen hours, there she was, standing, watching, waiting, and the moment he got out of his car she ran toward him, stopped, and stood

402

staring at him.

And he stared back. It was not entirely the physical change in Sally. She was still very slender, but the once-tangled flaxen hair was combed straight and fell only to her shoulders, bobbed straight across the front of her brow; she had developed breasts; instead of old, torn jeans she wore a cotton dress; and she had grown at least two inches. Yet more than these changes, it was the expression in the wide blue eyes, frightened, hopeful, wary.

"Hello, kid," Joe said to her.

"I wish I could have got rid of the stinking freckles, because then I might look all right, but there's just no way. How do you think I look?"

"You look fine."

"You don't look like a doctor. You look just the same as last year. Do you want to kiss me?"

Joe walked over to her and kissed her lightly on the cheek.

"That's some kiss," she said.

He shook his head despairingly.

"Well, what do you think? You think I don't know why you came back? Only you won't go near me because I'm jailbait. That's right. I know a lot more than you think."

"My word, Sally," he said desperately, "what do your mother and father think about all this?"

"They think I'm crazy, but they trust you. They know how stupid you are."

"Yeah, stupid."

"They said I could walk you around and show you the place just by myself."

"But I have to go inside," Joe said. "I have to say hello to your folks and your brothers."

"You can do that later. There's only about ten minutes of light left. We got a new truck and two new wells and a big new stainless steel aging tank. Don't you want to see that?"

"I guess so." Joe sighed. "I've been driving since six o'clock this morning."

"You talk like an old man."

"That's what I am. I'm an old man." He surrendered himself, and they began to walk along the dirt road that led up the slope. Now the sun had dropped behind the mountains to the west, and the hills had turned jet black, topped by a burning red fringe; but over to the east, on the other side of the Napa Valley, the setting sun still caught the hilltops, bathing them in a golden glow. Sally paused, and they both turned to look. They stood there in silence for a little while, and then Sally said, "I guess we'd better go back, because if I stay up here with you I'm going to cry or something the way I feel, which you couldn't understand in a million years, even if you're older than me, and I just finished reading *Sister Carrie,* by Theodore Dreiser, so I know how stinking men are, and I don't even care if you don't look at me again, because you'll be here all summer, and I can tell you this: men don't really know how to love anyone because all they're interested in is the flesh, and I'll eat a lot and stuff myself and get fat and sexy, and then you'll look at me all right."

"I'll be damned," Joe said.

"Oh, come on down," Sally said lightly. "I'll help you carry your stuff into the house, because you might just strain yourself. Anyway, it's getting dark."

"You are something," Joe said slowly. "You really are something."

Barbara had purchased a compartment for herself on the Paris - Berlin express, determined to make productive use of the hours on the train. She had armed herself with a French - German dictionary, an English - German dictionary, a Berlin guidebook, a French translation of Scherber's *Rambles in Berlin,* and a French translation of *Mein Kampf.* Since she had embarked on her journey without being possessed of a single phrase in the German language, she had little hope of any great progress, but since the French - German dictionary had an appendix that gave the modern equivalents of the confusing German Gothic letters, she hoped that she might at least progress to an easy reading of street and shop signs.

Actually, during the first two hours of the journey she did not even touch her books. Now that she had overcome her initial repugnance toward the idea of Germany and managed to put her trepidation in its proper place, fairly well convinced that she would face no real danger, the notion of a sort of secret mission into what she could only think of as "the lair of the beast" excited and fascinated her. Also, since she had been earning her living as a writer during the past several years, it was quite natural for her to think as a writer. Apparently, three publishers had asked to put her "Letters from Paris" into book form. How exciting it was to think of her name on the jacket of a book! And why hadn't she insisted on knowing the names of the publishers? Why did she always think of the proper thing to do hours after the time for doing it? That, she decided, was a character defect that she would have to remedy. In any case, now that she had taken the bit in her teeth and was actually on the way to Germany, she could appreciate the value it would have to her as a writer. On the other hand, Hitler had already taken over Austria; Czechoslovakia had been handed to him through the infamous betrayal at Munich, and when she left Paris, the papers had been full of the possibility of a Nazi invasion of Poland — and speculation on whether this would mean another full-fledged European war. For the first time, Barbara decided, she would have to pay some attention to politics, more, much more, than the cursory attention she had given it in the past, and she would have to try to do what her left-wing friends in Paris called "thinking politically." She didn't have a very clear notion of what thinking politically meant exactly, but certainly she must read carefully whatever French or English newspaper would be available in Berlin.

She was so filled with ideas and plans that she failed to notice a man who had stopped in front of the corridor door of her compartment, even though she was staring out of the train window, in which his image was faintly reflected. Then she turned and saw him and realized that he had been standing there for at least a minute or two. He was a tall man in his mid-fifties, impeccably dressed in an English tweed jacket, blue worsted vest with brass buttons, white shirt, and striped tie — thus on his upper half, which Barbara could see through the door. He had a long, narrow face, iron gray hair, a thin, long nose, and dark, curious eyes. The door window was down about eight inches, and once he caught her attention, he spoke to Barbara in German.

"I'm afraid I don't speak German," Barbara replied in French.

"Ah, then you are French," he said, speaking French easily, with only a slight accent.

"No, I'm an American."

"But your French is faultless."

"So is yours," Barbara said, smiling.

"Ah, no. I have a clumsy accent, about which I can do absolutely nothing. Am I intruding? Do you have a bias against speaking to strangers on trains?"

"That depends on the strangers."

"Ah, so. Of course. Yes, you are American. It becomes more noticeable when you smile. Europeans smile differently. May I come in, for a few minutes?"

Barbara said nothing, watching him thoughtfully.

"I am quite harmless. Let me introduce myself — Baron Franz Von Harbin. I am a refugee in the corridor. This wretched train has no club car, and my compartment is impossible. So until the dining car opens for dinner, I am exiled to the corridor, which is not only uncomfortable but boring."

"Why not?" Barbara asked herself. "On a train, nothing can happen, and while he does not look harmless by any means, he is certainly elegant, and a German who speaks French, which is a beginning." She was completely confident of her ability to discourage unwanted advances, and she did not mind the fact that he styled himself a baron. He might or might not be one. Titles were plentiful and fluid in Europe in the thirties.

He opened the door, and as if he read her mind, he reached into his pocket and handed her his card. Then he waited until she had read it before he seated himself facing her.

Staring at his card, Barbara said, "Your name appears very familiar, and I feel that I should recognize it, and I feel foolish that I don't."

"Why should you? I am not terribly important. I have served my government here and there, in an advisory capacity, but nothing of great importance. And you, Madame?"

"Mademoiselle. My name is Barbara Lavette. I live in San Francisco."

"How charming — that wonderful, beautiful city! But your French accent and your French name?"

"No connection. My grandfather came from France, and as for my French, well, I've been living in Paris for almost five years." She paused, wondering how much information to impart, and decided that her best defense from here on was no defense at all, but simply to be herself, which she felt was the only role she was fit to play. "You've been to San Francisco?" she asked him.

"I certainly have. I was consul general there for two years, twenty-seven and twenty-eight. Of course, Lavette. He was the man who married the lovely Jean Seldon." He clapped his hands together with pleasure. "What a small, delightful world! I entertained them. They are your father and mother?''

Barbara nodded.

''Yes. You do look like her. I entertained them at the consulate, and once I was at their home. Where was it — Russian Hill?''

''That's right. Russian Hill.'' Barbara was reassured, relaxed.

He switched to English. ''Why don't we talk in English. My accent is not great, but better in your own tongue, yes? Do you know, your father was planning a New York - Bremerhaven run for one of his ships. It never came about, but we discussed things like docking facilities at great length. And now you, here; what a pleasant occurrence!'' He smiled at her. His smile made his otherwise stern and fixed face almost warm. ''Don't you think so?''

''I certainly do,'' Barbara agreed. ''But tell me, why was your own compartment impossible?''

''A sudden change in plans and I booked too late to have a compartment for myself. I found myself sharing one with two Bavarian pigs."

"Bavarian pigs? I don't understand."

"Shopkeepers. Munich shopkeepers, a very loathsome and crude form of humanity."

"Oh? But," Barbara said gently, "that doesn't sound at all like a description of the master race."

"Yes. Touché." He appeared not at all disturbed. "The master race, as you put it, is by no means a homogeneous mass. I profess no disloyalty to the Führer by maintaining my own sense of discrimination and preference." He pointed to the books on the seat beside her. "I see you have been reading *Mein Kampf*."

"I bought it. I bought the whole pile to ease my way into Germany, but I haven't cracked one yet."

"You come as a tourist, if I may ask?"

"Oh, no," Barbara said bluntly. "I would hardly choose Germany as a place for a holiday. I do a weekly story for a New York City magazine, and my editor decided that I should do a few from Berlin."

413

"May I ask what magazine?"

"*Manhattan Magazine.*"

"Ah, a very fine magazine, perhaps the best in the States. But of course, B.L., Barbara Lavette — you sign with only your initials."

"Then you read *Manhattan?*"

"When I have the opportunity, certainly. It is witty, iconoclastic, and I enjoy the cartoons."

"Careful," Barbara said to herself, "careful, my girl. He knows too much about too many things."

"It's also anti-Nazi," Barbara said.

"Ah, so it is. Yes. But that is an affliction common to most American publications these days. However, if I remember your own writing, you don't dwell on that."

"The woman's touch," Barbara agreed. "I would be the world's worst political commentator, so I confine myself to the civilized aspects of life."

He looked at her keenly, smiling again, but thinly. "You interest me, Miss Lavette. One would take you, on the face of it, for a very average, very beautiful,

414

American college girl. One would be mistaken, I think."

"Yes. I left college five years ago."

"Of course. And tell me, if you will, what will you write in your 'Letters from Berlin'?"

"I haven't the vaguest notion."

"Then you must let me help you. I am prejudiced, being a Prussian, yet I regard Berlin as one of the most interesting cities in Europe, certainly the best organized and the most modern. Of course, much depends on how you approach it. You can approach it as a city of great avenues, of parks, gardens, lovely canals, splendid public buildings, theaters, libraries, museums, as the place of the Friedrich Wilhelm University, with its lineage of great teachers, such as Hegel, Schelling, Richter, the brothers Grimm, Helmholtz, Lipsius — the place where Schinkel created some of the noblest buildings in all of Europe. Or again, you can approach it with a closed mind and only distrust and hatred for people who attempt to right an old injustice."

"Baron Von Harbin," Barbara said, "I

approach it only as an American traveling in Europe. If I knew what I was going to see, I would not have to go there, would I?"

"Excellent. Now tell me, where are you staying?"

"I have a reservation at the Esplanade."

Harbin frowned and shook his head.

"I heard it was an excellent hotel."

"So — yes and no. You must stay at the Adlon, on Unter den Linden. That's the only place. Believe me."

"But I have no reservation there."

"Leave that to me."

Barbara's impulse was to tell him that she had no intention of changing her hotel at his insistence. She had never allowed herself to be dominated or directed by either the desires or directions of men, and she found this man repellent and in a strange way somewhat terrifying. It was not that she feared him, nor did she experience the slightest unease at being alone in the compartment with him. His manners were impeccable, even courtly, and his admiration for her was obvious.

An American male, traveling alone, would have been playing every card of the game; Harbin gave her the impression that he valued her company, and that any gesture beyond that would be obscene. At the same time, she had a sense of something totaly alien, totally different, from anything she had ever encountered. A Frenchman would have been praising her looks, identifying her perfume, commenting on the cut of her dress, pulling his every trick out of the bag to charm her. Harbin made no attempt to charm her or to be charming; he was simply himself, and it was his self that she found terrifying without being able to define or identify the source of the terror. Still, she felt that the meeting was invaluable, that there was more to Harbin than he displayed, and that he was a key that could open many doors. What a coup it would be to step into the inner circles of the Nazis, to do an interview with Hitler, or even with Göring or Ribbentrop! She could see Frank Bradley reading her copy and whooping with delight.

So instead of telling Harbin that she had

no intention of changing her hotel, she simply nodded and asked him why it had to be the Adlon.

"Because I think you should have the very best door into my city. You have never been to Berlin, but you will see that I am correct. Yes? And now, since I find you so delightful as a traveling companion, will you dine with me?"

Barbara said that she would.

John Whittier had been spending more and more time with Tom Lavette, pleased that now the once rather irresponsible young man had become a very serious and dependable banker. They lunched together at least once a week, and Whittier invited Tom to accompany him on a trip to Washington.

"If you're not afraid to fly," Whittier said. "I can't spare the time for the train."

Tom was very much afraid to fly. On the other hand, there was no one in his circle of acquaintances who had ever flown cross-country, and if he made the trip it would do wonders for his status as well as his self-esteem. And once the big, lumbering DC-3 was off the ground and into the air, circling over San Francisco Bay and then climbing to cross the coastal range, Tom's nervousness disappeared. He felt a sense of validity, as if this were his proper inheritance. He did not often think of his father these days, nor had he seen him in years, yet he could not help recalling that it was Dan Lavette who had established the first passenger airline in California. Dan Lavette whose Ford Trimotors had given Californians their first taste of air travel.

"Look down from here, Thomas," John Whittier said, inspired to what was for him almost a poetic flight of the imagination. "Take a good look at this California of ours." It was in deference to Tom that he used the plural; he would have been more inclined to say this California of mine, which was the way he often thought of it. "There's no other place like it on earth, and someday it's going to be the center of the country, not geographically, but in every other way. This is where the power is — food, oil, lumber, and land, and the men who run California will damn well run the country. That's something to think about, young fellow. We'll be talking to Harry L. Hopkins tomorrow, and I'm going to bring you with me. God, I hate the ground Roosevelt walks on — or rides on. That crippled bastard doesn't walk. You know, they hold him up when he speaks. He can't even stand erect, and that's where the malignancy of his nature comes from, but the fact remains that he is President, and now he needs us. That's why Hopkins made this appointment. When we were fighting that bastard Harry Bridges five years ago, Roosevelt didn't lift a finger to help, but he needs me now. He needs the ships, because there's going to be a war, and we have the ships. I can remember the last war, Thomas. Do you know what happened to shipping rates?''

''I imagine they went up.''

''Doubled, tripled, quadrupled — no end to it. And it will happen again. Roosevelt thinks he can control it, but power is a slippery thing. There is no separation of money and power. Now this man Hitler —

he's not all bad, not by any means. Lindbergh found positive things in him and Göring, but the trouble is, he doesn't know where to stop, and Roosevelt does nothing to calm him down. The point is, Thomas, that come what may, we function; the family functions and the enterprise functions. Right now, in the eyes of the Rockefellers, the Morgans, the Lamonts, the Vanderbilts, and the rest of them, we are Johnny-come-latelies. They still look upon the West Coast as a sort of colony. But they've had their day. If there's going to be a war, we'll come out of it a damn sight better than the eastern establishment. Now just when do you come into your control? When does your mother's trust expire?"

"January 1940."

"Half a year. That will give us time to plan and consolidate. What do you think of Martin Clancy?"

The question came unexpectedly. When Jean Lavette had given up the chairmanship of the board of the Seldon Bank, Alvin Sommers, the first vice president, had moved into her place.

Martin Clancy, the second vice president, had moved into Sommers' position. Sommers had been sixty-five then; he was now seventy. Clancy, six years younger, was a tight-mouthed, icy-eyed little man who had never displayed to Tom any trace of emotion, sentiment, or attachment to any living thing. His total attachment was to the bank.

"How do you mean that?" Tom asked Whittier.

"The way I put it. What do you think of him. Do you like him?"

"No one likes Clancy. But he does know banking."

"Al Sommers is going to retire in September. Clancy wants to be chairman of the board. That's been his dream all his life."

"What do you think?" Tom asked diplomatically.

"I think no. I don't like him. He started out as a little mick in the Tenderloin, and essentially this is what he remains. You will control the stock. I want you to assert yourself. Can you do it?"

"I think I can," Tom replied, pleased

and not a little amazed at his own self-assurance. Whittier's frankness with him had helped build this assurance. He had never opened up quite in this manner before, never taken Tom so wholly into his confidence.

"I've been thinking about this consolidation for years," Whittier told him. "There's no doubt in my mind that once our interests are joined, we'll hold the balance of power on the Coast. From there on, we'll call the plays. I don't know yet exactly how we'll do it. That has to be worked out. But I want no slip-ups with Clancy. If he remains, it means only trouble. We want him out. Do you agree?"

"He's been with the bank forty years," Tom said slowly. "He's sixty-eight or sixty-nine. We could put through a sixty-five-year-old retirement rule, which would make it a little less personal. I think I could manage that."

"Only as chairman of the board. Do you think you can manage that?"

"If I have the votes, yes."

"So it's a question of Barbara. Between you, you'll have three hundred and eighty-two thousand shares, seventy percent of the stock. What about Barbara?''

''I haven't seen her for years.''

''Do you correspond?''

''Occasionally. She's supposed to return next week — at least that was her plan the last time I heard from her.''

''I never asked about the split between you, never felt it was my affair. Truth is, I never quite got over that business of the strike. Was it over your father?''

''In part. Oh, we're not enemies. I can talk to Barbara. I can't think of any reason why she should stand in my way.''

''You might plan to spend some time with her when she returns, win her confidence. It's important, Tom. I don't want to upset you, but Clancy and Sommers hold enough stock between them to tip the balance if we were to have Barbara turn against us.''

''I don't think she would.''

''On the other hand, your mother holds enough stock to tempt Barbara. She must not be tempted.''

''I think you must let me handle it,'' Tom said.

"I have faith in your abilities," Whittier agreed.

The following day, as they stood at the gates to the White House, he spelled out that faith. "The trick, Thomas," he said, "for a man who intends to take up residence there someday, is to plan in advance. Not a month or a year in advance, but a lifetime. You have some of the qualifications, but it's a damn sight more than that. You have to establish a record. You have to calculate every move in your life, and one thing you damn well cannot afford is sentiment. Whether you're going to a toilet, a cathouse, or a dinner party on Nob Hill, you think of how it will look on the record. That benighted, crippled man in there will not live forever, and sooner or later our party will have its day. So take a good look at it."

"You're being very kind, John. But you're overrating me."

"I certainly am, Thomas," Whittier admitted. "At this moment, I don't think you have the qualifications for the state assembly, and that's pretty much the doghouse of it all. You've spent your

425

twenty-seven years sitting back and waiting for the Seldon trust to fall into your lap. If you think you can do something else with the next twenty-seven, I'll back you to the hilt." He paused and faced Tom. "When we go in there and sit down with Harry Hopkins, it can begin an association that can change some history. Do you like the idea?"

"I do. Thank you, John," Tom said, not humbly, but as a confirmation between equals.

"Good. Now let's get to work."

The enormous, ornate, two-room suite in the Adlon dismayed Barbara. "I don't want this," she informed the manager flatly, staring at the baroque furniture, the thick gold and blue rug, the gilted drapes, the huge vase of fresh flowers. A black Mercedes limousine, waiting at the station for Harbin, had taken her there — Harbin still the proper, reserved, avuncular tour guide and protector — where Harbin had whispered a few words to the manager. Already Barbara was beginning to regret the fact that she had committed herself to Harbin's cloying courtesy. To be on her own, to do as she pleased and go where she pleased, had become second nature to her. She told herself that she was perhaps the most poorly equipped candidate in the world for the act of dissembling. This whole venture, she felt, was both romantic and stupid.

"I don't want this," she said, "and furthermore, I can't afford it."

The manager's English was not the best. *"Bitte, sprechen Sie langsamer.* Slow, yes? I understand, but slow."

"It is too expensive."

"So? No. I agree with ze baron, price is the same as Esplanade. *Bitte.* You are important guest."

Her luggage was in the room, and she was too tired to carry on the argument. The manager left, and Barbara kicked off her shoes and sprawled out on the vast bed. What on earth was she doing in Nazi Germany, in Berlin? "If I had an ounce of intelligence," she told herself, "I'd be on the next train back to Paris and then to Cherbourg and home." Suddenly, she felt so wretched and lonely and aimless that she began to cry, and, still crying, she got up and walked to the huge mirror that took up most of one wall of the bedroom. Staring at the woeful, weeping face in the mirror, she burst into laughter, weeping and laughing at the same time. "Oh, I am a card," she told herself. "What a great undercover agent I have turned out to be!"

Enough of that, she decided. She stripped off her clothes and showered. It was still early, not yet midday. She dressed herself in a pleated plaid skirt, white blouse and light cardigan, and a good, solid pair of walking shoes; then she paced around her suite, studying it, and beginning, in her mind, the composition of her first "Letter from Berlin": "One discovers, immediately, a German gift for tastelessness. This is no inconsiderable talent. One would have to haunt the bazaars for weeks to discover a rug so garish and vulgar as that which covers the floor of my hotel living room."

She rejected it, annoyed with herself. She had hardly looked at the city, and she had no right to judge. She also realized that she would have to change the manner of her writing. There was something almost obscene about commenting on taste and manners and hotel furnishings in Berlin of 1939. ''No preconceived notions,'' she told herself, ''not even in this cesspool. You go out and you see, and you make no judgments until the facts are presented before your own eyes.''

It was just past noon when she came out on the street to a pleasant, sunny day, a cool breeze, and stretching before her, the magnificent reach of Unter den Linden. She knew from her guidebook that the university was on the same avenue, but she had carefully avoided mentioning it or asking about it. Now she decided to set out to find it on her own, after which she would find a restaurant and have some lunch. She strolled down Unter den Linden, studying the faces of the people who passed by. In all truth, she had to admit to herself that here on this lovely avenue there was no indication of what she had read about Germany. The people were well-dressed, cheerful, very

429

ordinary human beings. Men looked at her, but then, she was sufficiently aware of her own face and figure to accept the fact that men looked at her, even though she herself could not accept a picture of herself as a beautiful woman. It was all so normal, so very matter-of-fact a picture of life in a busy, prosperous city, that she had to keep reminding herself where she was.

When she reached the university, opposite the Zeughauess Museum, she had the eerie feeling that the unseen eyes of the Gestapo were fixed upon her, and she made sure not to slow her pace or give the university buildings more than a passing glance, which she felt was all their unattractive architecture deserved. Certainly, her reaction was based on nothing more than her own excited imagination, yet for all that, she felt naked and alone. She would not go near the university on her first day in Berlin, nor on her second; she had to have, in her own mind, a valid excuse, some pages in her writing that would deal with higher education. She wandered along and found herself in Leipzigerstrasse; she ate a sausage and drank a glass of dark beer at a food bar and then walked back to the Adlon. First things first. Bits and pieces of reading surfaced in her mind. If one went in for this sort of thing, one had to cover every movement. She picked up her copy of *Mein Kampf,* regarded it distastefully, and then began to read, thumbing the pages, picking up passages here and there:

"All the human culture, all the results of art, science and technology that we see before us today, are almost exclusively the creative product of the Aryan. This very fact admits of the not unfounded inference that he alone was the founder of all higher humanity, therefore representing the prototype of all that we understand by the word man —"

A knocking at her door gave her an excuse to throw the book from her in disgust. "Oh, no," she whispered. "There are people with a penchant for wandering in sewers. I am not one of them." Then she went to the door and opened it.

A tall, slender, thinly handsome woman

431

stood there, black hair in a close bob, high-bridged nose, and cynical gray eyes. She wore a flowered dress of red silk with a fur piece thrown across her shoulders. "My dear," she said, without formalities, "you are beyond question the beautiful, enchanting Barbara Lavette. Dutzi is quite right. You, my dear, are a knockout. In your own way, mind you." The accent was British, the voice high-pitched, confident, and touched with arrogance.

"Who are you, if I may ask? And who on earth is Dutzi?"

"Ah, so much for the famous — or for the infamous, should I say? I am the notorious Pleasance Rittford. Does it shock you, my dear?"

"Should it?" Barbara wondered, trying desperately to place the name. Certainly she had heard it — something British upper class and reasonably scandalous.

"My dear child, must I stand in your doorway? Even if you bloody well don't approve of me, you can invite me in."

"Please come in," Barbara agreed. "How do you know I disapprove of you?"

"Plaid skirt, walking shoes, cardigan —

all of it eminently sensible. Eminently sensible people do not approve of me. You see, I do not hate Nazis. I quite adore them, and I make no secret of it."

It fell into place, Lady Pleasance Rittford, wife of Lord Nigel Rittford, both of them eager and articulate supporters of Hitler's new order and very vocal propagandists against Britain taking up arms against Germany. Barbara's first inner reaction was cold shock, a kind of sick disgust and an impulse to burst out in a storm of righteous anger. This she controlled, even managing to maintain her expression of naive bewilderment. After all, she was not a tourist. She was a writer who had stupidly agreed to do a job for a cause she neither understood nor approved of; but she was also a writer whose editor would turn handsprings after reading the kind of story she could do on Lady Pleasance Rittford.

"I don't shock you?"

"Perhaps a bit," Barbara admitted, forcing a smile, studying Lady Pleasance carefully. "At least forty," Barbara said to herself, "neurotic, terribly thin, hardly

433

a sex object, and absolutely obsessed,'' trying to remember what she had read of Freud on the subject of obsession and compulsion. How wasted her two years of college had been; but again, how is anyone at age eighteen to know what educational necessities will arise a decade later?

"Poor dear, to come blasting in on you like this." She pointed to the great mass of yellow roses on the coffee table. "Dutzi's trademark. He is quite taken with you. You must thank him profusely. He's very sensitive and sentimental under that fish face Prussian mask of his."

"Who is Dutzi?"

"The Baron — Harbin, your traveling companion. His close friends call him Dutzi." She wet her lips with her tongue and leaned back, assessing Barbara. "Not you. It wouldn't sound right from you at all. It's that English schoolgirl look that has his heart dancing. Keep it. It's worth its weight in gold — or in yellow roses."

"What on earth are you trying to tell me? I barely know this man."

"Oh, he's not in love with you, my dear,

if that's what you're thinking. Men like Dutzi don't fall in love. But Dutzi has his Aryan image and ideal. He's quite nutty on the subject, and you fulfill it."

"Good heavens! Would you please tell him that I am a mongrel."

"That won't make a bit of difference. Aryan is as Aryan decides. They get rid of only the truly loathsome types. You wouldn't have a drink, would you, dear? I'm positively parched."

"I haven't had time. I only arrived this morning, and I've been wandering around Berlin. I'll have them send up something."

"I'll do it." She sighed. "Unless your German is good?"

"Nonexistent."

"I thought so. What will you have?"

"A white wine cooler?"

Lady Pleasance made a face, then went to the phone and ordered. Then she stalked around the living room, grimacing in disapproval. "You know, my dear, Germans have even less taste than the British. Dutzi says you're a writer. What do you write?"

"I do a weekly piece for *Manhattan Magazine*. Gossip, people, and fashion. Books and theater. My editor wants a few pieces from Berlin. But now that I'm here, I'm up against the language. I never had that problem in Paris."

"Gossip, people, and fashion," Lady Pleasance repeated, clapping her hands with pleasure. "Forget fashion. They don't have it. But gossip — dear one, we must talk and talk and talk. You're not political, are you? I mean, you're not going to pal around with that stupid group of American and British correspondents who pin virtue all over themselves by sitting around and hating the Nazis. But of course not. They write the dullest, dreariest things imaginable, and whatever Dutzi may appear to be, he has a nose like a bloodhound. You're very lucky that he approves of you. It's an open sesame."

"To what?" Barbara wondered.

"You name it, love. You could even get to the Führer himself, and he's not such a bad chap at that. No gentleman, like Dutzi and Papen and some of the others, but power is a heady drink, and one forgives.

And speaking of drink, where is it?''

The drinks came then. Lady Pleasance had ordered two double whiskeys, and she drank the first one neat, as if it were water. She mixed some soda into the second, and then launched into a rambling discourse on the character of the Führer.

By now, Barbara had had her fill of Lady Pleasance, and it occurred to her that perhaps she had also had her fill of Berlin. How had she ever gotten herself mixed up with this crew, and why didn't she put a stop to it? She knew the answer. Professor Schmidt and the university had dropped to the background of her mind, and like a child offered candy, she was composing, witty, cynical pieces for *Manhattan,* close-ups of these ''creatures,'' as she thought of them, journalistic scoops that might never have come her way under different circumstances. A door had been opened, and it needed only one angry, disapproving remark from her to close it; whereupon, she sipped her wine cooler and forced herself to make polite, leading remarks to a Lady Pleasance, who was rapidly becoming drunk.

"The Führer will like you," Lady Pleasance confided. "I wouldn't dwell on that mongrel business. What is it, a French father? Dutzi says your French is simply divine. Goebbels is somewhat confused about the French, whether to give them Aryan status or not, but with a woman who looks like you, it's not to worry about, not one bit. You don't have a few drops of Jew blood anywhere? No, of course not. Now, you're just about the Führer's height, love, if you don't go in for high heels. But don't be too chummy. I think Dutzi has his own plans. He had a wife once who died or something —"

"Died or something?" Barbara asked.

"Or sleeping pills. Who knows? Not that I blame her. Dutzi's great fun — but to be married to him? Heaven forbid. He's jolly good for an evening or two, a trifle kinky, but darling, they all are, and it's all good fun, you know, if you don't take it too seriously, and don't look at me like that. I don't kiss and tell, but I do draw the line. I drew it with Göring. He's a disgusting fat pig, and I told him so to his face. Anyway, his *Lüger* — good name for it, don't you think — anyway, it's so buried in fat that he can't do anything much, or so I've heard, and anyway, he's a bit of a dope fiend. Papen, now that's something else. There's a gentleman, only he's a bit stupid, and Dutzi thinks the Führer will find him a bit of too much. You don't want to chum up with anyone who's on the way out. It can get quite nasty. Well, Pleasance will mother you through the sticky places. I do hope you're here for a long stay, and don't be put off by this war talk. There won't be any war. Winston, Neville, Tony — the whole lot of them are a pack of sniveling idiots, and as for your Deladier, he's the toadiest of the lot. What Adolf wants, Adolf will get, and he'll get it his way — the whole bloody continent —''

And on and on. She returned to the phone, and the waiter reappeared with two more double whiskeys. Finally, at long last, she rose unsteadily, told Barbara, ''I must toddle, dear one. We'll have another darling chat very soon,'' and made her way to the door.

Alone, Barbara sat and shivered, and

then, moving like an automaton, she went into the bathroom and began to brush her teeth. Then she paused, thinking, What on earth am I doing here, brushing my teeth? Really, Barbara, you are behaving like a child.

She returned to the sitting room, which was now quite dark in the gathering twilight. She put on the lights, called room service, and in a mixture of French and English managed to order some dinner. She took out her notebook, and then she paused. She sat for at least ten minutes, pen in hand, staring at the empty page, and then sighed and confessed to herself that she was afraid. She realized that there would be no "Letter from Berlin." She could not remain here, and she could not write from here. She would do what she had to do, and then she would leave. Suddenly, it was not just Berlin, not just Germany; in her mind, the whole of Europe was turning into a miasmal nightmare, and somewhere inside her a voice was screaming to be let out of it.

That night, she lay awake for hours. "I want to go home," she told herself. "I want to go home. I'm so afraid and so lonely. I can't go through with this. I want my mother and I want my father, and I want to be able to see plain, ordinary people, who are not sick and not insane.''

She turned on the light, picked up the telephone, and asked for the overseas operator. It was one o'clock in the morning, and it took an hour more to get through to Dan's office on Terminal Island.

''Daddy,'' she said at last, ''is that you? Is that truly you?''

''Barbara? Where on earth are you? We've been trying to reach the ship.''

''I didn't sail, daddy. I'm in Berlin.''

''Berlin? No, you're kidding.''

''It's the truth.''

''God Almightly, what the devil are you doing in that filthy place? Are you all right?''

''I'm fine, daddy. Just a little homesick. Don't scold me. I'm here on a story. I wrote to mother. I know I should have written to you, but I knew how troubled you'd be.''

''Well, I am troubled. I can't tell you

how troubled I am. That's no place for you. All hell is going to break loose. Baby, please get out of there."

"How's Joey and May Ling?"

"Fine, fine. Joe's up at Higate. Where are you staying?"

"At a very posh hotel called the Adlon. I'm all right. And I'll be home soon, I promise you."

"It's been too long, Barbara."

"I know, daddy."

"When will you be coming back?"

"Soon, I promise. Very soon. Daddy, do me a favor."

"Anything you say."

"Call mother. Tell her I'm all right." Barbara paused. "Be kind to her, daddy. She's so unhappy."

Barbara felt better after that. A few minutes later, she was asleep.

She slept until ten the following morning, awakened slowly, and lay for a while in the luxury of her bed, lazy, comfortable in the thought that she had finally made a decision and admitted to herself that the whole enterprise was a mistake. In her mind, she worked out the steps: return to Paris, go to her apartment, pack her things, write a letter to the Limogets, confessing her cowardice and horror and her total ineptitude as an undercover agent, call the travel agency, get a room on any ship leaving for America, train to Cherbourg, and then be out of it forever. Dreaming this way, she heard the telephone ring.

There was a flow of German, in which she recognized her name, then a few words in English.

"Yes, this is Barbara Lavette," she said.

Frank Bradley's voice: "Barbara, for God's sake, is that you? Can you hear me?"

"Of course I can hear you Frank."

"Do you know, we've been calling every hotel in Berlin. I finally reached your father in Los Angeles. From here on, will you please, please let me know where you are."

"Frank, there's no need to get excited. I'm perfectly all right. Now I want to tell you what I've decided —"

"Hold on and listen to me. There's a

great picture of you on page four of the New York *Times*. Tomorrow's paper. I got a proof. Headline — beauty and the beast. The point is, I want you get to get to one of them — Hitler, Göring — and do an interview. I know it's not an easy assignment, but I got faith in you. And listen, just take notes. You don't have to do your piece until you get back to Paris. Then you can let go. We're ballyhooing this to the sky, so, baby, do your thing."

"Frank —"

"Whatever you need — money, whatever — just let us know. And listen, there's a feller by the name of Buck Crombie at the American Embassy. An old classmate of mine. I sent him a wire, so if you require a friend in need, he's there."

"Frank, what makes you think I can get an interview with one of them?"

"I told you. Faith. And take notes. You can do three pieces for us, and believe me, the publishers are licking their chops. So carry on."

"Frank," she pleaded, "I don't know. This is a strange place. I think I shouldn't have come here at all."

"Angel, don't go soft on me. You're there. You don't have to stay forever. Just get what you need."

She put down the phone, despising her own lack of fortitude, her weakness and indecision, admitting to herself that when the lines were drawn, she came off as a person of absolutely no character. "And no resolve," she said to herself. "Anyone can change what you so euphemistically call your mind."

While she was dressing, there was a knock at the door: two dozen fresh yellow roses, to replace the ones already in the sitting room. There was a note with them: "I've been up to my ears in the tedious business of politics. Forgive me for ignoring my most charming traveling companion. Will you lunch with me? I'll be in the lobby at one. If you do not appear, I shall be devastated." It was signed, Baron Franz Von Harbin.

There was no return address or telephone number. She could refuse by not appearing. It was only half past eleven. There was still time to pack and take a taxi to the railroad station. She was under no compulsion to obey the imperious demand of Frank Bradley, nor did she need to continue her association with *Manhattan Magazine* — both of which she presented to herself as reasonable arguments and then rejected them. Her earlier mood was gone, and she told herself that she would be a fool not to take advantage of the situation she had fallen into. She also told herself that living with herself would be difficult indeed if she simply forgot about Professor Schmidt and wormed out of her commitment to the Limogets with a letter confessing ineptitude and cowardice.

She got out her notebook and proceeded to put down as much of her conversation with Lady Pleasance as she could remember, pleased that she was able to capture the Englishwoman's tone and inflection. At precisely one o'clock, she went down to the lobby, defiantly dressed in a pleated gray wool skirt, a white cotton blouse, a gray cardigan, and her English walking shoes. If Dutzi wished to take her to lunch, he would take her as she was.

He greeted her with great formality, with only a slight, quizzical smile as a reaction to her costume. "We will eat here, yes? The food is French, but very good." In the dining room, the headwaiter almost collapsed in a fit of obsequiousness. It was a new experience for Barbara. The waiters behaved as if they belonged totally to the Baron, as if they were offering their lives and not just food. She had to restrain a desire to giggle.

She thanked him for the flowers. "But it seems wasteful," she said. "The ones already there would have been lovely for days."

"Possibly. But then I would be robbed of an opportunity to pay tribute to a beautiful American woman, no?"

"I don't think there's any need to pay tribute, as you put it. You've been more than kind to me."

"My pleasure and my indebtedness. Americans appear to harbor a — what shall I call it? — a native distaste for our system. Perhaps I can show you the more pleasant side of Berlin, of Germany. That's why I sent Lady Pleasance. I felt that a touch of your own tongue on your first day might be comforting. What did you think of her?''

"She was very informative," Barbara replied without enthusiasm.

"Yes." He smiled and shrugged. "She has been very useful to us. Her husband is a good friend. We need friends in England, just as we need friends in America. My dear, I hesitate to force myself on you, but you are alone, and the day after tomorrow there is to be a large reception — food, dancing — at Kunstler Halle. The Führer will be there, and others too. If I cannot entice you to allow me to bring you by, let us say, my own credentials, then perhaps I can lure you as a journalist. It will be an opportunity to meet some of the ogres, as you think of them.''

Barbara considered it for a while. He waited, smiling. "How do you know I think of them as ogres?" she asked.

"Ah. But I am not entirely insensitive. You offer no opinions. You simply listen. Even Lady Pleasance was unable to squeeze an opinion from you."

"I didn't know she tried." Barbara smiled. "Yes, I would like to go. I am very curious to meet your leaders. Will you interpret for me?"

"Delighted."

"Will I be able to ask questions? To have more than a few minutes of conversation?"

"Alas, it is not my charm that draws you."

"I am afraid not entirely," Barbara said bluntly. "As you remarked, I am a journalist."

"I shall make your opportunities." He studied her thoughtfully. "May I call you Barbara?"

"Yes."

"Then you will call me Franz, never by that ridiculous name that Lady Pleasance must have informed you of. Barbara, I will call for you then, day after tomorrow, seven o'clock —" He was looking at her blouse and sweater.

"I will not wear my walking shoes," she said, smiling.

He took his leave after lunch,

449

apologizing for the pressing demands his work made on him. It was a fine afternoon, with a cool breeze taking the edge off the summer's heat, and Barbara decided to explore the city further. She drifted along without plan or purpose, down Unter den Linden to the Tiergarten, where she watched children playing and listened to the music of a barrel organ, forgetting for a little while where she was and what she was there for. Back at the hotel, she finished a meticulous description of her experience up to this point, had a sandwich and coffee in her room, and then spent the evening working out a series of questions she would put to whatever leader of the Third Reich Harbin arranged for her to question. At the same time, her thoughts wandered to what she felt was an inevitable moment in the future when Harbin would attempt to make love to her. She was neither innocent enough nor sufficiently unaware of her own attractiveness to doubt that this would happen, and the very thought of it sent cold shivers up and down her spine. Nor could she analyze this response on her part as other than a total response to the existence of Nazi Germany. She had spent two days in a clean, well-run, and in parts very beautiful city. No one had been ungracious to her, and Baron Von Harbin had on every occasion been the soul of courtesy, concern, and impeccable behavior. Barbara was a very independent and self-confident young woman; she knew and accepted this quality in herself; and she also knew that she was very different today from the wide-eyed college student who five years ago had embarked on the Twentieth Century Limited for the journey back to California. But she also knew that since she had arrived in Berlin, there had been an undercurrent of fear in her that she simply could not shake off.

She went to bed without contriving any solution to the Harbin problem, telling herself that when it surfaced, she would deal with it. She awakened early the next morning, discovered that she was ravenously hungry, and ate an enormous breakfast of sausage, eggs, fried potatoes, rolls, and coffee in the hotel dining room.

Well, she had eaten almost nothing the day before, bereft of her appetite by the presence of the Baron and then content with a sandwich in her room. She felt more normal now, and, filled with purpose, telling herself, "Devil take the consequences. I said I would do it and I will," she strode along Unter den Linden to Friedrich Wilhelm University. There was nothing wrong, nothing curious, nothing suspicious, in what she was doing. Professor Schmidt had published two books, *Race and Religion* in 1936 and *Aryan Philosophy* in 1937. Neither book was obtainable in Paris, but she knew that *Aryan Philosophy* had been translated and published in New York, and she read a scathing review of it in the files of the Paris *Tribune*. The reviewer had found Schmidt's attempts to connect the Bhagavad-Gita with Hitler's theories of the master race and with the half-baked theology of Bormann, Rosenberg, and Himmler both childish and tasteless. Barbara's own impression was of a man undertaking an exercise in self-preservation, but this was only a guess, since she had not read the book. However, the book had created sufficient furor for her to be justified, she felt, in interviewing him.

At the office of the university, hidden in a Gothic maw, she found, happily, a young woman who spoke French well enough to explain that Professor Schmidt was not teaching the first summer semester. The young woman thought he could possibly be found in his apartment, which was on a street called Kurfürstendamm. If Barbara desired to walk, it was about three kilometers, off Unter den Linden onto Hermann Göring Strasse, then onto Potsdamer Strasse, and then it would be on her right. But the Fraülein, she was told, would be better advised to find a taxicab.

Barbara decided to walk. It was the only way to really see a city, to get the feel of it, and the day was still young. Past the looming bulk of the Kaiser Schloss, past the gardens and public buildings on Göring Street, past the chancellery, it was like walking through a dream or into the pages of a horror tale, yet it was all perfectly ordinary. Then she was in a street of shops, and there was a shop boarded over, and scrawled on the wooden boarding, JUDE; and how very strange and chilling that was, the first indication of the things she had read! She thought to herself, They are so competent and clean. They keep things out of sight.

Kurfürstendamm was a street of apartment houses. She had an odd sense of familiarity; there were streets exactly like it in Paris. She began to read the numbers, looking for the professor's building.

Then Barbara saw a small crowd on the street in front of her, and a barrier that diverted traffic into a single, narrow line. There were two men in the white uniforms of sanitation workers. They were standing by the barrier. On the sidewalk, a dozen onlookers watched in silence. Out in the street, a group of men and women were sweeping what appeared to be the remains of sewage, the overflow of what Barbara guessed might have been a broken or malfunctioning sewer line. As she approached the group, the strong smell of the sewage increased, and she could see on the street the damp residue of what appeared to be human feces, dark clumps and streaks of unidentifiable refuse that had apparently backed up out of the sewer. About fourteen or fifteen men and women were sweeping the offal into several piles. The men and women were not young. Most of them appeared to be in their fifties and sixties, some older; one woman was white-haired, very old, apparently feeble. They were decently dressed in suits and dresses, and several of the men wore spectacles. If she had met these people in the ordinary course of things, Barbara's impression would have been of a group of professionals and their wives — doctors, lawyers, storekeepers, teachers. Their work was being directed by four men, heavyset men who wore belted raincoats and hats in spite of the early summer weather. These four men shouted commands at the sweepers, pushed them, and snarled at them when their pace slackened. The two sanitation workers stood in silence, as did the onlookers on the sidewalk. Beyond the group, a sanitation truck and two black sedans were parked.

Barbara reached the group and stopped and watched, resisting the urge to avert her eyes and walk past quickly. She was trembling; she felt sickened; yet she could not tear herself away. She had read numerous accounts in the Paris newspapers of Jews summarily pulled out of their homes to clean streets, yet the fact was hideously different from the written account. It was not what they were doing that filled her with a kind of numb horror, but the blank-faced silence of the onlookers and the two sanitation men; and this, together with her inability to understand anything of the shouts and imprecations hurled at the sweepers by the burly men in raincoats, increased her sense of having stepped into a nightmare.

Now most of the offal had been swept into piles. The elderly men and women paused in their work, and one of the men in raincoats said something to the sanitation workers. In response, they walked over to the truck and returned with two empty metal cans, which they set down close to the mounds of garbage. They started back to the truck and were stopped by an order from the man in the raincoat. Then an exchange of dialogue. It appeared to Barbara that they were arguing with the man in the raincoat. Suddenly he raised his voice and shouted. The two sanitation men shrugged and walked to one side.

Now some of the onlookers turned and walked away. Other pedestrians walked past without pausing, without even glancing at what was going on. Some instinct told Barbara to go, to leave it alone, to get away before whatever was going to happen happened; a stronger force held her there. She had forgotten for the moment that she was on her way to find Professor Schmidt; she had forgotten everything except the drama that was being played out in front of her.

Now the same man in the raincoat who had argued with the sanitation workers turned to one of the sweepers. This was a man who appeared to be close to seventy; he was stoop-shouldered, scholarly in appearance, with a fringe of white hair around his bald head, and neatly dressed in a brown suit, a white shirt, and a dark tie.

The man in the raincoat pointed to one of the piles of refuse and gave an order. The old man looked at him without moving or replying. Raising his voice, the man in the raincoat gave the order again, pointing at the same time to one of the metal cans. His meaning was obvious. The old man was to pick up the filth in his bare hands and put it in the can, and now Barbara realized that the sanitation men had probably been going to the truck for shovels when they were stopped.

All sound, all movement on the street, stopped. Onlookers, sanitation men, sweepers — all of them stood frozen, watching the man in the raincoat and the old man. Now the three other men in raincoats moved toward the old man.

Again the order, this time quietly and coldly. The old man shook his head and sighed. The man in the raincoat took a step and swung his open hand across the old man's face, and the old man went down on the pile of filth. As he tried to pull himself away, the man in the raincoat kicked him so that he sprawled in the filth again, then he bent, dragged him to his feet by his collar, and drew back his hand to strike him again.

Barbara could stand no more. "Stop it!" she cried. "Stop it, you animal!"

The man in the raincoat paused with his arm drawn back for the blow, still clutching the trembling old man by the collar. He looked at Barbara. Everyone else stared at Barbara. The man in the raincoat grinned, disposed of the grin, and snapped at her in German. Then he struck the old man.

Afterward, Barbara had no clear memory of what happened in the next few seconds. She had never before in her life engaged in an act of violence, never been in a fight, never struck a blow or had a blow struck at her; so what she did was totally a response, without thought or premeditation. She flung herself at the man in the raincoat, swinging the leather handbag she carried at his head. The old man, whom he still clutched by the collar, was between him and Barbara, and the man in the raincoat was unable to ward off the blow. It caught him on the side of the head and staggered him. The three other men in raincoats leaped at Barbara and grabbed her; and then all reason departed, and she fought like a wildcat, biting at their hands where they held her, scratching, kicking. The fourth man in the raincoat let go of the old man, swearing and pressing his hands to his eyes. Then he joined the other three and managed to slap Barbara across the face, a heavy stinging blow, yet one that she hardly felt at the moment.

Then the fit passed, the rage drained out of her, and she stopped struggling and stood trembling and sobbing in the grasp of the three men; yet even in that moment of anguish and indignity, she noticed that no one moved a step to help her. No one but the men in the raincoats moved or spoke, not the two sanitation workers, not the onlookers, not the old people with the brooms. They watched in silence as the man she had hit with her purse raised his hand to strike her again. One of the men who held her barked at him, let go of

Barbara, and pushed the fourth man away. He then turned to Barbara, speaking quickly and angrily.

"I don't speak German," she managed to say.

The fourth man in the raincoat, the one who had been beating the old man — who now had collapsed on the pavement, blood running from his nose — the fourth man walked up to Barbara until his face was only a few inches from hers. One of the men holding her said something to him. He shook his head and smiled. Then he spat in Barbara's face.

The act had an electrifying effect upon her. She stopped trembling, stopped sobbing. She felt that something deep inside of her had turned into ice, and she said, slowly and precisely, "You filthy Nazi pig. I am not afraid of you. Not afraid of you at all. Do you understand me?"

His companion pushed him back and spoke to the other two. Then he turned to the sweepers and barked at them. The two men who held Barbara began to lead her off toward where the black sedans were parked. At first she held back. Then, rather than submit to the further indignity of being dragged across the filthy street, she walked with them to the cars. They opened the back door of one of them and motioned for her to get in. She felt cold, tired, weak, used up, but no longer half-hysterical, no longer afraid. One of the men got in next to her. The other went back to where her purse had fallen on the street, picked it up, and, returning, gave it to her. Then he got into the car and they drove off.

She took a handkerchief from her purse and wiped her face, then she looked at herself in her hand mirror. There was a red welt on her cheek where she had been struck, but her eye just above it was not bruised or swollen. Both the man beside her and the driver were silent. It was no use asking them where they were taking her. They either did not speak English or refused to. She leaned back in her seat, bereft of emotion. There was nothing she could do but wait.

They drove for only a few minutes, no more than a kilometer, she decided, then entered a narrow street and pulled up in front of a gray stone building. Over the door, brass letters spelled out: POLIZEIAMT. Barbara breathed a sigh of relief. At least they were taking her to a police station, not to some dreaded Gestapo house.

The man next to her got out and motioned for her to follow him; then, with a raincoat on either side of her, she was ushered into the building. Barbara had never been inside a police station, in America or elsewhere, so she had no measure of comparison. There was a wide entranceway painted dark green, with a cement floor, benches on either side, a staircase going up to a second floor, a wooden railing with a gate in the middle, and behind it a man in uniform at a desk. They went through the gate, and then she was standing in front of the desk, the men in raincoats on either side of her. One of them spoke to the man at the desk; Barbara stood there while the conversation went on, the man at the desk making notes on a pad in front of him. Then the two men in raincoats turned and walked out, leaving Barbara standing there while the officer behind the desk continued to write on his pad.

He finally stopped writing and looked up at her thoughtfully. He was a stout man, with a round face, tiny blue eyes, and a very small mouth, which he pursed constantly.

"Englisch?" he asked her.

"I'm an American."

"Ah, *Amerikanerin.*" It was evidently the extent of his conversation in English. He pointed to one of the benches. *"Sitzen!"* Barbara walked to the bench and sat down. A clock on the wall facing her said one o'clock. Where had the morning gone? It seemed to be a gap in her existence, as if what had happened out there on Kurfürstendamm had happened an eternity ago. The man at the desk picked up a telephone and talked into it. Then again silence. It was strangely quiet for a police station. Then a man in ordinary clothes came down the stairway. Barbara was looking at a large photograph of Adolph Hitler hanging on the wall alongside the staircase, thinking, as she had in the past, of how ridiculous the tiny Chaplinesque mustache was — and then she noticed the man on the staircase: no mustache, but nevertheless a striking resemblance. Did he realize it, she wondered? And then it struck her that, for some reason, she could not focus clearly on her present situation, in a police station in a foreign country, apparently under arrest, unable to speak the language — and sliding into some sort of daydream. Yet it was like a dream, vicious, stupid, impossible.

The man who looked like Hitler without the mustache walked to the desk and said something to the officer sitting there, who pointed to Barbara. He came over to Barbara and said, in English, "My name is Schlemer, Inspector Schlemer. What is your name, Fraülein?"

"Barbara Lavette."

"Yes. Good. Come with me, please." He had a heavy accent, but otherwise his English was fluent and grammatical. He led Barbara up the stairs and down a hallway, where he opened the door to a small room that contained a desk, several

465

wooden chairs, a bookshelf, a filing cabinet, and on the wall facing the door another picture of the Führer.

"Please, sit down, Fraülein," he said, indicating a chair. There was a window in the room. Schlemer switched on his desk lamp, evidently to increase the light, and he peered at Barbara's face. "How did you get that bruise?"

"One of your men enjoys striking women — and old men."

Schlemer walked around his desk and sat down behind it, facing Barbara. "They are not my men. My men don't enjoy striking women or old men."

"They arrested me — if I am under arrest. They tore my clothes and dragged me through the street," Barbara said coldly, angrily.

"Do you wish a doctor to look at you, Fraülein?"

"No, I'm quite all right. I just wish to know why I was thrown into a car and brought here."

"You are an American?"

"Yes."

"What is your business in Germany?"

"I'm a journalist. I'm here on assignment for my magazine. And you haven't answered my question."

"In time, in time. Where do you live, Fraülein?"

"I'm staying at the Adlon."

The expression on his otherwise impassive face changed ever so slightly. Barbara noticed this. "Am I under arrest?" she insisted.

"Please tell me what happened."

"I was walking down the street —"

"On Kurfürstendamm? Do you have friends there?"

"I was taking a walk."

"I see. Strolling."

"Yes. And then I saw these old people sweeping filth on the street. Four men in raincoats were supervising them. Then one of these men in raincoats insisted that an old man pick up the filth with his hands and put it into a metal can. The old man refused. The thug in the raincoat then began to beat the old man. I tried to make him stop. That's when he struck me. Then the other three grabbed me, dragged me into a car, and here I am."

"So. You should not have interfered, Fräulein. The sweepers were Jews, put to useful work for the common health of the city. They should be grateful that they are allowed to contribute in whatever way they can for the good of the Reich. When they become stubborn and willful, they must be disciplined."

"By beating an old man? By flinging him face down in that filth?"

"There are things you do not understand, Fräulein."

"Thank God!"

"Your own position is difficult Are you under arrest?" He shrugged. "I have no alternative. You interfered with security officers in the performance of their duties. You attacked them. You struck one of them."

"I don't believe this!" Barbara exclaimed.

"You say you are a journalist. It's very odd for a journalist to be living at the Adlon."

"I assure you, Inspector, that I did not choose the Adlon. But what if I did? Have I no right to stay at the hotel I choose?"

"Every right, Fraülein. But if you did not choose the Adlon, who did?"

"Baron Von Harbin insisted that I stay there."

The inspector stared at her thoughtfully, a long moment passing before he said, "Is the Baron a friend of yours?"

"Yes."

Again, moments of silence. Then Schlemer rose. "If you will excuse me for a few minutes, Fraülein —" He left the room, closing the door behind him. Barbara sat there, ill at ease, dissatisfied with herself, angry at herself for having mentioned Harbin's name, telling herself that she would rather rot in a cell than turn to Harbin for help. Right at this moment, Harbin symbolized everything that had happened to her this day, and she realized that she had lacked the courage to say, "No, he's no friend of mine. I have only contempt for him."

"Well," she admitted to herself, "there it is, Barbara. You are not the stuff of which heroes or heroines are made. You are scared." And then she whispered,

469

"Oh, God, I *am* scared, terrified. What if they put me in one of their jails, or a concentration camp. I never thought of that."

She sat there, pleading inwardly for Schlemer to return and tell her what her fate was to be. Would they allow her to communicate with the American Embassy? Would they allow her to reach her parents, to speak to anyone?

And then the inspector returned. She rose to face him.

"I am sorry for what has occurred, Fraülein," he said to her. "You must understand that those men were not my men, not Berlin policemen. I have arranged for a car to take you back to your hotel. I trust that you will understand that this is not the normal order of things in Berlin."

"Do you mean that I'm free to go?" Barbara asked uncertainly.

"Please. I will take you downstairs."

Back at the Adlon, Barbara went up to her suite and dropped tiredly into a chair. What a mess she had made of things! And what now? Did she dare go again to

470

Kurfürstendamm and seek out Professor Schmidt? Could she stay in Berlin? Could she sleep at night?

She looked down and noticed that her stockings and shoes were covered with filth. Why hadn't she noticed that before? Disgusted, she kicked off the shoes, pulled off her stockings, and then threw both into the trash basket. Again she sat down, closing her eyes, stretching out her bare feet. At least she was free, not in a police station, not in a Gestapo house, but free. That was something. No, that was everything. She had always been free; she had never realized the sweet taste of it. Even here in Berlin, even with all the problems facing her, the taste of freedom was as sweet as honey. And then her sense of relief gave way to the picture of the old Jew lying with his bleeding face in the sewage. She felt suddenly nauseated and ran into the bathroom, where she vomited. She hung over the toilet bowl, vomiting convulsively until her stomach was empty. The vomiting relieved her. She felt clean and empty for the first time since the incident began, and she went to the sink, scrubbed her face, and brushed her teeth. Just as she finished, there was a knock at the door.

"One moment!" she called out. She rinsed her mouth, dried her hands, and then went barefoot to the door and opened it.

Harbin stood there. "May I come in?" he asked her.

She closed the door behind him. Harbin walked slowly around the room, glanced at the wastebasket, where she had thrown her shoes and stockings, then at her bare feet. Barbara stood watching him. Then he walked over to her and touched her cheek gently.

"Does it hurt?"

She shook her head.

"Sit down please, Barbara." She dropped into a chair. "Have you had lunch? Do you want some?"

"I'm not hungry, thank you."

He placed his hat on the table where the yellow roses were, then sat on the couch, facing her.

"They called you, and you told them to

let me go. Isn't that it?'' Barbara asked him.

He nodded.

"Thank you. I was very frightened. I'm grateful to you.''

"Yes.'' Then he sat silently, staring at her.

"About my feet,'' she said nervously, "the shoes and stockings were filthy. I couldn't stand to touch them. I threw them away.''

"I understand. Your blouse is torn. Do you want to change?''

She glanced down. Why hadn't she noticed the tear in her blouse before? Or had she?

"Go in and change,'' he said tonelessly. "Put on shoes and stockings.

Her torn blouse was off and she was standing in her brassiere and slip when Harbin came into the bedroom. He stopped just inside the bedroom door. "Finish dressing,'' he told her. "We will talk while you dress and pack.''

She pulled on a fresh blouse. "What do you mean, pack?''

"You are leaving Germany. You have a

reservation on the four-thirty train for Paris. That doesn't give us too much time."

Strangely, she was not disturbed by his presence in the bedroom. He had erected a wall between them. "No," she said defiantly. "Why should I leave? I have things to do here." Then she added, "Is it because of what happened?"

"On Kurfürstendamm? No, that was childish and impetuous. The other thing was stupid."

She had stepped into her skirt and zipped it closed. "What other thing?"

"Finish dressing. The university."

She was taking stockings out of a drawer, and now she paused to look at him, the stockings in her hand.

"You play the game like a fool, like a child," he said harshly. "Are you a communist?"

"No," she whispered.

"No. Even a stupid communist would know better. What then, a sympathizer?"

"No."

"Well, it doesn't matter now. Did you think you could go to the university and make inquiries about Schmidt and have it end there?"

"I went there to interview him," she said hopelessly.

"What nonsense! Did your editor send you to Berlin to interview a fool who thought that by writing idiotic books he could pull the wool over our eyes? We have plenty of idiotic books, but they are written by idiots and not by quixotic fools. How did you even hear about Schmidt? His books were never published in France. You don't read German. Didn't you think of these things?"

It occurred to her to insist that she had read *Aryan Philosophy* in English, and then she realized that such a protestation would make no more sense than anything else she had done. She bit her lip and finished pulling on her stockings.

"And then you calmly walked to Kürfurstendamm. Luckily, you were arrested before you ever reached Schmidt's apartment. The Gestapo is still searching his apartment, taking it apart bit by bit. Oh, it would have been a fine thing for you to walk in there and ask for

Professor Schmidt. Because, my dear Barbara, Professor Wolfgang Schmidt died yesterday. He died after three days and three nights of questioning by the Gestapo. Let me be more brutally frank. He was beaten to death. And the same Gestapo, my dear, is waiting for you to try to contact Professor Schmidt. I am not saying that you would be beaten to death. After all, you are a correspondent and an American citizen and the daughter of a very wealthy family. As yet, they don't know what your associations in Paris were, but they can find out, believe me. And it would be damned unpleasant for you, very damned unpleasant."

He paused. Barbara said nothing, only watching him. "Put on your shoes and pack," he said.

She put on a pair of shoes, and then she opened a suitcase and began mechanically to put clothes into it. Harbin watched her. Then she stopped and turned to him.

"Why are you doing this? Why are you telling me all this?"

"Because unless you open your eyes, you will never survive in this world. You don't belong in Europe. Go home. Or else your insane innocence will destroy you. Don't you have any idea of what I am, of what this place is? Or what kind of a crazy game you are playing? Do you know why they chose you? Because you are an innocent, because it shines out of your eyes, because you are sick with the belief that people are good. Yes! Sick with it! It's no virtue today. It's a sickness. You talk so blithely of interviewing Hitler and Göring. Do you know what they are, what we all are? Do you know where I was yesterday morning? I was watching them finish off Professor Schmidt. That was my amusement for half an hour."

She finished packing, unable to speak, unable to respond in any way. When her bags were packed, Harbin phoned for a porter. Going down in the elevator, Barbara said, "I must pay my bill."

"It has been taken care of."

"No," she protested. "I can't let you —"

"It has been taken care of," he said severely. "We don't have any time to waste."

The same black Mercedes that had driven her from the railroad station to the Adlon was waiting outside the hotel. Harbin held open the door for her and then got in after her. He gave no directions to the chauffeur, who evidently knew where they were going; and when they were on their way, he reached into his breast pocket and handed Barbara her passport and railroad ticket. He said nothing at all while they were in the car. It was only after her bags had been checked through to her compartment and when they were standing on the platform next to the railway car, with no more than fifteen minutes before the train would depart, that Harbin faced her and said, "I am too old to be in love, Barbara, and too cynical and much too cold inside. I try to live with the illusion that I am a Junker, a Prussian gentleman, a person of character and honor. But my honor is a sham, and my pretensions are lies, and I serve a pig in a pigsty — which is not to say that I am any better than the other pigs. But I want you to know that if you had remained here, I would have behaved to you as a gentleman should. For a little while, you helped to feed the illusion that I could still feel, that I could love, that I could retrieve something of what men used to call honor. But that was as much a dream as the rest of my pretensions."

"Will you be all right?" she asked woefully. "They won't punish you for this?"

He shrugged. "I am still useful, I think. I am fifty-two years old, Barbara. I don't find life very enchanting. So it doesn't matter too much."

"It matters to me."

"Thank you for that. Now, get on the train."

He did not try to kiss her, and she could not bring herself to kiss him. She boarded the train and went to her compartment. Through the window, she saw him standing pensively, watching the train as it pulled out.